CLOTH
AND
DAGGER

JOHN H. HILTON

Jan-Carol
Publishing, Inc
"every story needs a book"

Cloth and Dagger
John H. Hilton
Published May 2024
Little Creek Books
Imprint of Jan-Carol Publishing, Inc.
All rights reserved
Copyright © 2024 John H. Hilton
Title page image: © Fantasy Maps/Adobe Stock
Cover images: Couple: Contributed;
Church interior © Wazir Design/Adobe Stock

ISBN: 978-1-962561-29-7
Library of Congress Control Number: 2024939872

You may contact the publisher:
Jan-Carol Publishing, Inc.
PO Box 701
Johnson City, TN 37605
publisher@jancarolpublishing.com
www.jancarolpublishing.com

To Claudia,
who always helps me do my best work.

INTRODUCTION

"Equality may perhaps be accepted as a right,
but no power on earth will convert it into a fact."
— HONORÉ DE BALZAC

Not so very long ago, a gifted and flawed young man rose to prominence as a Priest in the Episcopal Church. Within a shockingly brief period of time, he was considered by many to be the best preacher in town. He was serious about his calling but fell very short of leading by example. He was talented, charismatic, and warm, but he could be self-contradictory, and his critics would think him a narcissist — though, in this story, one is encouraged to view critics with a grain of salt. This young man was both loved and resented, as well as envied. It will be easy to like this man. It will be easy to resent him and sometimes be disgusted by his actions. What is out of the question is to be indifferent toward him.

Our tale unfolds where a life of privilege and frivolity have taken quite a serious turn. Michael Brandon was secure, for the moment, in his call to ministry in the Episcopal Church, induced by his mid-life crisis. It is his last year as a seminary student and six months shy of his 41st birthday. This is a story of a clergyman, a holy man, and an all-too-human man. In a sense, it is a statement of just how human we all are, including priests and pastors — and how so.

It would be no great stretch of the imagination to classify Brandon as an atypical seminarian. Most of the students were sensitive and introspective. Brandon possessed these qualities too, but at first glance he was what he had been his entire adult life — the consummate salesman/politician, living a life of worldly indulgence. Twenty years of jockeying for power and position in his hometown had not lived up to its promise of fulfillment, only a dissatisfying career and a failed marriage. At the moment, the quiet and reflective life of scholarship, spirituality, and friendships based upon honesty and genuine affection were a great relief to him.

Although Brandon's career change had been going well (he was on his way to graduating with honors and had received the highest recommendation from his faculty and mentors), his personal life was still the soap opera it had been for twenty years. As he is ordained and embarks on a hopefully brilliant ecclesiastical vocation, his private affairs and conduct will spin out of control, perhaps threatening to undo his second chance at a useful and fulfilling life.

Attempts to gain control over his seemingly contradictory persona are both rewarded and frustrated by his appointment as a Priest to a hugely important church, where Brandon soon finds himself the confidante of a parishioner the police like for several recent and well-publicized murders. Passions, both physical and emotional, overwhelm the priest as the police investigation travels down dark and mysterious corridors.

Set in the quaint and historic hamlet of Alexandria, Virginia within the greater backdrop of Washington, D.C., things are definitely not as they appear with the Reverend Michael Brandon II and his vocational journey. This story is about how the most gifted and well-intentioned of people fall prey to the contrary aspects of their own character. Brandon is seldom, if ever, defeated by others and has a gritty determination never to be defeated by circumstance. But will he be able to outwit and overcome the ever-looming threat of self-defeat which relentlessly haunts the man of passion?

CHAPTER I

On the cold and otherwise unimportant afternoon of January 12, 2009, the Hunter stalked his prey.

Observing his target and surroundings with a kind of controlled neurosis, no detail from earth to sky escaped his notice for those two late afternoon hours; not even as a steady stream of airplanes flew overhead, as the Hunter's position was in the flight path of Ronald Reagan National Airport, located on the Virginia side of the Potomac River across from Washington, D.C. This attested to the man's almost inhumanly calm nerves, for he never flinched for a second as his eyes peered through the lens of the high-powered Leupold scope on his Winchester Model 70 Bolt Action Rifle.

Just then, a conference was breaking up at the Hilton Hotel off Interstate 95, south of the airport. Limousines and company cars pulled up to the front entrance as dozens of men in suits were scuttling out the doors from a high-level meeting between Federal financial and housing regulators and a selected group of Washington area residential developers. One by one, the cars, carrying their dignitaries, pulled away from the hotel. As the Owner and Chief Executive Officer of the Open Door Development Corporation and his two aides arrived at their limousine, the Hunter pressed the speed-dial on his cell phone. Thirty seconds later, the concierge peered outside the front door and called the Open Door team back in. An important phone call at the desk for the CEO, or perhaps a private word with someone unknown?

It mattered not. All that was important was to delay them long enough to clear out the rest of the traffic in front of the hotel. Minutes later, an irate-looking CEO walked back out to the limousine with his aides. It was to be the last walk he would ever take. The Executive reached the rear passenger door held open by one of his aides, and then the Hunter did what great hunters do. He took absolute advantage of the perfect, split-second opportunity that both planning and chance provided. He breathed, gently exhaled, and squeezed the trigger.

The Executive never made it into the car; inches away from the seat and before he could bend into position for vehicle entry, his head snapped violently backward, and the man was dead before impact on the cold and blood-spattered pavement. In contrast to the horrific mess in the back of the victim's head lay a single and very precise entry hole near his left temple. This was a master shot, no doubt. But a master assassination? Not in your life. Unless the Hunter could make his escape without leaving any trace of truth to this terrible moment.

Within seconds, the shooter had his weapon collapsed and in a briefcase. He picked up the shell casing, a 7mm Magnum which is an intensely powerful caliber of rifle used to bring down large game, coupled with a 150-grain bullet to ensure that there was next to no drop with his 200+ yard shot. Placing the shell casing in a secure pocket of his trench coat, he left the vacant apartment of the rental building across the hotel on Seminary Road called Southern Towers. He had worn gloves, a shower cap, and a sock cap firmly on his head to avoid the shedding of hair. He did not eat, drink, smoke, or spit during those two hours. He had worn plastic bags over his shoes, a dark blue business suit, and a full-length trench coat to avoid any trace of the new carpet in the unit from clinging to him. He removed the shoe bags and the trench coat, rolled them up, and placed them in a laundry bag while in the foyer of the unit.

If anyone was paying attention for the next few moments (and nobody was), all they would have seen of the killer was a businessman walking down the street carrying a briefcase. The Hunter took a leisurely stroll to his gray Range Rover on the north side of an adjacent park. Without fear, or hesitation, he drove out of the car-packed commuter lot, which was unmanned, and sped away into traffic, hiding in plain site with the hundreds of other gray SUVs.

While the unfolding of a massive presence of police, paramedics, and the media in search of explanations and witnesses ensued, the Hunter was at home on his sofa with the news on. His briefcase was securely underneath a floorboard in his bedroom closet. The laundry bag and its contents were in the fireplace in the blaze (along with the gloves he removed before entry). Safe and secure in his condo not 6 miles from the killing zone, he continued to watch the events unfold on TV.

By nightfall, he would vacuum the ashes from the fireplace, and unde-tected and undisturbed, the Hunter made another short trip to his Range Rover parked in the building's garage with the vacuum cleaner and its contents ready for permanent disposal. With not a trace of evidence plac-ing him in the vacant apartment, nor any evidence in his own apart-ment except for the well-hidden briefcase containing the murder weapon which had been thoroughly cleaned, the Hunter was relaxed and assured as he drove away into the night, for he had gotten away with that one!

* * *

Michael Brandon, soon to be the Reverend Michael Joseph Brandon II of the Virginia Diocese of the Episcopal Church, turned into the parking lot on the grounds of the Virginia Theological Seminary in Alexandria. This much-esteemed institution dates back to the early 19th Century, producing numerous acclaimed priests, bishops, and theologians. It was Monday, February 20, and Brandon had two classes and an appointment to file his ordination papers that day.

While most of the students were very sensitive spiritually, even introspective and timid — Seminary can be great a place to hide from the world and oneself, which is of course both good and bad — Brandon was the son of a popular local lawyer and ex-congressman, and he himself a former politician. He was the consummate extroverted salesman. His good looks were softer rather than rugged, and although he was 6-foot-1 and had nearly 200 pounds of muscular frame, he had a defined baby face with a boyish grin that could be both endearing and deceptive. Brown hair, blue eyes, and a fair complexion at once betrayed his Waspish background. He was quick witted in discussion and a brilliant speaker, hence his brief political success.

Brandon had, in fact, ingratiated himself to many a fellow seminarian by writing and editing their sermons for Homiletics class, as well as helping them with delivery. Yes, this was a man on the move to remake his life using every tool he had been gifted and developed previously. Just two more classes with A-grades and he would graduate with honors. Just one more meeting with the Bishop and the Diocesan Committee on Ordination and he would be eligible for an early appointment to, hopefully, the church of his choice.

His first class that day was Ethics. Normally, students take Christian ethics in their first or second year, but Brandon found neither passion nor intellectual stimulation in the subject. As he reminded the professor and his fellow students aloud the first day of class, Oscar Wilde claimed that people are not so much good or bad, as they are either charming or tedious. And the study of morals and manners, though undeniably important, smacks of excruciating tediousness. The students were amused by the quip — the professor, not so much.

After coffee and some light food in the cafeteria, Brandon filed his ordination papers with his faculty advisor and went to his other class for the day. Systematic Theology was the series of classes that tripped up most students. One had to be a natural philosopher to breeze through the subject. As an undergraduate student, he had majored in political theory, so philosophical argument came easy to him. This final half of Systematics class part 2 would focus on what the Christian Church calls the "The Last Things," where one studies and contemplates the various church dogmas on heaven, hell, and purgatory. The Episcopal Church, as part of the worldwide Anglican Communion, does not officially endorse purgatory, the place where most souls go for purification after death according to Roman Catholic teaching, but some prominent Anglicans such as C.S. Lewis believed in it.

Brandon could not help showing off his classical studies knowledge by referencing Dante's "Divine Comedy," volume 2, entitled "Purgatory."

"Wasn't Purgatory where the action and the real stuff of life plays out in the 'Divine Comedy?'" said Brandon. In "Inferno" and "Paradise," the other two volumes, souls were either in torment or eternal rest. "Or was purification simply a metaphor for this life here and now?"

Despite his easy smile and demeanor, Brandon was consumed with dogmatic contemplation. Spiritual and theological matters were deadly serious to him, for they not only dictated where we go when we die, but they ultimately reveal the character of God Himself.

Brandon then went home to his laptop and to a well-deserved gin and tonic, where he put the finishing touches on his Master's Thesis. He was all set to graduate and assume ordination, but it was understood that he would turn in the 50-page paper on William Booth, the founder of the Salvation Army in England in the mid-19th century. To Brandon, the Salvation Army had a concrete spiritual influence, both in a practical and mystical sense. The Salvation Army is a church with Wesleyan roots

(Anglican Ministers John and Charles Wesley founded the Methodist movement in the 18th Century). Booth was a Methodist Minister, who believed in compassion, especially for the poor, and social holiness in a Dickensian sense.

Methodists and Anglicans (Episcopalians in America) have taught that the love of God prevails over all else, and that all theology must be subordinate to this essential truth. God does not will that some are saved and others not. No indeed! God passionately desires relationship and everlasting life with all of His creation. Brandon was convicted with this interpretation of Christianity to the point of obsession. He delighted in it and used every opportunity to share this good news with others; solicited or otherwise. In the temporal realm, he had been the Chairman of the regional Northern Virginia Salvation Army for 10 years and took particular delight in ringing the bells at the local supermarkets during Christmastime.

That night, he called his girlfriend in Miami, Florida. Bettina Vasquez was a bright and beautiful 35-year-old Cuban daughter of immigrants, who met Michael as an intern during one of his campaigns for local office. A casual drink one afternoon some time ago turned into an evening of walking in the parks and waterfront of the historic district in Alexandria. Driving her back to her home 5 miles away in Washington, D.C., near the Washington National Cathedral, he found himself interminably smitten. For the first time since he separated from his ex-wife, the shoe was on the other foot. How many countless romances with fine ladies had he burned through? It was as if the whole town's opposite sex were throwing themselves at him in a four-year span of time, and yet he could not bring himself to be close to anyone. Ironically, the older and more temperamental he became, the more female attention descended on him.

After just a few weeks with Bettina, he endeavored to pursue a meaningful relationship and be faithful to it. They had been together now since May of 2006, just before he entered the seminary. Though she was very intrigued at the thought of being Brandon's wife, her Catholic parents needed more convincing toward their daughter marrying a divorced Episcopalian, clergyman or otherwise.

"How's your mom today, sweetheart?" asked Brandon.

"She's out of surgery and resting," sighed Bettina. "They say it's a benign tumor but wanted to remove it because of where it is on the brain. I don't know any more detail than that. We think she will be okay."

"That's a relief," Brandon chimed in. "I've had everybody at the Seminary Chapel praying for her. Get some sleep, and we'll have our usual naughty conversation tomorrow."

"Haha!" a fatigued but pleasantly teased Bettina replied. "I'll be back in town this weekend. I love you!"

"Love you too," said the seminarian.

It had been a long but satisfying day all the way around.

CHAPTER 2

Friday, February 25

The Hunter finished his 2-hour workout: 1000 push-ups, 1000 squats, core mat exercises, full upper-body dumbbell lifts, and 40 minutes of heavy bag strikes. Punches and slaps. He then loaded a semiautomatic pistol with dummy rounds and drew from his belted holster, squeezing the trigger hundreds of times, mimicking a session at the shooting range called dry firing.

This training he did with an eerie religiosity as a matter of course. But today, he honed in on the pistol dry fire with peculiar focus, for his next victim was to die very shortly from a single shot to the head from an accurate and stealthy handgun. In his forties now, the Hunter was a Virginia local. His father taught him to hunt and shoot, just as his grandfather had done, and so forth. Old Virginia families are often a mixture of blue blood and back country frontier. Occasionally, there is some Cherokee Indian in the mix.

The combination of Army sniper school and service in Federal Law Enforcement had honed the Hunter's skills to that of a murder machine. He was trained well enough to throw anyone to the ground in the blink of an eye, break their neck, kill them with a knife — or preferably not to dirty his hands at all. Just one or two squeezes of the trigger, and lights out! His cell phone rang as he put his gun and boxing gloves away.

"Yes," he said. "I know the place well, but I'll not move until my install-ment from the last job has been received. It's there? Hold on, I'll check."

The Hunter pulled up a personal account on his computer, which showed the agreed upon money confirmed. Breathing deeply, he winked at the computer screen and smiled a sinister smile.

"Now," he said, "about this next assignment."

* * *

Christ Church Episcopal in Old Town Alexandria is a seminarian's dream. Located in the historic district, the church dates back to 1767, and served the Lee and Washington families among other notable Virginians. The grounds, buildings, and sanctuary retain their colonial charm, and after a solemn Eucharistic Service in the evening, you can feel a mystical presence about the place.

Michael was very much a product of this old Virginia culture. It cer-tainly helped matters that his family landed in Jamestown in 1699, and his grandmother's grandparents owned land in the city just west of the Virginia Seminary.

He and his parents still lived in the house in which he grew up.

"Thank you, Reverend, I'll see you Monday morning," said Brandon to the church's head Priest, Rector James Thompson, as he departed to his car, giddy with the enthusiasm of a child that got away with stealing the cookie jar.

All his past troubles, financial and work record, a political career ruined before it began were foremost in his mind. Now, Brandon's two-year intern-ship at the most prestigious church in the city had led to a stunning let-ter of recommendation from the Rector portraying Brandon as the most gifted and natural aspiring parish clergyman he had ever met.

Mixed emotions abounded as Michael drove away from the church.

He was grateful to God and to his mentors and friends in the church and the seminary. But he was also feeling the spite, and the antidote to that spite, of a man who knew he deserved what he wanted. He was self-aware of his gifts and his shortcomings but resented beyond description all the troubles and sufferings that life and other people had placed in his path. This was a young man born to privilege and he intended to live that life come hell or high water. And success being the only true revenge, he relished his newfound success in a career that was second to none in honor and prestige. Revenge gave way to euphoria, and he began to plot his next moves.

Peace of mind is a priceless commodity. In Brandon's case, that always involved getting what he was after. He had never felt so on top of his game and desperately wanted a transformation of life and vocation, assuming the theological and pastoral world would bring him escape from his previous life. Had he actually gotten away with it? *It appeared to be a safe bet,* he thought as he entered Bettina's apartment to await her return.

Michael was gently awakened by the tickle of a woman's hair on his face and neck. Pleasantly startled, he looked at his watch.

"You're early," he said. "How did you avoid the Friday traffic?"

"Got lucky today, clear shot from the airport," said the Latin beauty. "You are so irresistible when you're sleeping on my couch! I almost didn't wake you."

"This sofa is more comfortable than my bed, or anything else at my place," said Brandon.

Bettina put on her robe after a casual rinse in the shower. It proved to be a useless task, for Brandon's face and hands were inside that robe within seconds. He was down on his knees hugging Bettina tightly around the waist, kissing her stomach and her bosom for twenty minutes or more. Then he lifted her up with his right arm and shoulder, playfully and passionately depositing her on the sofa, still warm from his earlier nap. She was giggling and moaning at the same time.

Before Bettina received the first deep kiss and an "I love you" whisper in the ear, Brandon had sampled all the candy in his presence. Starting at her feet and working his way up, he caressed, licked, kissed, and sniffed every inch of her fantastically delicious body.

He hadn't even removed his pants, and already the woman he loved and intended to marry was in a state of nearly impossible ecstasy. Brandon was poised to take his turn, but as a man of superior gifts he paused, then he dove into Bettina again. His face was between her legs, and he did not see daylight for another half an hour. He held her as she quivered, and when she gathered herself, he penetrated. It was one of those encounters that shakes a couple to their core. Had it ever been that good before? Could it possibly be that good? Neither of them could remember, or even speculate. It was only possible to enjoy, and of course, not want it to end.

Brandon proved his chivalry with one final gesture. He gave Bettina a world class massage, knowing she needed the tender loving care to relieve her from her travels. He stared lustfully at her magnificent butt while taking care to ease her back and neck aches. It was only slightly after 8 p.m. when he carried her into bed, and she fell into a deep sleep.

As he awakened the next morning, he could smell bacon and other pleasantries coming from the kitchen. He looked next to him on the bed and saw Bettina staring at him.

"Don't burn the food, baby," Brandon joked.

"It's ready and served," Bettina said. "I've been watching you sleep, that's all."

"Again? I'm flattered."

The stunning lady replied, "I told you, you're irresistible when you sleep."

"Like a little boy, or a devastatingly handsome stud?" Brandon asked as he winked, yawned, and stretched.

"Both," exclaimed Bettina with an almost desperate sigh. "You are the best man I've ever met, Michael Brandon, by a wide margin!"

Not a bad way to begin the day, Brandon thought to himself. He pulled his girlfriend over to his side of the bed, thanked her for the marvelous compliment, and said, "Let's eat. And by the way, I could not possibly love you more. You're my girl!"

Smiling and slightly moist in the eyes, the two lovers sat down to breakfast. As Bettina got up to wash the dishes, Brandon just stared at what he knew was his greatest conquest — past, present, or future. Miss Vasquez was 5-foot-7 with more curves than an Alpine speedway. She had an exquisite face and big brown eyes that could pierce the psyche of any normal man. Although a professional woman, mindful of her career and image, her long hair descended halfway to her hips. Her sweet and intoxicating smile was simultaneously seductive and lovably endearing.

Brandon was used to being the stud in every relationship he had. Despite their break-up, his ex-wife thought he was the handsomest, most charming, and sexy man she had ever met. And his very long string of girlfriends literally flung themselves into his arms. *But now, what are the chances,* he thought, *that this perfect woman would think the same way about me?*

She told him she thought of him in the same way; the way that his previous ladies thought of him. And although he trusted her implicitly, he did not trust life. So, in the midst of this indescribably beautiful relationship with Bettina, Brandon was at the present condemned to share his euphoria with an unpleasant sensation that circumstance could be plotting against their mutual love and admiration.

And why not? Had circumstance not ruined his marriage and his political life? He was 40 years old and had not one business success to his name, despite usually being the smartest guy in the room. His parents were rich and respected, but that just put more onus on Michael to distinguish himself. He had chosen the ministry for mostly the right reasons. He was a believing and committed Christian, and passionate of all things theological. He relished the idea of a life of study, preaching and helping people with their spiritual matters. But he also loved turning the tables on society and circumstance, which until now had robbed him of the prestige and position that he was so sure he deserved.

That night, Brandon would accompany Miss Vasquez to her Catholic church for the Saturday evening Mass. After dinner, he polished off a sermon for one of his classmates who was to deliver the message at Sunday morning Chapel Service at the Seminary. To Bettina, although she respected Brandon's denominational faith and commitment, she never really knew how to express the differences between his Episcopal vocation and her Roman Catholic faith. They agreed to disagree, but Brandon downplayed the differences with great sophistication. After all, they are both Christian and the Mass is virtually the same. But he was far too emotionally intelligent to allow Bettina to see his intellectual snobbery predominate. He would handle this, and every other issue concerning the woman he loved with the utmost gentleness and care.

On Sunday afternoon and evening, they repeated Friday. As far as passion and tenderness go, these two were made for each other. The physical and emotional pleasures they heaped on one another were made for literature. Brandon, at that point, vowed that he would not let anything obstruct the happiness he had in store for Bettina and himself. It was one of those internal promises that a man made to himself that was so assured that Divine Providence had certainly been involved. By the week's end, he would formally propose to her.

Monday, February 28

The Deputy Chief stormed out of his office and said, "Where's Grimes?"

Detective Julie Grimes was on call, a twelve-year veteran of the Alexandria Police Department. She was brand new to the Robbery and Homicide Division.

The desk sergeant called her on her cell phone.

"The Chief says get over to Christ Church in Old Town now, Grimes. There's been a killing!"

"Got it," said Grimes. "On my way."

She arrived at the scene at 10:15 a.m. There were four people in the church: the Secretary, the Rector, seminarian Michael Brandon, and a dead man.

* * *

The night before had been cold and ominous, with a drizzly rain and winds that gusted every 20 minutes or so to intolerable levels that forced anyone outside to seek shelter and something hot to drink. Christ Church leaves the sanctuary open for anyone to come and sit and pray as a matter of course. As a taxicab pulled up, a man exited the car and pulled his raincoat over his head, making a mad dash to the door of the church. Despite the intense weather and poor visibility, he knew precisely where he was going for two reasons; first, he was a long-time member of the church, and second, he was to meet a man privately to obtain what he was told over the phone to be a considerable financial contribution to the Democratic Party.

As the party's finance chairman (or bag man, to be candid), he met the very large contributors himself. If they paid in cash, he would conveniently forget to report the donations to either the State or Federal tax authorities; and of course, pocket the difference himself.

He had arrived ten minutes early and was seated alone in the church sanctuary, where a chilly breeze was running from the window just to his right. The party operative expected a brief encounter with one man holding a large envelope full of money and a name and phone number where he could have a particular politician contact him to discuss the favor that he sought in return for the donation. Due to the darkness inside and outside, it took him a few minutes to notice that the cold draft was caused by the window on his right being open at the bottom several inches.

"Hello," the man muttered as he saw a shadow lurking outside the window. "Hello, is this who I am to meet?"

There was silence and no movement from where the man stared. Irritated, he rose from the pew and walked toward the window.

"Listen, if this is a game, I am out of here, got that?"

The party operative dropped like a fly with a single bullet hole in his forehead. Cloaked in the rain and darkness, the figure outside gently pushed the window shut and left.

* * *

"Harry Penrose," said Rector Thompson. "How tragic."

Detective Grimes needed some more information, but Michael Brandon knew quite well who Harry Penrose was. Brandon and his father had been two of only a handful of successful Republican politicians in that part of Virginia within an hour's drive from Washington, D.C.

His father, Michael Brandon Sr., was now a retired lawyer and former Congressman. He had known Penrose when they served together in Virginia's General Assembly. Both men belonging to the "old school" of political machinations, they had a cordial relationship. Michael II had always thought Penrose oily and a typical political hack.

"So, what's the story?" Detective Grimes chimed in.

The Rector briefed her on Penrose's bio and church membership. A lawyer and Finance Chairman for the Democratic National Committee, Penrose was single and had no family in the area. He was well-to-do and gave generously to the church and had served on the vestry (the church's governing body). Brandon had to pretend to be upset, and thought it odd that he, as a priest to be, could say to himself, *I don't really give a tinker's damn about this guy.*

He thought this a momentary reaction because he never liked the gentleman. However, Michael found himself in this state of pretense to care for longer than he would have thought.

Detective Grimes asked to interview the Rector and the Secretary, and afterword Brandon. About thirty minutes later, the Crime Scene Unit showed up in order to sweep the sanctuary. As they labored methodically, Brandon and Detective Grimes went into a conference room, and she closed the door. They would stay there for nearly an hour, which was odd, for Brandon, after all, was only a seminary intern. Both the Rector and the Secretary thought it strange too, for they only had to endure 15 minutes or so of questioning.

As Brandon and the detective exited the room, there was silence and bewilderment.

"Obviously, this a murder investigation," said Grimes. "Don't leave town until further notice. Crime Scene Unit may have some questions before they leave, so please cooperate. I'll be back here around 4."

As Julie Grimes drove away from the church toward the police station a couple of miles away, she smiled for the first time that morning.

"What a cute clergyman," she said to herself. At that moment, she had little idea as to how intense that attraction would become. And even less of an idea how it would compromise her, personally and professionally. But for now, there was a murder to solve. Two if you count the high-profile builder killed at the hotel down the street.

Because of the peculiar circumstances at the hotel killing, the Governor of Virginia had ordered the State Police to investigate immediately. But after several exhaustive weeks, the State investigators had come up with nothing. Nothing! Not the slightest evidence of any kind, save the fact that now, the two victims were middle-aged white men of considerable wealth and obvious political connections. Once the detective reported the identity of the second victim, she and her superiors all had their curiosity peaked. These two killings must somehow be linked, but none of them could apply science or reason to the speculation.

* * *

That night, the Hunter returned to his 2-bedroom furnished apartment, turned on the TV news, and watched the local broadcast featuring the two recent murders.

"Both state and local police are telling us it is too early in the investigation to determine whether or not the crimes are linked and if there are any solid leads in the cases," a voice martially blurted over the TV. "Although both victims were shot with a single bullet, there is an obvious discrepancy. Mr. Robert Martin of the Open Door Development Corporation was killed with a high-powered rifle at well over a hundred yards, while the second victim, a Mr. Harry Penrose of the Democratic National Committee, was shot at close range with a .22 Caliber bullet that police think was fired from a handgun."

"And that is the entirety of the evidence they will uncover," said the smug assassin to himself.

Confident in his operational prowess and execution thus far, he had next to no concerns about being found out. Then, in a fever pitch of highly creative and precise brain activity, the Hunter began to draw up his next plan.

CHAPTER 3

Tuesday, March 1

Brandon arrived at his parents' home, where he had been living since his divorce and before entering Seminary. It was 4:45 p.m., and the cocktail hour was upon him. His mother, Patricia, who was a very gracious and doting parent, kissed her son of whom she was so proud and told him to take his time washing up for dinner.

As he ascended the winding staircase leading to his bedroom, he caught a glimpse of his imperious father fixing a drink in the parlor. The older man shot him a disapproving look as if he somehow should have arrived for the daily regimen of drinks and dinner promptly at 4:30 p.m., and properly attired.

Michael smirked and tuned out the gesture, for he had stopped trying to please his father years ago. The two had a loving relationship as father and son, but there were ever lurking those recriminations so common with young men of privilege.

"Why are you such a playboy, and a slickster salesman? Why didn't you go to law school like me, or medical school? What about working your way up in one of the many Fortune 50 companies in the area? And now, a clergyman! An honorable vocation indeed, but you're pushing the envelope if you think your mother and I are. Well, if I'd had your advantages in life."

And so, Michael Brandon Sr. would rant at least twice a week at the family cocktail hour.

As Michael Junior put on a polo shirt and blazer, he thought to himself, *At least the old man doesn't control what I do for a living now.*

He was right, for the Brandon family worshipped at St. Paul's Episcopal Church, also in Old Town Alexandria. And though he wouldn't know his exact church appointment for a couple of weeks, he did not ask for St. Paul's to be in consideration. Dinner at the Brandon house had a Jane Austen quality to it; the full-time house keeper was a superb cook and Mrs. Brandon spent very full days tending to the upkeep of the home and the grounds with an exceptional garden. Four lush acres presented on a hill. The Georgian-style home had six bedrooms, and the first floor was full of 18ᵗʰ and 19ᵗʰ Century antiques. The Brandons would entertain many guests throughout the years, particularly when Mr. Brandon was a congressman.

As an only child, Michael knew that he stood to eventually inherit in excess of a $300 million estate, but his parents were healthy and only 70 years of age.

"So, tell me what's going on at Christ Church, Michael," said Mrs. Brandon nervously.

"What a way to end up my two-year internship," replied the son. "No drama the entire time, and then..."

"Yes, bad business," said Congressman Brandon. "That fellow Penrose made no few enemies over the years, I tell you."

"I'm more interested in what kind of recommendation you'll have from Rector Thompson," Mrs. Brandon said. She had an old school charm and a gifted way of tuning out the horrors and sufferings of the world, getting down to the brass tacks of what is actually important — family, religion, education, and the humanities. Unlike her husband, she could not be more pleased with her son as an Episcopal Priest.

"The Rector is a little shaken up about the killing," Michael said. "In 250 years, our parish has not witnessed so much as a nasty quarrel, and now on his watch, a murder. He asked me to do the sermon this Sunday at the 5 p.m. service. He says he will give me the highest recommendation. That, plus my graduating with honors should do the trick for the long haul."

"Oh, how delightful!" Patricia said. "I will make it my business to attend. Joe, how about you?"

Mrs. Brandon was one of the few people who called the Congressman Joe, Joseph being the middle name of both him and his son.

"Allow the young man some space, Patricia," the Congressman said. "He needs to carve out his own niche. We will go hear him at wherever he is in a few weeks."

Brandon senior grunted as he guzzled his goblet of Chardonnay.

"Perhaps you make a good point, dear," Patricia said. "Anyway, you shall email me a copy of your remarks, Michael."

"Mom, you know I just write a few notes and then wing the rest of the sermon, just as I did with my campaign speeches."

"Listen, you are now truly educated, and doing the Lord's work when you speak. I expect more discipline and formality going forward."

"Yes ma'am," said the seminarian affectionately. "I am quite certain of a brilliant position shortly. But I have other news which will dominate the dinner conversation; I am going to propose to Bettina."

Mrs. Brandon jumped up from the table and smothered her son with hugs and kisses, while the Congressman drank a toast and gave Michael the rare paternal approval.

"That's a fine choice, my boy!" said Michael's father. "I don't know any man who wouldn't be green with envy at your walking into a room with that temptress on your arm."

"Pop, you're talking about my wife-to-be."

"Take it easy, son, you know what I mean. Bettina is as beautiful as, well, a Spanish Elizabeth Taylor."

At that moment, Mrs. Brandon chimed in, "Let it end there, Michael. That's as tactful a compliment as you'll get from your father tonight, especially with all his drinking."

"Aww, Patricia, loosen up," Michael Sr. said.

"It's a wonder you ever got elected to anything," Patricia said. "Unlike our beautiful and charming son."

"Who wouldn't have been elected at all but for me pulling some fairly slippery strings?" snorted the Congressman.

A slightly uncomfortable but usual pause engulfed the dinner table due to some unpleasant family secrets yet to be revealed.

For the rest of the week, Brandon attended his classes, had lunch with the Rector and secretary, and prepared his sermon. He had visited the Alexandria high rise condominium community called Marina Towers, an exceptionally located property on the Potomac River, just minutes from Reagan Airport and the bridges into Washington.

Securing a charming 2 Bedroom, 2 Bathroom with a den unit, he and Bettina would be moving in together in a couple of weeks. Brandon always worried a little about Bettina living in the city of Washington. It was more dangerous than the suburbs. Not to mention, the traffic ordeal; just crossing the river during rush hour was a new dimension in stress agony. Michael was now fully enjoying his coup de tat on the world.

Four years ago, he had no job, no political office, large debts, no relationship, and no direction. Now he was about to be ordained an Episcopal clergyman, marry the best woman on the planet, and live large in his waterfront luxury condo. His fortunes had indeed changed for the better.

* * *

Conversely, Detective Julie Grimes had it rough. Divorced with a 5-year-old daughter, she rented a small house in Fairfax County about 10 miles outside Alexandria. Real estate prices and rents had risen sharply over the previous decade, and her meager detective salary was just enough to keep her out of the slums. Her ex-husband, a Staff Sergeant in the Army, was stationed at Fort Lee near Petersburg, Virginia, a little over two hours to the south. He did pay child support, which combined with her income, helped to make things tolerable. She was the only female in the Robbery and Homicide Division, and though her male colleagues befriended and supported her, she knew she was not one of the guys. Thus, with the exception of her child, Julie was living a rather unfulfilling and insignificant life. This was about to change.

CHAPTER 4

One Month Later
Tuesday, April 7

It was a day to savor; impossible to forget. If any of us have just one day like it, we may count ourselves among the most fortunate of souls. This blessing was certainly not lost on the newly ordained Reverend Michael Brandon II as he walked out of the ordination service at Virginia Theological Seminary Chapel with his vestments and his fiancé.

Bettina had said yes to Michael's proposal with an emotion and authenticity that would make a grown man cry, and it did. She had also moved in with him at Marina Towers. As they approached his car, Brandon looked back at the buildings and grounds of the institution which nurtured him intellectually and spiritually. This seminary had made him a priest in the church of his birth, the church of his parents and many generations of Brandons. His mother was in tears, and even his father could not maintain a dry eye when they emerged from the chapel. The Congressman signaled to Michael to meet them at the house for drinks and dinner, and more drinks.

As the two lovers got into the car, Brandon checked his phone messages and prepared to pull out of the parking lot when the Provost of the Seminary approached the car. As Brandon rolled down the window, the Provost told him, "I wanted you to be the first to know that all clerical appointments are on hold for six weeks due to administrative matters which require further resolve."

"Further resolve, what does that mean?" Brandon asked.

"We're handling each case individually. Are you able to remain at Christ Church for a little while longer? The Diocese will pay all of your salary and benefits until such time as your new parish assumes them."

Brandon was unsure of things as he attempted a response.

"I've already cleared it with Rector Thompson, no problem," declared the confident Provost.

"Then I suppose it's business as usual for a bit," said the partially frustrated new priest. Bettina assuaged him as he drove off down King Street to his parents' estate. Brandon resolved not to let timing of this news disturb his perfect day. It really was no big deal, just a bureaucratic hiccup. But he possessed a probing mind, one that imagines everything. And those imaginings could produce anxiety before he was even aware of it. In reality, the news from the Provost was a mole hill, but Brandon had the propensity to turn it into a mountain if he didn't restrain himself.

In the center of the vast, circular tri-state sprawl of the Washington, D.C. metropolitan area; an area of more than five million people, the old part of Alexandria comprising Christ Church, the Seminary and the Brandon estate felt like a small hamlet. Any nice weather day in the town was an exceptionally gorgeous day. In April, King Street, Seminary Road, and the cross streets were lined with blooming dogwood trees, the occasional magnolia and weeping willow, and hundreds of oak trees.

"Sounds like your friend has your back, Michael," observed Bettina.

"Yeah, he could easily have just let me find out when they notify everyone else," Michael agreed. "Perhaps they have something special in mind for me. Oh, well, just don't let my folks in on it. I just got our condo, and the old man will be sure to give me the insufferable living beyond my means lecture."

"Haha, very well then," Bettina said. "Let's eat, drink, and be merry."

"That's my girl."

Friday, April 10

Rev. Brandon answered his cell phone at 8:30 a.m.

"Michael, it's your mother," the voice said. "Bring Bettina over to the house on Sunday around 4 p.m. I want to talk about the wedding with her. And of course, stay for dinner."

Imagining what else his parents might have in store, he kept the thoughts to himself and gladly accepted. He arrived at Christ Church at 9:00 only to be greeted by Detective Grimes, who looked more than eager to monopolize his morning.

"The bullet that killed Mr. Penrose was a .22 Long Rifle," Grimes started. "And as most civilians are unaware, that caliber can be fired from a handgun as well as a rifle."

"Yes, I'm well aware of that, detective," Michael said. "I grew up hunting with and shooting .22's, and many other firearms."

Realizing that he was being unnecessarily forthcoming, he anticipated her next question: "Yes, I have several rifles and one pistol of that caliber."

"Crime Scene Unit has Penrose being shot at less than 25 feet," Grimes said. "There is a faint trace of gunpowder on the windowsill where he was facing when he was hit."

Grimes couldn't help and perhaps did not realize that she shot him a subtly accusatory glance.

"Are you suggesting I had something to do with this?" asked Brandon in a muffled voice. "I've been more than forthcoming, perhaps too much."

"Take it easy," said the detective. "We checked out everyone who works here at the church thoroughly. None of you are as of yet persons of interest. And, by the way, we know you and your father are avid hunters and gun collectors, so don't worry about incriminating yourself. You haven't."

"A private word please, Detective Grimes," insisted Brandon.

They went outside into the courtyard when Brandon confronted Grimes: "Why are you acting like two different people with me? I mean, one minute you're all cop and give me high blood pressure with your questionings, and when I get the slightest bit exercised, you pour on the reassuring charm like you're on my side."

"I am on your side," insisted Grimes.

"Why? You hardly know me," asked Michael.

Grimes's mind was all over the place by then, with thoughts of Brandon paramount. It was at that very moment she longed to tell him that she would do anything to look after him. In a motherly or sisterly way? No, more than just that.

This young, strapping, and very well-mannered, sophisticated authority figure with his white clerical collar staring down at her had captured Grimes's desires to a boiling point. At that moment, in her unconscious mind, she would trade her career and status as a detective to be the Pastor's paramour.

Brandon had a gifted foresight into knowing when any woman was interested in him in the slightest, and immediately pounced.

"I think it would be advantageous to both of us if we took a ride in your police car," he suggested.

Almost stunned, Grimes agreed. As the two approached her vehicle, Grimes had no idea what to expect, and Michael slyly removed his clerical collar when he entered the vehicle as the two sped off.

Sunday, April 12

Michael and Bettina went over to her Washington, D.C. condo. She had kept the property and was renting it a colleague of hers. She picked up the monthly check and did a once-over to make sure all was well.

It was almost 3 p.m., and they were due at his parents at 4 p.m. in Alexandria. As they approached Wisconsin Avenue, Brandon turned onto a street adjacent to the Washington National Cathedral.

"Why are we going here, Michael?" asked a curious Bettina.

"To hear a guest organist play Mozart," Michael said. "Come on, it starts in a few minutes."

"What about your parents?"

"I called Mom at your place and said we'll be there just before 5 p.m."

Anyone who has ever been to the Cathedral in Washington will understand Brandon's impulse. With over ten thousand pipes, situated in a virtual echo chamber due to the marble and concrete in the floors, walls, and ceiling, any competent player of this exceptional pipe organ will put an audience into an ecstatic trance. If the organist is distinguished, and the program is Mozart's "Requiem," then a musically astute listener will believe that he or she is in the presence of absolute beauty.

As the couple sped off to Alexandria, they remembered nothing of the petty arguments of the day, for they were both in that ecstatic trance until they reached the Brandon home. Bettina was more than content with her Sunday, enjoying its lovely simplicity with her man. Michael, however, couldn't help thinking about how he had tried to get a clergy position at the Cathedral last summer. With his grades and connections, he thought it would be a cinch to get a job on the Dean's staff. Three times he had tried, and three times he was politely turned down.

"What are you thinking, Michael?" Bettina asked. "I know that frustrated look when I see it."

"I knew it was a long shot getting on that Cathedral staff right out of seminary," Michael said. "But to get sidelined three times with no proper explanation galls me. Worse still is that dad offered to put in a word to the Dean. Apparently even ministers of the gospel owe him favors."

"Why don't you take him up?" Bettina said.

"Say what?"

"Really, Michael, you need to get past this thing with your father. So what if he helps you and rubs it in a little? At least you get what you want, right?"

"You're too smart for your own good, honey. I'll mention it at dinner tonight, but you have no idea what you're asking."

"Swallow your pride and get the job done, my stubborn, gorgeous man," the lady said as she kissed him at the stoplight.

* * *

"How did I know you'd come back to the old man?" said a slightly drunken Congressman Brandon.

"Come on, Pop, don't make this hard," Michael said.

"Didn't I tell you that if you want to jump ahead of the pack, it's who you know that counts?"

"Yes, you've said that...all my life."

"For two reasons, boy. First, because it's true, and second, because I know! When you applied the last time, did you interview with the Dean's office?"

"No, just the Human Resources Manager," Michael said.

"I'll call the Dean myself tomorrow and get you an interview," said the Senior Brandon. "Be convincing!"

"All right, all right. I'll get it done," Michael replied, feeling both gratified and defeated at the same time. He knew deep down that in a town like Washington, nobody gets anywhere following the regular rules of procedure, despite the protestations of the popular culture.

Monday, April 13

Brandon knew he was about to enter a new world as he finished his phone call with the secretary of the Dean of Washington National Cathedral.

She had called him at the behest of his father to schedule an interview for Thursday afternoon. As Canon to the Cathedral, he would be a priest in the Episcopal Church working for the Dean and the Bishop of Washington. Despite his father's intervention, Brandon chose to postpone his excitement until after the meeting.

As he told Bettina over the phone, "You don't have it until you have it."

After classes, he drove to Christ Church for a meeting of the Vestry. He was tight-lipped about the Cathedral but couldn't help telling Rector Thompson.

"Congratulations, my boy, provided you get it," Rector Thompson said. "I've never heard of them taking someone straight out of seminary. By the way, that detective was over here this morning again. I'm not sure what she was doing."

"I wouldn't worry about her," said Brandon. "She's pretty zealous about her job but assured me that no one here is a suspect or person of interest."

"She told you that privately?"

"Yes, go figure," said Brandon opaquely.

"Be careful with this, Michael," Rector Thompson said. "It's quite obvious she wants something from you. Remember, you have a bride-to-be."

Brandon thanked the Rector as he left, concealing the truth as successfully as the Hunter concealed his crimes. He had gone off with the detective in her car that day. But instead of going to the police station for a chat, he had Julie Grimes drive them south down the George

Washington Memorial Parkway to the secluded grounds of the Mount Vernon Estate, the home of George Washington — where people come from all over to tour the mansion and grounds.

They pulled up in the north parking lot and slipped through the gate to walk the grounds alone, thanks to Brandon's membership which granted him daily access. After walking through the house and gardens, Brandon stopped them against a large Poplar tree out of the view of any mansion staff.

He grabbed Julie's hands and kissed her cheeks and forehead. When he put his arms around her waist, he could feel her shaking with a nervous panic. Despite her trembling, Grimes put her arms around him and squeezed tightly. Brandon cupped her face in his hands and gently kissed her lips, many times, until he grabbed the back of her head and deeply kissed her in what would seem to any passersby 30 minutes of outrageous public displays of affection.

"I haven't been kissed like that since...maybe never," Grimes said as she stuttered and trembled.

"You're the sexiest cop I've ever seen, Miss Grimes," Michael said. "Now, listen to me very carefully. I am about to marry someone whom I love very much, and this can never amount to anything more than it is now. And nobody can know anything about it, agreed?"

"Of course," said Grimes, "I would never complicate your life that way. I just... I've never met anyone like you before. I'm lonely so much of the time. I need a friend like you to speak words of wisdom to me and hold and comfort me now and again."

She appealed to Michael simultaneously as a priest and as a man.

"I can do that, as long as my boundaries are enforced," said the Reverend.

Brandon then pulled her close and kissed her deeply again, this time caressing her back and slipping his hands down the back of her pants.

The two would not stop caressing each other until another 30 minutes passed, enjoying an intense mutual pleasure against the big tree in the woods.

As they made the 12-mile drive back to the church, Julie was very much at ease. Brandon, not so much. He had cheated many times on his ex-wife, but that was only after their marriage had gone south. This time, he'd had his first illicit sexual encounter since telling Bettina he loved her 3 years ago. Despite finding Detective Grimes alluring, his conduct that afternoon had been primarily about survival.

The Brandons had not retained power and wealth by observing the Boy Scout code of honor. Michael sensed that Grimes was unusually willing to look into his past as well as that of his father. He also knew from their first meeting that she wanted him romantically, and as the murder investigations dragged on, there would be much tension between them. He decided that very day that he had better take control of the circumstances, and of Detective Julie Grimes.

As they pulled up to the church, the coast was clear, and Brandon exited Grimes's car with his clerical collar in place.

"Thank you for your cooperation, Reverend," said Grimes. "You know, I can get you into our restricted pistol shooting range any evening you'd like."

"Consider it a date, Detective," said Brandon, as he struggled to maintain his countenance.

As Michael drove home after the Vestry meeting, he thought back to that day, and was now convinced that Rector Thompson had seen him get into Grimes's car.

Brandon would have had a terrible weekend with Bettina at the Cathedral concert and at his parents' home had he not put his overdeveloped libido with Julie Grimes to what he compartmentalized as good and proper use.

He was not just keeping the Local Police off his family's back, but potentially the Federal Bureau of Investigation (FBI) as well. But as such, he could legitimately go home after his church meeting and make love to his fiancée without considerable remorse.

He had used his charm as a defensive weapon against a looming threat to himself, his parents, and Bettina. After all, they were now in everything together.

CHAPTER 5

Thursday, April 16

The Right Reverend John Stoneham had been Dean of the Washington National Cathedral for nearly 4 years. A conservative Episcopalian from South Carolina, he was an anomaly within the Washington Diocese.

The Episcopal Church had been moving steadily to the left on almost all cultural issues of the day: gay marriage and ordination, transgender recognition, gun control, and heavily pro-choice on abortion. Michael Brandon, just like his parents, was on the conservative side of things, but he had the human touch that could traverse the cavernous differences between the factions. He had friends on all sides of all issues in the church. Despite this, he and Dean Stoneham reinforced each other's views during Brandon's interview.

The Dean was quite impressed with Michael's suggestion that the priests in the Cathedral when sermonizing or leading prayers for the nation replace their current language of "gun violence" to simply "violence."

"Should the church be less outraged if innocent people are thrown off buildings as opposed to being shot?" quipped the young priest.

"Very perceptive, young man," chuckled the Dean.

The interview was very obviously going well for Brandon. He couldn't help wondering, though, why it took his father to get him in to see a man who seemed like he would give Brandon the job of his own accord.

"Don't look a gift horse in the mouth," he said to himself.

Then, the Dean spoke, "The position of Canon to the Cathedral is just what it says on the job description, Michael. You will have an office, and you will participate in and eventually lead daily worship and special events. You will read scripture, teach Bible study, and deliver the sacraments. Your references at the seminary and at Christ Church tell me that you are an exceptional preacher. I want to let you warm up for a while before you do a Sunday sermon, perhaps two months."

"Does this mean I have the job?" asked a very eager Brandon.

"Indeed, it does, sir," replied Dean Stoneham in his southern patrician tone.

* * *

Meanwhile, 120 miles away in the most scenic and historic Blue Ridge Mountains near Charlottesville, Virginia, the Hunter stalked his prey yet again. It was Spring Wild Turkey hunting season in the state, and the killer had been seated next to an oak tree camouflaged to the hilt, since 5:30 a.m.

His movements were restricted to lifting his right arm up to his mouth, very slowly and very deliberately, and blowing into the turkey call twice at a time. The call is roughly the size of a short and fat cigar, camouflaged of course. The scenery could not have been more majestic. The Blue Ridge Mountains are called such because from a distance on a clear day they have a blueish tinge in the backdrop. The city of Charlottesville is famous for housing the University of Virginia, founded by Thomas Jefferson, who just happened to have resided at a nearby grand estate he called Monticello. This plantation lies east of the city in Albemarle County in Virginia's Piedmont region. The beauty of this region cannot be overstated, and to someone unfamiliar with it, adequate description is an impossible task.

The sunrises and sunsets will envelope visitors in a landscape of such primitive sophistication. Only an hour from Virginia's capital city of Richmond and two hours from Washington, D.C., visitors will be transported to another world — one of natural magnificence and stark historical presence. One may escape the 21st Century and the urban/suburban hustle and bustle with a vengeance. With working farms, wineries and vineyards, huge estates, and wildlife preserves, these several counties which comprise the Virginia Piedmont regulate mass development with an authoritarian zeal. This is naturally a splendid state of affairs for the hunters and sportsmen.

BANG! One crack of the Hunter's rifle was all it took to bring down a very large Tom (a male wild turkey). It was a few minutes before 10 a.m., and the unfortunate bird had shown itself about 90 yards from its killer.

He paused for a moment to take it all in. The smell of the gunpowder was nothing short of delicious. You cannot eat or drink it, but at that moment of such heightened sensation, the smoke from a rifle or shotgun in the field will intoxicate you. You want to breathe it in and savor the scent. And its dissipation is most unwelcome.

As he placed his game in the back of a pickup truck, the Hunter washed his hands and checked his phone for messages. There were several, but not the one he expected. The Hunter was unaccustomed to being played with. He had killed two individuals for his current employer and had received instructions for further operations. He knew the generalities and the targets, the details to be forthcoming. But communications were the riskiest part of his profession, even more so than the killings themselves. So, if the Hunter receives word that he is to impart or receive information on a specific day and time, that information must be imparted or received accordingly. These protocols must be religiously followed if a hitman and hirer are to operate in a low stress and trustworthy atmosphere.

As fortune would have it, he received the call on his way home. He was ordered to stand down and not to proceed with his preparations for the next hit.

"Stand down and await further instructions," a quiet voice insisted.

"You know how to reach me," said the Hunter. "I'll be in the area until conclusion of business."

"Very well. Apologies for the late call," said the voice. "For the time being, we operate within a one-hour window instead of a precise minute. Notices will continue to be sent by secure email, and the detailed instructions will continue at dead drops. New locations."

"All good," said the killer who knew his job well enough not to ask why or what was in store in the near future.

He had been paid exceptionally well in advance for several kill jobs and was due a very large bonus if and when all were done to everyone's satisfaction. That bonus, plus his reputation as a professional, would keep the Hunter in forthright cooperation with his handler. Neither side had much fear of treachery from the other.

CHAPTER 6

Sunday, April 19

As Reverend Michael Brandon stepped up into the pulpit at Christ Church to deliver his final sermon as a seminarian, the sanctuary was full. The next time he would preach would be at Washington National Cathedral.

He had definitely carved out a niche for himself here during the last two years. Rector Thompson had been an affectionate and competent mentor for the young priest, and the congregants took to him immediately with his charisma, booming and deep speaking voice, combined with passionate erudition. These qualities grew over time, and he knew that he not only had the gifts, but he could envision his victory over everything in his way.

His critics could not touch him in any way that mattered now, for he knew how much better he was than they. Privileged or not, defeats both personal and political melted into history with his appointment as Canon to the Cathedral, his impending marriage to the most magnificent woman he had ever met, and the fact that he owned any audience he opened his mouth in front of. These personal and vocational victories helped backstop his confidence immeasurably.

Brandon's parents were true to their word and didn't crowd him, but they slyly sat in the back corner pew out of sight. They simply had to hear their boy perform. Bettina was in the front seated next to her younger sister, Nora, who had just arrived from Miami for a visit and to help Bettina and Mrs. Brandon put the finishing touches on her sister's wedding to take place during Memorial Day weekend.

"Oh my!" Nora whispered to her sister. "Look at him, he's so gorgeous up there! I could not be more jealous. Look how regal he is."

Nora had done some modeling in Miami and was the party girl in her conservative family. She had been arrested by Brandon's charms at their first meeting. Truth be told, she may have been his biggest fan. During their sisterly chats over the previous 3 years, it had been Nora who encouraged Bettina to marry Michael when she and their parents had doubts as to their religious compatibility.

As Brandon concluded his opening prayer and began his sermon, both sisters stared, eyes transfixed on the priest and man they both thought hung the moon. Bettina held a close-mouthed smile and sat with legs crossed, contented and overwhelmed with pride as Michael reached the crescendo of his message:

"Now, my friends, I will conclude with a poem I wrote in honor of this farewell occasion. It is inspired by the verse and style of an aged T.S. Eliot, my favorite modern poet, as though he were reflecting on his spiritual life and poetry in the whole of his lifetime. It's called 'Beyond the Journey.'"

Then, Michael proceeded to speak his poem to the congregation:

"Now the Journey is at an end,

Not that the Journey ever really ends.

But it leaves me with joys unspeakable to comprehend. But I should think the Christian life

Has more to offer than struggle and strife. I could say I have earned this peace,

But that would profane the free giving of this gift.

For the Author of peace has made it impossible to boast or earn,

Or do anything but gladly receive the gift and cease

This self-reliance only, but lean on God and his blessed church.

Church of England past and present, upon this rock my faith takes leap,

And I toss the meaner theology of my youth on history's ash heap.

Calvinism and Puritanism in my heart do yield to the via media of

Lancelot Andrewes and the Elizabethan shield.

Dominus vobiscum

Et cum spiritu tuo

April is not the cruelest month after all, it simply belongs to the season,

To the cycle of life where rhyme and reason, are subject to the Divine Will.

And that will which renders all manner of things well, makes possible the stillness

Of mind and soul. A calm before the storm, a calm during and after the storm.

The Dry Salvages and the Mississippi, I traded for the Dover Cliffs white,

Where the water breaks also, but in England, my country and that light,

That fires my pistons and charges my soul, inspiring the verse I write.

In nomine patris

Et fillii

Et Spiritu Sancti, Amen.

Either one is Catholic or Puritan, tis true.

I will not turn again. I will not turn again

From the ancient faith of our ancestors, for under the sun

There is nothing new. And island I am not, a part of history I am.

Tradition, tradition, tradition provides the identity

Of the worshipper and the writer, no island me.

To simply add to the tradition has been my profoundest wish.

And when this life is done, the journey marches on,

To the Purgatorio, or dare I wish, to the Paradiso

Where all shall be well, and all manner of thing shall be well.

Where the soul's dark night is negated by the Light

Of He who on humanity pours out His Love. Why worry, why fret

At all about our common destiny? Tis needless, for in the end,

God is Love Incarnate, we shall be all together, forever.

My friends!

Gratia Domini Nostri, Jesu Christi

Et caritas. Dei

Et communicatio Sancti Spiritus

Sit cum Omnibus vobis,

Et cum Spiritu Tuo."

Michael concluded by saying, "God is love, ladies and gentlemen. And the church is a fellowship, a community of loving and reconciled people. We are on this journey of the Christian faith together, and we will all somehow get to where we are headed; to where we belong. Our Lord will have it no other way. Would you please stand as we recite together the words of the Nicene Creed?"

It was a home run, and he knew it instantly. So did the congregation, especially his soon-to-be wife, and sister-in-law. The good Reverend then presided over the Sacrament of Holy Communion, delivered the final prayers and blessings, and dismissed the congregation. Most of the people in church lined up to shake hands with Brandon and wish him well in his new endeavors.

That night, turning down dinner with his parents and an evening with Bettina and her sister, Brandon went for a drive alone. It was the best way to absorb the sense of thrill and accomplishment that morning had delivered to him. For the first time since his election to public office, he felt like a star. But not the phony star of political celebrity this time. No, he felt like the hero in a Hemingway story. The bull fighter; a real star, a real hero. Never in his life had Brandon been able to piece together in his mind what he so desperately was in search of, and have it happen. He was now an ordained priest, a vocation he had chosen for its own sake — not some hack politician or celebrity lightweight.

But he had been using this calling to fulfill himself as well. This morning at church, he commanded the atmosphere and audience in a way that even his worst competitor or critic would have to bow in abject surrender. Finally, he was on that high road to prestige, influence, dominance, and satisfaction.

"Stuff my past, stuff my failures, and stuff my critics," he said to himself as he drove ever faster down the Parkway toward Mt. Vernon, his favorite place of solace. "I showed the old man, too."

Despite his father getting him his impending job at the Cathedral, he knew that he outshined the Congressman in all the classical ways: in oratory, poetry, literary skill, and emotional appeal. The younger Brandon could charm human beings better than his father could ever dream of.

As he pulled up to the Mt. Vernon estate, this time at the south parking lot, which was more secluded, he would end this victorious day by charming a certain Detective Julie Grimes, whose squad car he spied at the back of the lot.

"How's your daughter, Julie?" asked Brandon as he entered Grimes's passenger seat. "How's everything at home?"

"It's going," said Julie. "Tina is fine, but this investigation is taking me away from her too much."

"That bad?"

"Yeah, we have...I could get charged with obstruction just for telling you this."

"Tell me what?" Brandon asked as he put his hand on her cheek.

"We know that Robert Martin and Harry Penrose are linked," Grimes said.

"Yes, Martin was a major political contributor and Penrose a bagman," said Brandon.

"It goes deeper than that, Michael. We're now looking into a Virginia land deal that took place back in the 1960s. I think it's called Tuscarora."

Brandon's blood pressure rose to the ceiling as he struggled to maintain his composure.

"What is this deal all about?" he asked calmly.

"We think Penrose and Martin's company were knee-deep in a shady deal, which involved bribing several public officials that turned a $300,000 investment into more than $50 million. We just can't fill in the timeline and details."

"Details?" Michael said.

"We can't prove the names and the exact times and places of the bribes," Grimes explained. "The Chief asked for help from the FBI, from their forensic accountants, but they turned him down. They view these crimes as local for now."

Brandon pinched his right thigh very hard in order to remain calm. "Julie, I'm worried about you and this case. Can you handle being in charge of it?"

"I want to desperately," she admitted. "It's my big chance to make my career take off."

"Then I will help you handle it," Michael said as he gave Julie a tender hug.

She sighed, looked at him, and said, "You're just a little too perfect. Why couldn't I have met you before your fiancée did?"

"Because you were married, Miss Julie."

"I would have left him," Grimes said.

"But you have a beautiful child with your ex," said Michael. "Anyway, as I told you before, I'm your special friend. Understand? With me, you get friendship, affection, free counseling, and even spiritual advice."

"How about my hugs and kisses?" Grimes smiled.

"That comes with affection, my dear," Brandon quipped. He hugged Julie tightly again and let her know they could stay that way for another 30 minutes or so.

Detective Grimes slowly and reluctantly exited the warm embrace and bid Brandon goodnight, for she had to get home to her daughter. Michael blew her a kiss as she drove past his car, got into the driver's seat, and closed his eyes and breathed very hard. He then made two phone calls, the first to Bettina and the second to his father.

"Stay at your parents' as long as you want, baby," said the gorgeous and dutiful lady when Michael called. "Nora and I will be up all night digitizing our family photo albums."

"Sounds delightful," Michael said. "I'll be home in a couple of hours."

Michael hung up the phone and dialed his father. He waited for him to answer before saying, "Pop, it's me. Listen, I'm coming over now. Not on the phone; wait until I get there."

Brandon had never in his life seen a look of helplessness and horror on his father's face. That night when he arrived at the estate, there it was.

Father and son had a chat, and some drinks.

To explain, in 1962, Dulles International Airport opened in the southeastern corner of Loudoun County, Virginia — a rural county 25 miles northwest of D.C. It took nearly two decades for the eastern portion of the county to transform into a suburban enclave. What did not take as long is for a certain 300-acre parcel of rural land to be zoned industrial commercial just before the airport opened for business.

This land was located less than ½ mile from the runway and hangers of the airport and was owned by none other than Congressman Brandon. As a young lawyer and member of the Virginia State Senate, he had prior knowledge about the exact location and dates of the airport's building and debut. He borrowed a large sum of money from a bank, bought the 300 acres from a retired farmer for just over $250,000, and bided his time.

During the next few years, two hotel chains, three airlines, and six moving and storage companies bought up the Congressman's land. By the early 1980s, land around Dulles Airport was selling at premium prices. The senior Brandon had profited over $100 million and still received annual royalties from those deals. It was all perfectly legal and above board, except for the fact that Congressman Brandon and his silent partner who did the legal work bribed 3 zoning commissioners, who in turn expedited the up zoning of Brandon's land years in advance before the rest of the county was up zoned. Then, when a lawsuit was quietly filed by some neighbors who had gotten wind of what was happening, the two business partners bribed the judge in the case.

The lawsuit was dismissed, the farmer and the judge died years ago, and the local public officials never appealed. The matter faded out of any public consciousness.

The junior Brandon knew all of this. His father had told him when he decided to run for office himself. Thus, this was the big family secret Reverend Brandon was trying to keep hushed. And for good reason; had he been caught and prosecuted, Brandon Senior would have faced jail time, disbarment as an attorney, and public disgrace of himself and his family, with no chance of holding public office ever again.

What the Congressman had neglected to tell his son was that his lawyer and silent partner was Harry Penrose of the Democratic National Committee.

"Penrose?" blurted out a startled and disgusted Michael. "The detective told me the police consider Penrose and Martin to be linked."

"I wouldn't be surprised if they had sleazy dealings with each other, but I never did any deals with Martin," the Congressman said. "Get that anxious look off your face, Junior!"

"Martin was in no way involved, nor had any knowledge of Tuscarora?" the Reverend Brandon asked. At this very moment, he needed to hear it from the horse's mouth. To hear that his father was not involved in these two killings.

"No, son, of course not! Besides, Martin was never involved, and if he found out about it, I never knew. Penrose was a rising star in the Democratic Party, but he was homosexual, and he knew that I knew."

"Dad!"

"Relax, I never threatened to out him, but back in those days, his career would have been destroyed, even in Democrat circles. When I bought the land and became a State Senator, the Democrats controlled the Virginia legislature by a wide margin, with conservatives down state and liberals up here near Washington. I needed a Democrat who was in on the secret talks with the Feds concerning the airport. I had gotten to know Penrose well. He was a first-rate lawyer, and he loved to wheel and deal and make money. Our senate districts were adjacent, and we cooperated with each other on vital community issues. When I ran for Congress, he of course endorsed my opponent, but he never helped him and never got in my way. When he moved over to the Democratic National Committee, we maintained our mutual cordiality."

Michael's thoughts raced at a fever pitch. It was a good thing he had Detective Grimes where he wanted her. Congressman Brandon didn't get where he was by not being able to read people. He glared slyly at his son and paused.

"You are fucking that lady detective, aren't you, son? Still up to your old tricks I see."

"Almost, but not quite that far yet, Pop. I can't stand the thought of stepping out on Bettina, but when Detective Grimes questioned me last month, I had a sense that I had to get control of this thing, or something like tonight would happen. I just found out they have been talking to the FBI. Holy shit, what are we going to do, Pop?"

"You're going to do it, son! Do you have this detective's trust?"

"Yes, for the moment."

"Keep it and find out everything that's happening with the investigation. There are only three documents which exist with the Tuscarora deal. I have them all where nobody can get to them. I'll do a brainstorm and make sure there are no loose ends. I'm sure, but I'll scrub it again. In the meantime, use your considerable charm and your wits to keep our family secure, Junior!"

Michael took that as a compliment as well as a command. He said, "Don't worry... I will, Pop. How much does Mom know?"

"Only the legal part, and we're keeping it that way."

"Understood! Call you tomorrow," Michael said as he set down his empty drink glass and headed out the door.

There was no time, and no mood for Michael's priestly judgment and recriminations upon the sins of his father. He had known of these peccadilloes (Brandon much preferred this terminology to what they actually were, which is major crimes) for over 10 years, and when he made the decision to go to seminary and answer the call to ordained ministry, he promised to preserve the family skeletons. But he told his father emphatically to remove him from the inheritance of any money or property resulting from the Tuscarora deal — an admirable act given the millions of dollars involved.

He still stood to gain his mother's estate, the Brandon house, and other properties and holdings, though, which had nothing directly and very little indirectly to do with the crooked machinations of the Congressman. So, Brandon got to have it both ways again. He was set for life financially but also enjoyed the privilege of dignified outrage at his father's misconduct and how he had sequestered himself from it all.

Michael got home late, but as expected, Bettina and her sister were up messing around with the family photographs. He kissed his loved one and bid Nora goodnight as well. He then went to his den to grab a set of books to read himself to sleep. His new job was to begin after the honeymoon on June 15. Brandon was exhausted from the week of sermon preparation, wedding plans, and trying to stay on top of a police investigation, which just took a distressing turn. His father's disclosures that night, although disturbing, put his concerns to rest temporarily. He knew he could now focus safely on his wedding and his Cathedral job, but to do that successfully, he had to rest well for the next two weeks.

He changed and cleaned up for bed, closed the door, and began reading Ernest Hemingway's short stories and the plays of Oscar Wilde, for he needed both escape and irreverent humor that night, and most likely through the week. Brandon had become a voracious reader in his thirties, owing much to his mother, an English teacher and amateur writer herself. She had smothered him from a young age with "all things western civilization," as he later told Bettina on one their first dates. From plays to poems to the textbooks, Mrs. Brandon was the ideal parent in the instruction of a son's classical education. She would not, however, enjoy the fruits of her labors until Michael entered seminary. In high school and college, he was a party animal and athlete, with exceedingly average grades.

After college, he became a Real Estate agent and messed around with local politics. His goals back then were simple — to make easy money as a salesman, date as many beautiful girls as possible, and get elected to a political office to prove to everyone he could do something on his own. What he failed to understand at the time was that his looks, charm, and pleasing personality could not compete with political machinery, favor trading, and money. His father warned him from the beginning that there were over 10,000 real estate agents in Northern Virginia, and no one would give him any business simply because he was the son of a soon-to-be ex-congressman.

"You've chosen a flunky profession, Junior," the father told Michael more than once.

Brandon could have allowed his mind to travel to his success in getting elected to the Virginia House of Delegates when he was in that flunky profession, but he decided to relax with Hemingway and Wilde. He also had a pen and note pad in his bed where he wrote out his reading schedule for the week. There would be no Bible, no theology, no philosophy, or political theory — only literature, such as Shakespeare, Jane Austen, John Donne, William Faulkner, Mark Twain, Charles Dickens, and of course his favorites, Oscar Wilde and Ernest Hemingway.

He would decompress this week with story, humor, and superior language, and by so doing would serve two simultaneous purposes: pleasure and good mental health for himself, and a very keen competitive edge in his vocation. The job of a priest requires a high degree of emotional intelligence for purposes of counseling and offering spiritual advice, often in a life-coaching fashion. When preaching sermons, one's literary skills are indispensable. Approaching the age of 41, Brandon had finally recognized and developed both his emotional intelligence and literary brilliance. In seminary he had written his first poetry and had positively fallen in love with the world of ideas, and of the written and spoken words which communicated them.

Yes, Brandon had his tonic and his narcotics with him now — his books. Bettina was under strict instructions to let him sleep late in the morning.

He would do nothing the entire week but rest, read, and exercise. It was fortunate for him that he had family money, for Brandon had to know that he was very ill-equipped for a humdrum everyday life. He would have been shocked, had he really understood how few of his fellow clergymen and clergywomen had the luxury of taking off weeks at a time to decompress and read for their mental health.

In fact, he never really understood how shockingly, psychologically incapable he was of getting up early in the morning, commuting in heavy traffic to a 10-hour job, coming home to a very rushed dinner with the wife and to bed early, only to do the same thing again the next day, having the weekend in mind as his only solace. Throw in a couple of children and you would have a catastrophic meltdown in Michael Brandon. How this privileged young priest could connect with and relate to parishioners who lived exactly these kinds of lives is almost beyond explanation — yet he did.

* * *

The Hunter was as competent an assassin as you will find for hire. He did have one shortcoming which had stood in the way of his advancement; he would only kill people who needed killing. Collateral damage was unacceptable to him. Harming an innocent person just to throw off suspicion was out of bounds as well. He had turned down a lucrative job in Las Vegas because a poor hotel maid and her son would have had to die in order to kill the high-profile target. He recalled to this day how the telephone conversation had gone:

"I thought you were a professional, Mr. Jones."

"A professional, not a scum bag. Apparently, *you* are a scumbag. And since you were stupid enough to let me know who you are, I will make it my business to check Las Vegas news daily. If any hotel personnel should happen to be injured or killed during the time frame you just described, I will kill you! Do you understand? Nothing you do will be able to stop me from killing you."

The man on the other end of the call gulped nervously, cleared his throat, and complied with, "Understood."

The Hunter was a man who was old enough to know how the world really works, and young enough to do the dirty work of survival himself. For he only had three things on which he could rely — his skills, his reputation, and his anonymity. In time, the skills would fade. The more jobs he did, the more he would jeopardize that precious anonymity and perhaps his reputation, so the trick was to literally make out like a bandit with a couple of more jobs. All this had been in his mind since the killing of the Real Estate Developer at the hotel. And with the recent back and forth going on concerning his next hit, he determined to finish his work for his current hirers and retire early. He had been advanced the money for three kills, with a possible fourth for extra loot, and decided that very day he would do the final two and get out.

Friday, April 24

Bettina left her hibernating husband-to-be in their condo, knowing full well that he would have nothing of value to add to dinner and wedding plans at the Brandon estate that evening. As she and Nora pulled up the driveway, Congressman and Mrs. Brandon were walking out on the lawn with their wine glasses in hand, offering some much-appreciated libations to the two young ladies.

"I'm damn proud of my boy, and yet I never tell him," sighed a slightly drunken Brandon Senior at the dinner table. "He's a lucky sailor to be marrying you, Miss Vasquez. I can't say it plain enough."

"Joe, you're embarrassing her," an annoyed Mrs. Brandon chimed in.

"Thank you," laughed Bettina, knowing exactly what he meant to convey.

"She's lucky too, Mr. and Mrs. Brandon," said Nora. "He's such a dreamboat."

Bettina poked Nora's knee under the table to stop her from carrying on about Michael.

"Got you charmed as well, I see, Nora," Brandon Senior said. "Well, that's par for the course. That kid has been mediocre at most things he's done, mostly because he won't put in the time and effort. But when it comes to matters romantic, let's just say it's a good thing he never got elected to a high office as a single man. John F. Kennedy times three!"

Red with embarrassment, Bettina and Patricia hurried to change the subject. Nora sat back in her chair, drank some wine, and gave a naughty smile.

"Anyway, I'm proud of Michael redeeming his education and for seeing this new career change through," the Congressman boasted, drunker by the minute. "He'll do wonders with that Cathedral job. And how about that stemwinder of a sermon last Sunday? He is a natural orator; there you go! Nothing mediocre about his public speaking!"

"I have always been proud of our son, and no mother was ever prouder of her son than was I on Sunday," said Patricia. "How about you girls?"

Bettina reminded the group that no woman alive was prouder of her man than she was. She had spotted Brandon's gifts when they first met and marveled to herself that Michael was maturing emotionally. After all, he would rather stay home reading books than be at the fawning fan club meeting that was this gathering at his parents' home. Nora just continued smiling quietly.

Brandon's fan club included one more member that night: Julie Grimes. For the foreseeable future, the priest had to keep the detective close. His motives for seeing her were more than understandable in his mind, but one aspect of this lurid relationship began to eat away at him; he was enjoying it. Brandon had the love of his life, the redemption of career and spirituality, and an earnestness toward God and other human beings that he'd never thought he would possess.

He loved his life, but he liked this other thing too. No one except his father knew what he was doing, so his secret was safe. But now, for his own peace of mind, he had to apply boundaries with Julie Grimes. He figured that if they did not actually have sexual intercourse, and all physical activity ceased after he and Bettina were married, then, yes, he could maintain friendly contact with Grimes for as long as it took. Whatever the conflict, he endeavored to it until he and his family were in the clear concerning these homicide investigations.

Shortly after Bettina and Nora left for dinner at his parents' house, Brandon called Julie. She had the night off and wanted to see him.

"I can't get out this evening," Brandon said. "Tomorrow afternoon?"

"Why don't you come to my place for an early dinner?" replied the very hopeful detective. "Promise to have you home at a decent hour."

Brandon's gut reaction was to make an excuse for not accepting the offer, but he acquiesced within seconds. "Sure, that sounds lovely. Thanks!"

"Four in the afternoon then. I'll email you the address."

"Goodnight then."

"Goodnight, handsome!"

Saturday, April 25

Brandon awoke violently around 8 a.m. the next morning. Sweating and breathing heavily, he looked over at Bettina. To his relief, she was sleeping soundly. To his horror, he was certain he had yelled out the name of Julie Grimes in his sleep. As he plopped back down on his pillow, Bettina began to wake. Brandon gently grabbed her and hugged her back to sleep for a few more minutes. He did not dare go back to sleep himself. Shortly thereafter, he woke her.

"You know I love you more than anyone or anything, Bettina," said a sweet and sorrowful Brandon.

"Considering the fact that we're getting married next month, I approve!" a playful Bettina replied.

Always attentive to Michael's needs, she grabbed her robe as if to go make him breakfast.

"Not so fast, you tasty dish," said an aroused Brandon.

"Shhhh, you'll wake up Nora," Bettina laughed.

"She'll live. Anyway, it's our home. Come here."

Brandon made love to his wife, his mind being mostly on her, but partly on the dream he had about Julie Grimes.

"Mmmm, I sure hope you're this attentive when we're old and gray," purred Miss Vasquez.

"I'm already gray, a little," Michael said. "Anyway, you have nothing to worry about. I belong to you — lock, stock, and barrel. You are the most beautiful, the most dangerously sexy woman there is."

"Is that you or your stomach talking?"

Michael laughed. "I could use a bite," he quipped.

Brandon made coffee while Bettina cooked, and he drank it feverishly as he stared out the window.

"Nora, coffee's on," Michael said to his almost sister-in-law. The three drank coffee, ate Bettina's exceptional omelets, and the two ladies teased Brandon mercilessly about how his parents were trying to outperform each other the previous night in their praise of him.

"Now you know why I refused to go," Michael said.

"No, no, you're just lazy," said Bettina with Nora laughing and nodding in agreement.

"I've got to go to a parishioner's house at 4 p.m. today. Counseling! I should be home by 9:30 or so. Okay?"

"Of course, honey," Bettina said as she made some more food. "It's your job. Nora and I are going to my tenant's house for dinner and drinks, then it's home for girls' night on the TV."

"Let me guess," Michael said. "Cuban soap operas on Telemundo?"

"Hey!" Nora and Bettina each threw a slipper at Brandon simultaneously. Then they had a long laugh together.

Modern psychology is instructive here. The human mind is not a single, all-cooperating unit. Rather, it is a series of compartments that are often at war with each other. Try not to pass too quick a judgment on our friendly neighborhood priest. His love for Bettina is real, as is his intention to be a loyal and faithful husband to her. Of course, he did not like the evasion. Bettina was so endearingly trusting, and Brandon literally could not live with himself if he knowingly betrayed that. Hence, the justification schemes he played back and forth with himself. The only thing that kept him functional and composed was that he was doing this for the good of those he loved most, which was true. But at the same time, he could not shake the feeling that he was indeed up to his old tricks.

One thing was certain, though — he would have to go to Grimes's house thoroughly exhausted sexually. Then, nothing could happen. To this end, he whisked Bettina back to the bedroom twice more before they departed to their respective dinner engagements.

Brandon pulled up to Detective Grimes's home at the end of a cul-de-sac. It was the perfect police officer's house, with some woods and a creek behind it, and tall pine trees on either side, obstructing any nuisance neighbor watching from the houses next to hers. Spotlights and flood lights surrounded the structure, and her unmarked squad car SUV was in the driveway for all to see. Grimes's neighborhood was both secluded and proximate to commercial areas, health care facilities, and schools.

Brandon was looking forward to meeting her daughter, Tina, but was met at the front door by Julie, who gleefully informed him that Tina was with her father for the weekend.

"Welcome to casa del Julie," she said.

"Thank you again," said Brandon, his radar flapping around inside the devious sector of his mind. She had told him over the phone that little Tina would be there. Now, he was preoccupied by what she might have in store for him tonight.

"I have something to show you," said the detective as she grabbed Michael by the arm and led him to a locked closet near the laundry room.

"Wow," said Brandon, as he eyed the impressive collection of hand-guns in the closet. "Beautiful and a gun lover? Your ex is a moron!"

"You're sweet, but I threw him out!"

"This one's a nice replica, the Colt Peacemaker," Michael said.

"Not a replica, darling. The real thing, made in 1890."

"You're kidding," a startled Brandon said. "Here, wipe it down and put it away. Don't bring that one to the range... I would feel guilty even cocking that gun."

"Not to worry," Grimes said. "I have enough range pistols, as I'm certain you do as well."

"Of course!"

As they finished dinner, Brandon helped Grimes clean up and braced himself for the temptation that was certain to be upon him when, to both his relief and astonishment, Julie informed him that there had been some office chatter about the murder cases being temporarily sidelined. That the Virginia State Police may want to repossess the cases and work them themselves. Being ever the detective, Grimes peppered Brandon with questions about the two of them possibly being seen together, plus her acknowledgement that her initial interview of him at the church was noticeably long.

Julie was getting too policelike in her questions for Brandon's comfort, but he played it off like a pro.

"Relax, Julie, my dad is good friends with the Superintendent of the State Police. He helped him along during his career. I'm sure he could garner a favor, like including Julie in the investigation to bolster her credentials. Meanwhile, I will make an inquiry of my own into the possibility of us having been seen."

"You're a very easy person to like, Michael," said Julie.

Of course, this wasn't quite true. Congressman Brandon's influence was still a reality, but he had never even met the current Virginia State Police Chief. Brandon poured them both another glass of Pinot Noir and walked Julie over to the living room sofa. They drank and talked with each other intensely for about an hour when a text came over Brandon's phone.

He had asked Bettina to page him so he could leave from his parishioner call while the evening was still early. "I have to take this call outside."

After the pretend phone call, Michael returned to the living room and said, "I have to go. My apologies! But thank you for dinner, and for a lovely evening. The Rector asked me to counsel with a parishioner. I'm going to do it on my ride home."

"Oh, don't apologize," Julie said. "I know how seriously you take your job, just like me."

"On that note, I will consult my father and see if we can kill off any nasty office politics on your behalf," said Brandon as he walked to his car.

As he drove off, Julie, who had just enough wine to clear her head, walked into her home office and sat down to retrace the steps of her investigation. It would be a long night for her, but richly rewarding!

The detective leaned back in her chair and allowed her mind to travel back to the Monday morning of her first call to the church where

Brandon and the rest of the staff found the body of Harry Penrose in the parish sanctuary. CSI had confirmed what she had speculated from the beginning. Penrose had been seated in the pew toward the right corner's back window the previous night. Fibers matching his raincoat were in the seat, and mud from his shoes on the floor by the kneelers were discovered directly below where he was sitting. Two very crude shoe prints were found by virtue of the mud from the rain. They suggested he got up to peer towards the window, due to the fact they were pointed in that direction. When the bullet hit him in the forehead, he either dropped to his knees or fell directly on his side and onto his back. This was no idle speculation, for the autopsy confirmed that Penrose was killed instantly by the single shot and the distance had to be within 25 feet.

But since there was no powder residue on the window and no small hole in the glass, Grimes had determined that the killer had been outside and fired through a slightly opened window. The trajectory of the bullet was slightly upward. No prints were found on the outside windowsill, and the heavy rain would have washed anything away.

Wait a minute, thought Grimes.

"Trajectory!" she announced.

She called her boss.

"Chief, it's Grimes. When State Police briefed us on the hotel killing, what was the angle of the rifle bullet?"

"Can't this wait, Julie?" said the Deputy Chief. "It's Saturday night. Are you closing in on someone now?"

"Don't know yet," she said. "Can I get the report from you? I think their investigators may have missed something."

"Meet me tomorrow, my office, at 5 p.m.," the Deputy Chief replied.

"Will do."

Grimes was getting places now. Places where she wanted to go. It had been her intention all along to not only solve the crime at the church, but also to discover linkage between that killing and the one in February at the hotel. Neither she nor anyone else in the Alexandria PD could believe that there were no leads. The only thing that the Virginia State Police investigators could say for sure was that the shot came from across the street at over 200 yards.

Grimes had also been wise to Brandon's scheming. Her ex-husband played her the fool, despite her intelligence and police training, simply because her emotions got the better of her. She knew he had been cheating. She knew where he was doing it and with whom. Grimes allowed it to continue as long as her love for him and her dignity could tolerate it. And now, she had fallen for Brandon, a man with a fiancée and a clerical collar.

Perhaps she thought Michael a safe encounter, a spiritual authority figure; someone who had his act together and on whom she might lean for strength. *The times we were together were real*, she thought. She knew the chemistry was mutual, but she also immediately spotted his treachery. Her emotions were not so raw that she failed to notice his interest in her was primarily due to the murder case. This time, she resolved to be a cop first and a schoolgirl with a crush second. That night at Mt. Vernon, Julie had given Brandon false information about her department talking with the FBI, partly to prove to Brandon she could be useful to him, but mostly to see how he would react.

There you have it. Brandon, the priest, was feeling guilty for deceiving an honest cop and lovely woman, and Grimes was feeling guilty for deceiving the priest for whom she had tender feelings. Both people certainly had dignified motives. Grimes, whose police instincts led her to closely watch Brandon; and Michael, who felt the need to protect his family. But Julie could not focus on the investigation without thinking about Brandon romantically. She decided that the only way to combat that was to rule him out entirely as a person of interest.

* * *

Meanwhile, Brandon contemplated the fact that someone had intentionally killed that "rat bastard Robert Martin" at the Hilton Hotel. The same Robert Martin who had engineered his defeat for reelection to the legislature. In 2005, Brandon was elected to serve a 2-year term in the Virginia House of Delegates. His father had strongly advised him not to run, but when the younger Brandon insisted, the Congressman counseled him every step of the way — the right moves to make, who to trust, and who not to trust.

"Northern Virginia Real Estate Developers are an unprincipled lot, Junior," the elder Brandon said. "With few exceptions, do not trust them, and whatever you do, don't let any of them know what you are thinking, ever."

The senior Brandon began to wax philosophical, telling his son that nothing mattered to these people — not historical preservation, not the environment and beautiful landscape, not pleasant and livable neighborhoods. Not even the property values of the region's lush suburban enclaves. No, they were naked in their greed for what is termed in the developer community as the highest and best use of the land. This is, of course, euphemistic lingo for the cheapest and easiest profits.

The younger Brandon failed to heed this sound parental advice when Martin's Open Door Development Group made public their plans to build a mixed-use project of office and retail, and residential condominiums just north of the town of Middleburg, the capital of Virginia Piedmont Hunt Country. The Congressman and Mrs. Brandon owned a farm just west of Middleburg, in addition to three other rural tracts of land in the Piedmont counties. These properties were all in rural jurisdictions with no intention of allowing any dense urban development.

But Middleburg was in Loudoun County, the same county of the infamous Tuscarora deal. Intense growth had overtaken the county by the 1990s, and Brandon feared for the Middleburg area. He and his friends went to Polo matches and wineries there. He knew many of the shop and restaurant owners in the town. He hunted and fished in Western Loudoun County, and although his district was in Alexandria, he gathered in full force all of the Piedmont Delegates from the legislature. They put intense pressure on the County Board of Supervisors, who voted not to approve Martin's project. Martin swore revenge and garnered much money from the builders in the area and during the next election cycle managed to knock off one of the politicians who had harmed his interests.

Delegate Michael Brandon lost his bid for reelection by just 246 votes out of more than 15,000 cast. But a loss is a loss, and Brandon was too personally affronted to mount a comeback the next time around. To add insult to injury, he had to acknowledge to himself that he was wrong, and his father was right. It did not take him long to lick his wounds and then to determine that business and politics were beneath him. He was disgusted with the ways of the world and the people who ran it. From a practical standpoint, Brandon as a freshman legislator should not have stuck his neck out so publicly on a deal that was miles from his constituency.

There were only two real pleasures he treasured from his 2007 losing campaign: first, his burgeoning relationship with Bettina Vasquez, and second, a phone conversation he had with a threatening caller, who clearly was a representative of Open Door Development.

"I urge you, Mr. Brandon, not to continue speaking against the Middleburg Project if you value your career," the caller said.

"Are you threatening me, you cocksucker?" asked an emboldened and agitated Brandon. "Tell your piece of shit boss to have a heart attack. His project is toast."

This, of, course, was pre-seminary language coming from Brandon.

But the same colorful metaphors circled through his mind on the day Robert Martin was killed.

"Priest or not, I hope that clown rots in hell," Brandon said to Bettina on that homicidal day.

Bettina, assuming that Michael was just being dramatic and was spiritually incapable of that kind of hatred, replied with, "I thought you liberal Episcopalians didn't believe in hell, like us Catholics."

Brandon glared at her, affectionately and philosophically. "I'm re-thinking my position on that. The Robert Martins of the world need somewhere to go after they die."

He entertained the same thoughts when he and the staff at Christ Church found the body of Harry Penrose.

Sunday, April 26

This was a day of no particular significance for Michael Brandon. He had agreed to preside over the liturgy and sacraments at the 5 p.m. service at Christ Church, with the Rector delivering the sermon.

In typical leisurely fashion, he slept late and read his books until such time as he had to get ready for the church service. Bettina took Nora to the airport that morning to return to Miami. Before he left the condo, she reminded him that they would be having a late dinner and watch a French movie she had been wanting to see, *Summer at La Goulette.*

"Subtitles, seriously?" he said to her.

Bettina shot him a classic glare, which clarified that he will watch the movie with her and like it! Brandon knew the look well and was wise enough to appear happy when he said, "Yes, dear."

He gave her a rather long kiss goodbye, and she hugged him for at least two minutes.

"What did I do to deserve that?" Michael said.

"Just love you, that's all," she said.

"Aren't I the lucky one?" winked Brandon.

"Remember it well," said Bettina.

On the other hand, Detective Grimes was having quite the significant day. And little did she know just how her meeting with the Deputy Chief would make its contribution to that significance.

"The State Police bigwigs don't want the Martin case anymore," the Chief said. "They say they're exhausted and it's making them look bad to the Governor's Office. And if there is any linkage to the Penrose case, they sure as hell don't want to take the fall if one or both go unsolved."

"What's that to us, Chief?" asked Grimes. "Typical cover-your-ass bullshit?"

"It means I'm giving you lead on both cases. You're in charge. You report directly to me, and CSI and the other squad detectives work for you. Can you handle it?"

"Yes, sir, I absolutely can," said Grimes with a guileless enthusiasm.

"I'll keep all the higher-ups at bay," the Chief said. "You just do your job, and no mistakes, Julie!"

"Thanks, Chief. I'll make you glad you did this for me."

"Well, get to work, Grimes, and I'll need a report every 48 hours."

"Yes, Chief."

As her boss departed the station, Julie grabbed a coffee in the break room where she was alone. She yawned and stretched and began sipping the coffee that came out of an old Keurig machine.

"This is good coffee," Grimes said to herself. It was good coffee that evening, for it came as a night cap on top of the most extreme professional satisfaction which she knew existed but had always felt out of her reach.

A half hour meeting with the Deputy Chief had elevated the 36-year-old detective beyond what she could hope for at this stage in her career. Yes, it was simply the best cup of coffee she had ever tasted. On her way out, she saw two of the junior detectives in her squad, both men, who would be reporting to her now.

One cannot blame Julie for taking delight in saying, "My office, guys. Tomorrow at 3 p.m."

Grimes did not care that she was the only woman in the Division, or that she was the first woman to lead a murder investigation in the history of the department. She didn't care about politics at all; she just wanted to be an exceptional police officer. Her daughter was due back home from her father's at 8 p.m., and it was 5:45 p.m. now.

"I think I deserve a little celebration — just me, myself, and I," Julie said.

Just off King Street, a block from the Potomac River, was Neptune's, the best seafood restaurant on the Virginia side. They had an old-fashioned bar with the mahogany woodwork, cushioned bar stools, and dark, romantic lighting. A few drinks and an entrée were considerably more expensive than the same thing at her favorite police-frequented pub. But she knew she deserved the treat, and before she hit the bar stool, she ordered her first of three Cosmopolitans. Halfway through the second drink, she glanced around the bar and at the lobby, secretly hoping Brandon might walk through the front door at any minute. He had told her some weeks prior that he and Bettina ate there sometimes.

But why would I want to bump into her? Julie thought. *No, Julie, don't be like that. She seems nice enough.* Grimes remembered seeing the soon-to-be Mrs. Michael Brandon at his farewell sermon at Christ Church. Julie had stayed hidden from Brandon and everyone else.

"She's gorgeous...I hate her!" Grimes remembered saying to herself in jest.

Grimes was a woman with confidence in herself; her retired military father had made sure of it growing up. But she never fully comprehended how attractive she was. Most men were too intimidated to approach her, and when she received compliments and attention, she would wonder what all the fuss was about. And although she was floored by the intensity of her moments with Brandon, she still could not half believe that this smooth-talking Romeo thought her beautiful.

She was wrong. In reality, Julie Grimes would be considered drop-dead gorgeous wherever she went, even in her detective street clothes. When she dolled up, however, she could have any man she wanted. Julie stood about 5'5" and had curves that an oversized trench coat couldn't hide. She wore glasses on her very pretty but strong, determined face. Dark blonde hair with green eyes, she was like that sexy librarian you always checked out a book from...one you never had any intention of reading.

When Brandon called her the sexiest cop he'd ever seen, it was in a passionate moment, but he meant what he said. Julie did not have to be single or lonely. She had proven her steadiness as a cop and a mother. After tonight, her professional identity would take on new life. But would she be able to remain focused and steer clear of a still very powerful temptation?

"Why don't we elope?" an exasperated Brandon said to Bettina after their movie ended. "To the Florida Keys, say hello to your folks in Miami, and call it a day? All of this planning, and your mom can't travel yet due to the surgery."

"Stop, mi amor," Bettina said softly. "Your mom has already paid for the winery."

"I know, I know. In Charlottesville. That's a two-hour drive, it's hot, and—"

"—And we're going to love it, Michael," interrupted a perturbed Bettina. "We're going to Miami in the fall, sweetie."

"I'm the man here. It's my duty to bitch and moan about duties."

"Duty?" Bettina repeated.

"I didn't say that," a remorseful Brandon said with his arms around his lady. "You know, I don't think I ever told you how grateful I am to you, Bettina."

"For what, honey?" she asked.

"Not only for agreeing to marry me, but for being my girl in the first place. Ours is the most important relationship I have ever had, or ever will."

"I've known that since the beginning; every time you look at me, I know," Bettina said. "But it's lovely to hear you say it. I thank God for you."

Brandon, hugging her, couldn't help but joke, "Boy, you're easy to please. Some sweet words and a French movie. That's all it takes?"

They both laughed and cuddled, and they slept in very late that next morning.

CHAPTER 7

Nearly One Month Later
Sunday, May 22

Brandon woke that morning to the smell of bacon and very expensive coffee.

"It's 10 a.m., you lazy American," joked Bettina as she jumped into bed and into Michael's arms.

"What did I do to deserve all this?" inquired a very pleased Brandon.

"Nora called me early this morning. When she got home, she didn't like the way Mom looked and took her to her doctor. They are running more tests on her this afternoon. They keep assuring us it's not cancer, but I'm too worried to stay up here. Would you mind terribly if I go to Florida and help Nora and Dad for a while?"

"How long?" Michael asked, surprised.

"Four to six weeks, I'm thinking."

"Of course, baby, and that settles what we talked about last night," Michael said. "We will postpone the wedding and the honeymoon. I'll square it with Mom today."

Bettina began to cry as she hugged onto Michael. She had secretly been dreading the conflict between her mother's needs and her marrying the man of her dreams. In a strange but quite wonderful irony, Bettina felt she was with a man who could have anyone he wished to be his wife.

She was fortunate beyond measure to be that woman. And that is exactly how Brandon felt about being with Bettina. They had, during all their time together, both been endearingly insecure.

As her palms began to sweat and her body began to shake, Bettina was comforted and reassured by Michael's passion and sensitivity. As he held her hands tightly, he gazed into her eyes and gave her his unqualified blessing to go to Miami indefinitely — with one caveat.

"I have the marriage license in that desk drawer," Michael said. "And Judge Callahan down at the courthouse is one of Pop's best friends. I'll bet he could marry us this week. Will you do that for me? For us?"

Brandon was smothered with kisses as Bettina said, "Yes, yes, yes! Oh, Michael, you are too good to be true. But I want to get down to Mom as soon as possible."

"I'm sure I can have it arranged by Tuesday at the latest."

The couple then cuddled in bed and stared at each other without speaking, and let their breakfast get cold.

* * *

Only two days had passed since Brandon learned how the City of Alexandria Police Department had closed in on Unit 906 of the Southern Towers Condominium as the likely place of the shot which killed real estate developer Robert Martin.

Julie Grimes had informed him that police would be questioning all of the owners or tenants in the building. The 9th floor was the top floor of the property and only four units faced the hotel. Police ruled out the roof due to the fact there was scaffolding and tar for renovations which had been going on since the previous November.

It would have been impossible for a gunman to stand, crouch, or lie down and see over the construction to make the shot, according to investigators. After speaking with the residents of the four units, they discovered the ones at 906, a young married couple, were recent purchasers. They informed Detective Grimes that the unit had been vacant for some time before. Grimes immediately ordered her junior detectives to obtain a search warrant for CSI to sweep the place. The new owners were less than thrilled, but when the warrant arrived, they would comply.

Brandon was grateful for the information and was more than a little shaken up. He knew that his father had owned units in Southern Towers, and his father added to that concern when he told Michael that he had owned and sold unit 906. The timing of the whole thing left something to be desired as well. Brandon had served his last Sunday one week ago at Christ Church, and he and Bettina were readying themselves for their upcoming nuptials.

Although Grimes assured him that there was nothing she knew of that could involve him (she questioned him over the phone in great detail), Michael knew he had to carry this information in his head during his impending courthouse wedding, but although he longed to share his burdens with her, Bettina needed an untroubled departure to Florida and her family. So, he kept it to himself.

Tuning out unpleasantness came easier to Brandon than to most people. He had always possessed a secretive and deceptive side, which contributed to the demise of his prior marriage. To be frank, this deceptive side harmed him in other relationships as well, both romantic and professional. Despite, however, his recent reversion to his old ways, he resolved to begin his second marriage the right way, in every way possible. Upon her return, he would tell Bettina all about his and his family's concerns.

As for his liaisons with Grimes, that was another story. He would be content never to tell his bride about that, owing mostly to his eerie ability to compartmentalize. Just as he reconciled his calling as a priest with lying to numerous people closest to him, he viewed his infidelity as a practical necessity for himself and those he loved. In these endeavors, he would act upon demand and then wash his hands — just like that. Did he really have a choice?

Bettina Vasquez was a woman who prized honesty and trust in a relationship above all else. When she fell intensely and perfectly in love (which she had with Brandon), she was someone you didn't ever have to worry about. She stayed in love and would do anything for the man who gave her his heart. You might say that Bettina made an ideal clergyman's wife, and you would be right. None of this was lost on Michael, who was everyday fully and frightfully aware that he could never replace this jewel of a lady, should he ever do something unfortunate. No, this impending marriage was Brandon's to take and make wonderful and happy; or to utterly ruin.

It would appear that a poor, honest cop was getting the break she so richly deserved but did not welcome. Grimes and her team had finally discovered what Michael had already found out; that the Brandon family trust had been the true owner of Unit 906 during the time of the Martin killing.

It took police forensic accountants over 50 separate steps to untie the knots put in place by the Congressman and his attorneys. The Light Horse Investment Corporation was the owner named on all of the public records, including the sale of the unit a month after the Martin killing. After thorough computerized analysis, one document was found with Congressman Brandon's signature, and two more were found listing the Brandon Family Trust. When all the forensics were done, Grimes could prove that the Trust was the owner and the Light Horse company the dummy corporation.

She also would not abandon her hunch that the Martin and Penrose killings were somehow linked. But the trail appeared to have gone cold on all fronts...with one exception.

"I don't know how I could have missed this," said Grimes to one of her junior detectives.

"Missed what?" said the puzzled detective. "We have a meeting with the Deputy Chief tomorrow. He's gonna cream us if we don't bring something."

"We do have something," said Grimes. "In fact, I'll do this one alone. Reverend Brandon owes me a visit, and I need to ask him just one question. I'll call you tomorrow morning so we can prepare for the meeting."

"Roger that," chimed in Grimes's teammate.

Grimes left a voice message for Brandon to call her. The question that had entered her mind, literally 15 minutes before, now seemed so elementary that she was reddening with embarrassment, thankfully alone in her office.

"Why," Grimes said to herself, "would Brandon just jump in my car and whisk me away like that? A man was killed in his church, Harry Penrose. Both he and his father knew the man. And now the Brandon family owns the condo where the murder took place. And Brandon is good with guns..."

Suddenly, Grimes became sick in the stomach. Had she overlooked the obvious? Granted, her new assumptions were logical, but they amounted only to limited circumstantial evidence at best.

"All those sweet words...those hugs and kisses, the gardens at Mt. Vernon!"

Grimes knew she had been played a little but chalked it up to Brandon being secretive about his family. She also knew they had a genuine mutual attraction. But now, she was aware that she may have found the killer — or someone protecting the killer.

Just then, her phone rang. It was Brandon's number.

"Get ahold of yourself, Julie! Breathe."

She could not satisfactorily compose herself, so she let the call go to voicemail.

When Grimes entered the ladies' room, she was sweating beads. She splashed her face with cold water, and as she looked into the mirror, her thoughts and emotions became unusually clear. She was in love with Michael Brandon and had very obviously suppressed her analytical investigative mind when it came to him. Any rookie detective would have pressed Brandon much further due to his being present in the place where a murder had been committed. But he was her golden boy, a priest. He carried himself with such regal and honorable demeanor.

She had been smitten from the beginning but now understood just how much she had idolized, perhaps even mythologized, this man. He was a knight on a tall, white horse, and his lips had touched hers with intensity and feeling. Now, she had to call him back for another meeting, and this white knight could be an assassin, or something just as bad.

Grimes had no earthly idea what she would tell the Deputy Chief tomorrow, but in her mind, Brandon was now at the top of the suspect list. And it was killing her inside.

CHAPTER 8

Tuesday, May 24

The elegance of the Brandon estate, four acres on a hill with magnolia trees and every color of azalea under the sun, was overpowered by the radiance of the lovely couple as Mrs. Patricia Brandon sat them down on the patio for drinks and an early dinner.

Bettina, wearing a simple French blue dress and black stilettos, was a portrait painter's dream. Her beauty, poise, and overwhelming sweetness that afternoon was extreme and almost unbalanced her new husband, the Judge, the Sheriff's deputies, and even Patricia. The ceremony was quick and simple, and Michael Brandon now had his wife. He actually had her. He would grow old with this exceptional woman.

"Your father is still under the weather," said a sorrowful Mrs. Brandon. "He told me to wish you a happy trip, Bettina."

"Oh, can't I kiss him goodbye?" Bettina asked.

"Better to wait until you get back, darling."

Brandon composed himself in a cool manner but was clearly troubled because his mother had not mentioned to him that the Congressman was ill. When Bettina excused herself to the powder room, Brandon whispered to his mother, "What's going on?"

"You two have had enough to worry about," Michael's mother said. "It's nothing, really. Your father has been fatigued and achy, that's all."

Michael somehow did not entirely believe her, but he knew she would take a bullet for her husband and trusted her emphatically with his well-being. So, he let the matter drop.

After dinner, Michael and Bettina bid Mrs. Brandon goodnight and headed back to their condo. Bettina began to pack for her early morning flight, and Brandon turned on the television until he heard the shower running. This was the signal to what he was fantasizing about all day; he was about to make love to his actual wife, for the first time. They were as good together as they or anyone else could imagine, and they got very little sleep.

Wednesday, May 25

Morning came, and Michael and Bettina grabbed the latter's bags and entered Brandon's SUV. He got to the airport 20 minutes early, intentionally, so they kissed and pawed each other like teenagers before he had to watch her disappear into the mass of people inside the terminal.

Brandon looked at his watch and saw that it was almost 8 a.m. Rector Thompson should be at Christ Church by now, and Michael sped over there to ask the senior Priest to lead them in prayers for his wife's safety and wellbeing, and that of her family.

With Brandon married, secure in his upcoming Cathedral job, and convinced that God's blessing and protection were firmly upon his loved ones and himself, he resolved to rest, read, and exercise for these final two weeks. He would check in on his parents, of course. He read the Bible and the Episcopal liturgy, especially the High Mass. He practiced these readings in front of the mirror so he could simulate a sermon or reading in worship. Though it would be weeks before he was allowed to do a sermon, Brandon was resolved to be ready. For when he was duly prepared, Brandon could literally preach the paint off the walls with one of his stemwinders. He could also be soft, solemn, and poetic, at times reducing many of the congregants to tears.

It is uncommon for someone of Michael's ability and gifts to be unaware of them. But when he was at his best, it required other people to tell him just how good he was. Not that he wasn't plenty confidant, but the Reverend Michael Brandon was as brilliant a preacher as any the Virginia diocese had seen in many a year, something Washington National Cathedral would hopefully soon discover. And it was customarily his wife, Bettina, who would make him understand that he was not just good, but great.

The 5 p.m. briefing with Alexandria Police's Deputy Chief went better for Julie Grimes than expected, even though she had decided not to throw Brandon under the bus.

She merely reported the findings of the forensic team that uncovered the owner of the 906 condo where the shot was fired. Thus, she had to admit that she and her detectives had hit a slump in the investigation. Even so, the Chief knew his lead detective was good and the right fit for the case. Throughout her career, Grimes had exhibited not only a quick mind, but an exceptional emotional intelligence. She knew human beings, and she knew what made them tick.

"I'm not happy about this case and its lack of progress in general, Julie," the Chief said. "But I still think you're the one for the job."

"Thank you, sir, that means a lot coming from you and in context of my extreme frustration," Julie said.

"Don't mention it. To be blunt, do you want new subordinates to replace these guys?"

Grimes looked at her two junior detectives and then back at the Chief.

"No, these are my people. They're doing outstanding work."

This statement was indicative of Grimes's character as a police professional and as a person. She knew that politics would always demand scapegoats when things got rough, and she was not about to let her people suffer. They had been working as diligently as she had on what now seemed like an impossible case. If another person or persons were killed who had any linkage whatsoever to Martin and Penrose, then the FBI might be persuaded to assist the investigation. With their vast resources and capabilities, they would no doubt uncover some vital pieces of evidence. But the last thing Julie wanted was another murder, and she was incurring much anxiety over the fact that despite the lack of hard evidence, she believed the two killings were linked. Grimes's capacity to handle stress would very soon be tested to its limits.

Julie had been able to finally reach Brandon and set up an interview. Michael had allowed her to think he was out of town, as he was supposed to be on his honeymoon. He was due to start his job at the Cathedral on June 15 and asked Grimes if she would agree to a 6 p.m. meet up on Thursday the 16th, to which she agreed. She was tired and needed to rest, anyway. And she did not want her other detectives to sit in with her and Brandon. They might pick up on body language or some other giveaway that she was so favorably disposed toward her now chief suspect.

Julie would go home Tuesday evening and rest and collect her thoughts (and emotions) for most of the next day and Thursday. She would return quite fit for duty on the weekend, and with her mind fresh would be determined to have all evidence possible in her hands when Brandon returned for his June 16 interview. But it would never occur to her to check public records on Brandon and discover that he and Bettina were already married. If confronted with the revelation by Grimes, Brandon would simply admit they were married for expeditious reasons and were in Miami. Thus, Brandon's several alibis and explanations bought him a restful two weeks.

Brandon's concerns about Grimes and the investigation were abating. He had too much faith in his father's intelligence and operational prowess for anything dangerous to happen within the short term. He could lay low very easily until Sunday, June 12, when he was scheduled to return to Alexandria in preparation for his upcoming job. Just then, he had a thought and called his mother.

"Mom, it's me."

"Hello, Michael, dear," answered Patricia Brandon.

"Are there tenants at the Keswick property this month?" Michael asked her.

"As a matter of fact, the place is vacant until September," she replied. "The utilities are on."

"Can I go there tomorrow? I want to clear my head for this new job... get away from the investigations and the news."

"Of course, honey, just come by and get the keys," Patricia said.

"I'll be by tomorrow at around 10 a.m. Thanks, Mom. Love you!"

"Me too, darling. Goodnight."

Keswick, Virginia (pronounced Kezik) is a small hamlet surrounded by rolling country, the Blue Ridge Mountains, and huge estates with vast tracks of land. The Brandon farm was about 30 minutes east of Charlottesville, and a little less than 15 miles from where the Hunter bagged his wild turkey. This oldest of the family's farms was just what Brandon needed to hide from Julie Grimes and to shake off all of the unpleasantness in Alexandria. He could hunt and shoot, fish, workout and run for miles, read and study, and see next to no other human beings until Sunday, June 12th, when he would come home.

He was liable to bump into his eccentric but harmless neighbors, and the general store folks along with the pub and restaurant owners and patrons nearby. And that was all well and good. His parents being at table for a late breakfast when he entered the house, Brandon grabbed the keys and inquired as to his father's health. He got a thumbs up from a man with a mouth full of sausage and eggs, and his mother blew him a kiss.

Michael was on the interstate heading southwest in minutes, unable to obey the speed limits; he was like a man possessed in his resoluteness to escape the city. Miraculously, he was not pulled over by any of the dozens of State Troopers keeping watch in their speed traps.

Brandon wasted no time. Entering the house, he dropped his luggage and headed for the enormous back yard. From his truck, he pulled out two portable steel pistol targets and assembled one of them at 50 feet and the other at 25 feet from a line drawn a yard from the back porch. He took out a Ruger Bull Barrel .22 caliber target pistol and loaded the magazine. He took careful and lengthy aim at the 50-feet target with the first shots, hitting the head of the silhouette every time. With each additionally magazine, he shot faster, hitting the head again every time. With 90 shots fired, and all of them on target, he emptied the last magazine in the chest of the silhouette, with a circular grouping less than three inches in diameter.

The next exploit would be the 25-feet target. Michael fixed a holster to his belt and the inside of his blue jeans. In that holster sat a Sig Sauer P226, a full sized 9mm semi-automatic pistol with custom grips. Brandon began this exercise with a practice of stance and grip and drew the pistol from the holster slowly and smoothly. After 20 or so draws, he fired into the head of the target, hitting it left center. Left center meant that as a right-handed shooter, Brandon had pulled the trigger slightly to the left. The next shot hit the head dead center due to his slightly tighter grip of the gun and smoother trigger squeeze. Next came the double-tap, a fast two shots in the same body area. Brandon drew faster this time and, *bang, bang.*

Two nearly perfect chest shots almost on top of each other. He would repeat the single shots and double taps for the next 45 minutes, using two dozen magazine loads of ammunition, 15 rounds a piece.

Hungry and thirsty, Michael ate the sandwich he picked up from a food mart and gas station and drank about a half-gallon of water. He then walked 300 yards, three football fields in length, and set up his rifle target, a simple bullseye target. Arriving back at the truck, he opened his rifle case and pulled out a beauty. Brandon's 7mm Magnum was his prized hunting possession. No animal on the North American continent was safe from this luxury death instrument at the proper range. Michael and his father and their hunt club friends had killed moose, elk, deer, wild boar, and black bear over the years. And this gun had done more damage than the rest of the gang put together.

"I've created a monster, gentlemen," the Congressman said during a club hunt 20 years ago. The elder Brandon had always marveled that the hunting and shooting sports was the only area of life where Michael had seriously taken his father's advice and direction.

BOOM! The rifle pounded its lethal projectile into the target. Brandon looked through his binoculars and saw a high and right shot just above the bullseye. Smiling, he knew from experience that a simple adjustment on the Leupold Scope would do the trick. He took a dime and set it inside the groove of the top adjuster and turned ever so slightly left. He then repeated the step with the side adjuster, relaxed, and took aim. Brandon steadied his body and hands, breathed and exhaled, and squeezed the trigger.

BOOM! Nearly two feet of flame shot out of the muzzle of the exceptional rifle, and upon examination, a bullseye. A very pleased Brandon would shoot another 20 times, with each shot dead on target.

"Enough for today, pal," said the good Reverend to himself. "I'm damn proud of you."

He wiped his guns down and put them in the house. He would clean them thoroughly after he used them for the final time of the trip. He kept a .45 semi-automatic pistol in his truck and would sometimes carry it on his person.

The one drawback to the Cathedral job, he thought, was that the city of Washington had very strict gun laws. He could carry a concealed handgun into church in Virginia if he wanted to. He generally felt safe enough to just leave it in the vehicle. But Washington is a more dangerous place for robbery, assault, and murder. Since the Cathedral had its own police force and was located in the embassy row part of town, there was a constant presence of police and security. But the young priest who took vows of the utmost integrity would not quite obey the Washington gun laws. He would fix a superb hiding place in his truck for the large caliber pistol and plenty of ammunition.

Brandon made a trip to the local grocery store, where he was greeted in that wonderful country manner. But he did not bump into anyone who appeared to know who he was. He returned with enough food and drink to last him the week, and then showered, ate dinner, and called Bettina. Everything was fine in Miami, and Michael read himself to sleep on the sofa. Brandon would repeat this routine, coupled with running, weightlifting, and kickboxing with a heavy bag he had in one of the out-buildings on the farm.

Owning a farm in the Piedmont hugging the Blue Ridge Mountains was a sublime privilege that was not lost on very many people in Virginia. The nation's short history shows there was much contention for this ground. During the Civil War, both the Union and Confederate armies used these mountains to screen their troop movements, and the towns and rural counties of the Piedmont and Shenandoah Valley changed hands dozens of times during the conflict.

Toward the end of the Revolutionary War, Governor Thomas Jefferson was nearly kidnapped by the British Legion under the command of Lt.

Colonel Banastre Tarleton. Jefferson was tipped off by a local and escaped from Monticello down Carter Mountain to safety.

Brandon, ever the history buff, had the capacity to almost channel these events spiritually. He was perfecting his marksmanship in full view of Carter Mountain. When he walked the property, he would imagine himself as the Virginia patriot riding through the night to warn Jefferson. And although he was so proud of his Virginia and southern heritage, he would always imagine himself in command of a Union Army Calvary regiment. Brandon was a proud southerner but believed the confederacy was a terrible and tragic mistake. And though he admired Generals Robert E. Lee and Stonewall Jackson, his head hurt trying to understand why both of those great men fought for the Confederate side when they were on record opposing slavery and secession.

Oh, well, such is history, Michael thought.

One thing was for certain with him, though. And that was that Virginia Piedmont life should not change; not now, not ever. The ground there was hallowed, historical, exceptional in its natural beauty. Every type of river, creek, stream, and lake imaginable was present. Promontories jutted out into many of the larger bodies of water. The fertile soil gave rise to magnificent rows of corn and other crops, and the fields and woods teamed with an unimaginable array of wildlife.

Upon his final group of rifle shots, Brandon's mind had been on the preservation of the vast region of the state where he was shooting.

"That bastard Martin got what was coming to him," he muttered to himself.

Not a very priestly thing to say or think, but it was businesses like Open Door Development that were the enemy of everything Brandon loved. Sure, he despised Robert Martin for torpedoing his reelection to the legislature, but that paled in comparison to Martin's ruinous contribution to the Northern Virginia commercial culture of mass growth and sprawl. This was a mortal threat to true Virginia living, to history, nature, and hunting. An endless list of things of the utmost value to families like the Brandons were at risk with ever-expanding, high-density development. Brandon, the priest, might be directed to stay politically neutral as much as possible, but Brandon, the man of the gentry and guardian of tradition, would be compelled to fight in this battle.

The political operator seldom ceases to be an operator. Once firm convictions intersect with the smallest taste of power, the victim is infected severely, and usually carries the affliction to the grave. Though Brandon was a committed priest, part of him would never cease to be a soldier in the political battles that inflamed his passions. That being said, he spent much time and focus those two weeks to ready himself to spread God's loving kindness to the world around him. He was deep enough into the theological world to know that as he ministered to others, as he preached and presided over the sacraments and led worship, the chief beneficiary would be himself. Not because of a selfish opportunism, but because doing those things and doing them well would feed and service so many of his own needs.

For two years, he had been a priest intern at a world class church. He had visited the sick and prayed with and for them. He had assisted the Rector in counseling families, healing marriages, and making sure the poor and hungry had food and shelter. Each time he had done these works of mercy, he had stepped outside himself, and the experience had strengthened his own faith and given him a joy and peace inside that was rare in his prior life. Perhaps what he loved most about being a pastor was sharing his knowledge of Christian philosophy and theology, and the Bible, and educating people as to what he deemed the "correct theology." And that is the message of God as Love — loving and desiring relationships with every person, and for people in the world to be reconciled to God and to one another. Every human being was created a child of God. The principal job of the church is to bring this sublime message to people everywhere. Brandon discovered the depths of this truth while taking an introductory course at seminary. He fell in love, wholesale, with the Christian message and with all things theological. It strengthened his faith and gave him purpose. And he vowed never to be otherwise.

The next few days were spent in that reflection, in days of activity and nights of study. Brandon spoke to nobody except for the daily call to Bettina. On the morning of Monday, June 6, however, Rector Thompson from Christ Church was compelled to disturb Brandon's peace.

"Rector, it's Michael," Brandon answered. "I just got your message. Everything okay there?"

"We are all doing quite well, thank you," Rector Thompson said. "I have a parishioner in the waiting room who says he has something to confide, and he oddly has asked for you. The trouble is, I don't know this man."

Michael paused for a second and replied, "I thought our church didn't have a sacrament of confession."

"We don't, officially," Rector Thompson said. "But I have encouraged congregants over the years to do it anyway. It often times brings them tranquility."

"But, Rector—"

"Michael, I know you are resting and preparing for your new assignment, but...I feel a sense of foreboding with this. Will you do me a favor and meet with this gentleman the day after tomorrow here at the church? I will be here as well, but over in the sanctuary. We can discuss the whole matter after he's gone."

Rector Thompson had more to do with Brandon's tutelage and rapid rise in the priesthood than anyone else, save his father. And he was a true friend to Michael. "Of course, I'll come home tomorrow. Anything else you can tell me in preparation?"

"Be careful about promising silence about what he wants to tell you," Rector Thompson said. "If you do that, then I am the only one to whom you can divulge anything. Except you have to tell the police if you think a crime is about to be committed. Those are the rules. Be at the church on Wednesday at 4 p.m."

"Will do," replied the young priest.

CHAPTER 9

Wednesday, June 8

After a week in the country, Michael was certainly refreshed, his mind clear and his sense of direction singular. But he had no idea what to expect from the impending confessional.

"Hello, Michael, and thank you again for doing this," said the Rector.

"No sweat," Brandon replied. "Did you get the guy's name?"

"It's John Gauge, pronounced Gage," the Rector explained. "He maintains he's a member of the church, but I've never seen him before."

"No worries, I've got this," Brandon told his friend with a confidence he had not yet earned. Michael proceeded to engage the stranger.

"Mr. Gauge...Michael Brandon," Michael introduced himself. "Good to meet you."

"The pleasure is mine," said Gauge.

"So, what brings you here today?"

"I come to worship here sometimes," the man said. "I guess you could consider me a kind of backbencher. I never mingle, and I don't remember meeting any of the clergy. But I was quite moved by your sermon some weeks ago."

"Really, which one?" Michael asked.

"The one where you quoted T.S. Eliot and read a poem you wrote, I think," Gauge replied. "Yes, it was that sermon. Very eloquent."

"Thank you, Mister...?"

"John, call me John, please!" the man said.

"All right. Thank you, John."

"I need to get something off my chest now, before I lose my nerve," said the mysterious middle-aged man. "The police are interested in me."

"Interested," said a puzzled Brandon.

"Yes, interested. I own a small security firm and do much of the executive protection myself. I was in the State Department, you see. Diplomatic Security Service. The man who was killed at the Hilton Hotel some months back...you remember?"

"Yes, I remember," Michael said.

"That man, Martin, had hired me to protect him. He had been receiving death threats for several weeks, and I guess it unnerved him. At first, I didn't think a Real Estate Developer was important enough to be a target. But he was very wealthy and active politically. He told me that he had enemies."

"Why are the police looking at you?"

"I'm getting to that," the man went on. "A Detective Julie Grimes called me and ascertained that I was Martin's bodyguard. The police had the bank records, and I had nothing to hide on that score. But I believe that the detectives on the case think I'm involved in the killing."

"How?" Michael asked. "Wasn't he shot from across the street?"

"Yes, but you see, I had gotten to know Martin a little and had done my own background check. A man of low character, to say the least. On the day at the hotel, I overheard Martin tell his aide not to pay the remainder of my bill. Apparently, he was no longer scared or was dissatisfied with my protection methods, or both. That was the last straw for me, so I walked off the job, then and there."

Brandon paused and said, "Sounds like a reasonable thing to do given the circumstances."

"That's not all," insisted Mr. Gauge. "I was almost at my car in the side parking lot when I looked up at the building across the street. I looked at it for no particular reason, but I saw a flash of light. Then I saw it again. When I saw it the third time, I knew what it was. In my profession, a flash of that kind signals a telescopic sight attached to a rifle."

"What did you do, Mr. Gauge?"

"I had a split second to react, then I didn't. That is what I am here to confess. I know myself, and deep down I did not want to get in front of that man, Martin, and a sniper's bullet. I could have perhaps saved his life, but it was more than just self-preservation at work. I think I actually took pleasure in knowing he was about to get clipped."

Brandon tried to look pastoral, but he, like his parishioner, was battling mixed emotions. He knew it was wrong to wish a man murdered, but he just couldn't garner the requisite sympathy in this case.

"I grew up Catholic but never used the confessional before," Gauge said. "How do I get absolved of this, Reverend?"

"The Episcopal Church does not have a confession sacrament," Michael said. "What I can do is pray with you on this matter. We believe that if people ask God to forgive them, and are sincere, then He grants absolution. Why depend on a mere mortal when you can go straight to the top?"

The two men had a laugh, and Michael escorted Mr. Gauge into the sanctuary. They used the kneelers in front of the pew, and Brandon prayed for Gauge. He crossed himself and said, "In the name of the Father, and the Son, and the Holy Spirit. Lord, we pray earnestly that you forgive your servant, John, for any transgressions he may have committed in this matter. Heal and comfort him and fit him spiritually for the rest of this life and the life to come. Amen."

Gauge prayed a few minutes silently and ended with an Amen.

"Thank you, Reverend Brandon, you've been quite the help to me today," John said. "Before I leave, I wanted to ask you something else."

Seeing the Rector and the Secretary enter the sanctuary, Brandon took Mr. Gauge back to the office and closed the door.

"That fellow who was killed at this church not long ago...the Detective I told you about grilled me concerning him, too," John said. "I take it she's questioned you and the other people here?"

Brandon was in a tight-lipped mood and almost dodged the question. But his curiosity got the better of him, and he told Gauge that Grimes had aggressively questioned everyone there.

"Don't trust her too far," John said mysteriously.

"What do you mean?" Brandon asked.

"I read people for a living, and she's got an agenda."

"Don't we all?" Brandon asked.

"Let me guess, she promised that if you were cooperative, especially if you had something to offer to help her solve the case, she would go easy on you. Not investigate you or people you care about too hard?"

"As a matter of fact—"

"I thought as much," John said. "Be careful if your paths cross again. Thank you again, Reverend. You just might see me in church one of these Sundays."

"Goodbye, John," Michael stuttered.

Michael then approached Rector Thompson and told him the entire thing, except the part about Detective Grimes. How could today's visitor have been so insightful about a detective he only briefly spoke with?

Strange, thought Brandon. *I'm sure I have this woman figured out.* The Rector told him he did exactly the right thing toward Mr. Gauge and not to worry about any of it. Hopefully, the man would return and attend services. Brandon could not help thinking that there was more to this whole situation.

Mr. Gauge had been forthcoming, but the man who looked despondent before the prayers in the chapel cheered up awfully quick. And why would it concern him so much how Julie Grimes conducted herself in investigating him? Whether John Gauge would return to the church was a matter out of Brandon's control, but he did have some control over a certain lady detective. And he decided it was time to up the ante.

Wednesday, June 15

The Washington National Cathedral is a magnificent gothic church, which took more than 80 years to build beginning in 1907. It is situated at one of the highest and most enviable location points in the city of Washington, at the intersections of Massachusetts and Wisconsin Avenues.

One can leave the Cathedral grounds and walk to some of the truly magnificent, old-money neighborhoods. It is walking distance from embassy row, Georgetown, and the Naval Observatory and Vice-President's mansion. It is just a few minutes of a drive from the White House, U.S. Capitol, and other top government buildings, not to mention the Kennedy Center for the Performing Arts, the Lincoln and Jefferson Memorials, and countless other monuments. The outside of the Cathedral is reminiscent of the Cathedral of Notre Dame in Paris at the front, and the Cathedral of Canterbury in England from the side.

The church serves two simultaneous functions. It is the house of prayer for all people, the nation's church in the capital city. But its official name is The Cathedral Church of St. Peter and St. Paul.

This is because a cathedral is named after the Latin, *ex cathedra*, which means, "From the Bishop's Chair." Thus, this cathedral is the home of the Washington Diocese of the Episcopal Church and its Bishop. It takes a staggering sum of money to support the church, but the diocese and staff always seem to make it work. Full participation in the fundraising efforts of the Cathedral would be a major part of Brandon's job. His parents had given untold thousands of dollars over the years, a fact that had not escaped the notice of the Dean.

Brandon arrived at his job at 9 a.m. on the 15th of June. To his surprise, the Dean with whom he interviewed was out on family business. So, the Vicar and Human Resources Director welcomed him and had him sign his remaining onboarding forms. The three of them then toured the offices where Brandon got to meet nearly everyone who would be a colleague of his. Then the three went out to lunch, per the Dean's instruction. And they treated Michael.

Afterword, they all went to hear the new organist practice. Brandon was as entranced as when he and Bettina attended the Mozart concert.

"Very nice and impressive group of people," said Michael to the Vicar and Director, back in the offices.

"Yes, they are," noted the Director. "Everyone in town seems to want to work here. We get hundreds of quality resumes for every position."

"The Dean will be back on Friday, late," said the Vicar, who was second in command at the Cathedral. "He wanted me to give you some liturgical and historical readings to do. Now that your paperwork is done and you've met almost everybody, there is no need for you to be here until Sunday morning. Get here about 7 a.m. to prepare for the first service, which starts at 8 a.m. You can spend the next few days studying the material. I will have you do the Gospel reading and assist with Holy Communion."

"Nice," said a well-pleased Brandon. As he said goodbye and walked to his car, Brandon had that feeling of someone who had arrived at a superb place and felt deep down inside he could remain there for a long time.

As he drove over Memorial Bridge to his parents' house, Michael called Bettina from his cell phone.

"It went great, honey! I just have that feeling it's going to work out really well."

"I'm so excited, baby," Bettina said. "I know you're going to be important and happy."

Bettina's parents had come over from Cuba. Both were educated, but they had to work several jobs between them over the years to support Bettina and her sister, Nora. Unlike Bettina, Michael was born with a silver spoon in his mouth. He was looking for spiritual and intellectual enhancement even more than power and position. The Cathedral's beauty and majesty impressed him more than the fact it was a prime place and assignment in the nation's capital.

Bettina would have married Brandon had he been a bartender, but she could not help enjoying the immediate prominence and prestige she herself had worked so hard to get in Washington.

"Tell your folks hi for me," Michael said. "I can't wait to see you, sweetheart."

"Tell your parents the same, Michael. Talk to you tomorrow."

"Don't forget to watch the church service online, honey. I'm doing the Gospel reading...live!"

"You better believe I will," said Mrs. Michael Brandon II.

The elder Mrs. Michael Brandon was clipping some roses in her garden as Michael pulled up in his parents' driveway.

"It went very well," Michael said. "I'm going to love it there, Mom. I get to do the Gospel reading and serve Holy Communion. It will be on TV and the internet."

"I'm so pleased, darling, and so proud of you," Patricia said. "Your father is upstairs resting. He won't be joining us for dinner."

"What's wrong with him?" asked the concerned son.

"Let's go into the house. There is something that I haven't been telling you."

The two went into the parlor, and Brandon made himself a drink. Patricia did not drink often, but that afternoon, she was sporting a large goblet of Merlot. "Daddy has had several mini strokes over the last year."

"What?" Brandon spit a mouthful of gin onto his shirt and down onto the hardwood floor. "What possible reason could you have for not telling me sooner? Is he okay?"

"He has been able to stay functional and live at home, but he has been hiding his discomfort and his worry from you for a long time," Patricia explained. "He didn't want you distracted from graduation and ordination. Not to mention your engagement and marriage to Bettina."

"Mom, what the hell caused all this? He's as healthy as a horse."

"I'm afraid not, Michael."

"But he laughs and drinks like usual, Mom."

"And I am beside myself over that," said a heartbroken and disgusted Patricia. "He isn't supposed to drink at all. It interferes with his medication."

"Mom, what caused all this in the first place?" Michael asked.

"I'm not sure, he hides his stress so well. But I know it's had something to do with finance and business dealings. I've overheard several conversations outside in the garden that I wasn't supposed to overhear. I can't remember any exact words, but his tone of voice alternated between rage and anxiety."

Brandon's mind went immediately to the Dulles Airport deal that Julie Grimes had brought up. With this news concerning his father, he was not about to tell his mother about his upcoming interview with the detective.

"He's on medication that will most likely prevent a major stroke that could kill him or paralyze him completely, but his good health seems a wreck," said a now crying Mrs. Brandon.

Michael teared up, kissed his mother, and made himself a double gin and tonic. "I'm done for the week at the Cathedral, Mom. I just have to study some liturgy for Sunday. Let him rest tonight, and I'll come back and see him tomorrow."

"Come over around lunchtime. That's when he has the most energy. Now, let's go eat dinner before it gets cold."

Patricia Brandon was fortunate in her rare ability to compartmentalize even better than her husband and her son. The Congressman was in bad shape, yet she had Michael, and it was dinnertime in this southern home. Despite the agony of her circumstances, Mrs. Brandon would not allow supper to be ruined.

Thursday, June 16

Brandon walked into the police station at 6 p.m. as agreed.

Detective Grimes offered him a coffee, and the two sat down in her office with the door closed.

"Do they make a habit of leaving you here all alone?" asked the Reverend.

"No, there's always a Sergeant and several officers downstairs at all times," answered a puzzled Grimes. "Now, down to business. I'm this close to putting you at the top of my suspect list."

"You're joking!" cried Michael.

"Look, a man was killed at your church, and a month before, a man was shot from the building your family owns a unit in."

Grimes was almost stoic in her disposition as she demanded an answer. To Brandon, it looked as though she was impervious to his charms at that moment. He had to employ another star quality he possessed — deception. During the subsequent conversation, Brandon would tell Grimes all about his father's family trust, and the ownership of Unit 906 during the shooting of Martin.

"I have additional information to tell you which might help your investigation, but only on one condition," Michael said. "You do not involve the Feds in anyway. No FBI, no IRS, no federal dog catcher."

Brandon leaned in across the desk, and with the most serious and piercing look, told Grimes, "I can, and will, help you with these cases, provided we have this understanding."

Grimes was unmoved during most of the conversation, and Brandon knew he needed to close this out with a little surprise package. He excused himself and went out to his truck and came back with his 7mm Magnum rifle, two .22 Caliber rifles, and his .22 Caliber target pistol.

"Run your ballistics tests on these and see if I'm not telling you the truth," Michael said.

Julie Grimes was now impressed. Brandon could have disposed of these guns, refused to give them up without a court order, or simply denied that he had them.

"I'm going to hate myself for this, but as long as you cooperate and we make some progress, I will keep the Feds out," Julie agreed. "We will meet regularly at times of my choosing."

"Very well."

"I'm not quite finished yet, Michael," said the inquisitive detective. As she paused to gather her next round of sentences and questions together, Brandon braced himself for impossible demands. But to his astonishment and delight, Grimes asked him if he knew a Mr. John Gauge.

Brandon, under a priestly edict of silence on the matter, had his opening, and he played it masterfully: "Yes, Mr. Gauge has come to Christ Church now and again. I don't think he ever joined officially."

"Can you tell me what he was doing there last week? We've had him under surveillance."

"Why have you been watching him, Julie?" Michael asked.

"I'm asking the questions here," Grimes replied. "Why was he there? And you too?"

"Mr. Gauge had a spiritual matter he wished to discuss," Michael said.

"And why not talk to the Rector?"

"The Rector called me and said that the man asked to see me. He told me it was because of a particular sermon I recently preached on the Love of God. He must have been there that Sunday. Anyway, this subject, I'm afraid, is out of bounds for you."

"If there's the slightest chance of future criminal wrongdoing—"

"There isn't," insisted the priest. Grimes was getting more aggressive by the second.

"I still need to know what his connection is to a church where a murder was recently committed," Julie pressed.

"Why don't you tell me right now why he's a person of interest, and maybe there is a way I might be able to confirm or deny?" suggested a sly Brandon.

Grimes took the bait and repeated almost verbatim to Brandon what he heard from John Gauge concerning the first victim, Robert Martin. She added that she and her junior detectives all thought it odd that he would abandon his client minutes before the shot. As if maybe he was in on the crime — a set up. Brandon would only reply that Gauge said nothing beyond what she already knew.

"One last thing," Grimes said. "Do you or your father possess any more guns of these two calibers?"

"No," replied Brandon without a second's hesitation. "You have them all."

Grimes would not put a major lie past Michael, but somehow, she believed him. Moments later, a smug Brandon left the police station with not only a massive concession from the detective, but confirmation that his parishioner had probably been truthful with him. There would be more to John Gauge than prior assumptions would suggest.

And Julie Grimes and her team would continue to surveil the man. They would also keep watchful eyes on Brandon.

CHAPTER 10

Michael could not help thinking that his mother was keeping something to herself. She had deliberately kept him in the dark about his father's true condition. That night, his cell phone rang.

The area code was 804, which covers the central part of Virginia, including its capital, Richmond. At first glance, he ignored it. Then, mainly because the Episcopal Church Diocese of Virginia offices were there, he curiously answered. A very long, 2-second pause ensued, and just before Brandon hung up, a voice said the following: "Tuscarora."

"Come again?" directed Brandon.

"If you care anything at all about your family name and its well-being, talk to your father. He knows the score."

"Who in the hell are you?" Michael asked. "And what do you want?"

Brandon was shaken to his core in an instant, a toxic blend of rage, fear, and desperation.

"Tuscarora, Tuscarora!" said the voice. "Talk to your father."

The man on the other end hung up before Michael could get his next words out.

"That was no call from the bishop's office," Brandon said to himself.

Friday, June 17

The next morning, Brandon had a late breakfast with his parents. He waited for his father to retire upstairs for more rest. The Congressman was more stable in his vitals than the other day, but his overall constitution had been diminished, along with his energy. Now, Brandon confronted his mother with a gentle ferocity.

"Is somebody out to hurt Dad?" he asked.

"What do you mean by hurt?" asked Mrs. Brandon.

"I know someone is trying to get Dad, maybe all of us. Stop pretending, Mom. I know you know something."

Patricia was losing her Southern composure by the second. "Oh, Michael, your father is being blackmailed."

"I figured as much," Michael exhaled. "For how long?"

"Going on 10 months now."

"Who is doing this, and why?"

"No, Michael, your father and I made the decision to keep you out of this."

Brandon was now beyond frustration and made it clear that he was in a position to help and demanded to know everything.

"Sweetheart, you're a priest, and such a sweet and gentle man," Patricia said. "It's my job to protect you."

"Protect me?" Michael snapped. "Dad is sick, and I am the man of this family."

Brandon stood up from the table with a presence more akin to a professional brawler than a clergyman. "Tell me everything."

He apologized to his mother and sat down beside her. For the next hour, Mrs. Brandon told Michael about Robert Martin and Harry Penrose threatening to supply the police and the media with evidence of the bribery in the Tuscarora deal if Congressman Brandon didn't pay them $5 million each.

"But both of these men were rich as Croesus," Michael said.

"Not Penrose," Patricia said. "He squandered his wealth over the last 15 years or so. Your father gave him money when he first got into trouble. I suppose Mr. Penrose saw a permanent cash cow, since he and your father were in on the whole mess."

"Mom, you know about Dad bribing the judge and the zoning people?"

"Of course, darling. Your father always said that my uncanny ability to keep a secret was one of my most attractive qualities."

At this point, Brandon, although he was endeared by the steely loyalty shown between his parents, wondered if there were truly any incorruptible people in this world. Possibly Julie Grimes? His wife, Bettina? Yes, definitely her. The Brandons were as respected and prominent an Episcopalian family as in all of Virginia, and yet they had brought this sorry blackmailing episode upon themselves.

Be that as it may, Michael idolized his parents, and in the face of this new revelation would overlook his father's indiscretion and his mother's complicity. He would overlook it not reluctantly, but with rather a sense of entitlement. Whatever his parents did was for the family's good, as were the morally questionable actions he was contemplating himself. To Brandon, there was one crime only in this whole saga, and that was the extortion of his father to the point of rendering him ill.

"Okay, Mom, so that takes care of Penrose," Michael said. "Why would Martin bother with this, and how did he know about Tuscarora?"

"I took Harry's word that Martin knew. I had no choice in the matter," said the Congressman, startling his wife and son as he hobbled down the steps.

"Pop, go back to bed," Michael said.

"I'm all right, Junior," the Congressman said. "Coffee please, Patricia. If you're making strategy on my behalf, I will damn sure be in on it."

"We're not making strategy, dear," Mrs. Brandon said as she poured her half-infirmed husband some coffee.

"So nice to be kept in the dark about this," said a perturbed Michael.

"It would have done you no good to be involved," chortled the Congressman.

"So that low life Harry Penrose could have taken his $5 million share and convinced you to give him Martin's bum share as well?"

"Looks like it could have happened that way," the Congressman said. "I couldn't possibly have afforded to approach Martin. We despised each other, and if he knew about the whole thing, he could have done a lot worse to me than $5 million."

"So, you don't really believe Martin knew?" Michael asked.

"No," the Senior Brandon replied. "If I had to guess, it was all Penrose. But like I said, I couldn't risk confronting Martin or anyone else. Tuscarora has been the best kept secret in the whole state for years. Penrose was a high roller for most of his career. Then he made some poor investments, and then that homosexual rumor started circling around. I wouldn't be surprised if he had to fork over a king's ransom just to keep everyone quiet. Then, I paid some of his bills to be charitable to an ex-business partner in trouble. But he came back for more."

Michael hugged his mother and with a coffee cup in his left hand, placed his right hand on his father's shoulder.

"It's all good," Michael said. "I have the ear of the detective better than ever. No part of this investigation will lead back to Tuscarora. Do not worry about a thing. We're all going to be okay. And besides, I pray about it every day...God looks out for compassionate souls!"

Brandon swiftly departed to his truck and headed back to Marina Towers. His balcony overlooked the swimming pool, which he stared at as he poured himself a brandy much too early in the day and sat outside.

Marina Towers had a history that Mrs. Bettina Brandon knew about, and a history that she did not. Michael had met his ex-wife there. She was living in a unit on the first floor, and Brandon met her at a Christmas Party in the building. Bettina knew the story; they met and fell in love at the party, and Michael divided his time between his parents' estate and her condo. After two years, they married and got a house together. They divorced a few years later.

Having made few friends during his time at Marina Towers, Brandon reminisced about the six or more other women he had relations with who happened to live in the building. The affairs included a high-powered lobbyist who owned one of the penthouses, a congressional aide from Capitol Hill, a recent college graduate interning for an association, and several ladies who were considerably older than he. Every time he looked at the pool or the hot tub, he fondly recalled the memorable encounters, which had taken place usually at night in violation of the condo rules.

"I still can't believe I got away with all that, and in this building," he said to himself. As far as he could figure, none of the lovely women found out about the others. Perhaps they would have cared if they did, perhaps not. This was the Marina Towers history unknown to Bettina Brandon. *Better keep it that way.*

Getting up from his balcony chair to retrieve a second brandy, Michael noticed his cell phone flickering. It was a voice message with an unknown number: "Don't forget about Tuscarora."

This time, Brandon was cool and collected instead of out of sorts like the previous day. He called Julie Grimes.

"Hello, Reverend, everything okay?" said the courteous and professional-sounding detective.

"Good, Julie. Remember when I told you I would help you with this case any way I could?"

"You know the answer to that," Julie said. "What is it?"

"Trust my hunch on this," Michael said. "Please find out where this cell phone number came from: 804-555-3456. Can you run it now?"

"What's this about?"

"I don't know yet. Please run it and maybe I can find out."

"Okay," Julie said. "Wait a minute."

Five long minutes passed before Detective Grimes came back and said, "It's not a cell phone. It's a private landline belonging to the Republican Party of Virginia, the Vice Chairman's office."

Brandon struggled not put his fist through the wall. He was beyond livid.

"You okay, Michael?" Julie asked after a moment.

"Yes, fine, Julie. Thanks for the favor. My hunch was a dead end. Let me get through Sunday's Cathedral service, and we'll talk about the case some more. I really am sincere in helping with this."

"I know," said a tenderly guarded Grimes.

"Bye, beautiful," said the sincere but scheming priest. Brandon had lied again and got exactly the information he wanted.

The Vice President of Virginia's Republican Party, James Smalls, was an attorney by trade. In college, Brandon had interned for a conservative political organization and worked for Smalls there. The two disliked each other.

Brandon, the privileged golden boy who everyone instantly liked, rubbed Smalls the wrong way at the outset. According to Brandon, Smalls was a typical low-life social climber who licked the boots of his superiors and pissed on all his subordinates. Yes, Smalls was appropriately named. He was a small man, physically and character-wise. He had his political office in Richmond, but he lived in Fairfax, about 15 miles from the Brandons. His law office was just down the street from his house.

About 5 p.m. that evening, a gray truck pulled up in back of the low-rise office building. The offices were condos, and each had a front door. Brandon scoped out Smalls' office and upon determining that he was alone started to unfasten his clerical collar. Then, he stopped and fastened it back.

"This man is going to see a white collar deliver some well-deserved ass-kicking," said Brandon to himself as he walked into the waiting room of the office.

Smalls came out, and upon seeing Brandon, froze in total fright.

"You should learn to disguise your voice, you maggot."

Brandon had not only recognized Smalls' voice in the message, but his mind had also gone completely clear as to the time when that same voice called to threaten his career if he didn't back off on the Middleburg deal with Martin's development company.

Brandon, as he pulled the blinds and locked the front door, informed Smalls that he had no more than two minutes to tell him all about his knowledge and involvement in his father's dealings regarding Tuscarora.

When Smalls made a move for the desk phone, as if to call 911, Brandon lunged speedily forward, grabbed the phone, and smacked James Smalls across the chin. Smalls fell to the floor, and before he could scream, the priest palm-struck him in the center of the face four times. The lawyer, only half-conscious, tried to reach for a drawer in the desk.

Brandon opened the drawer and saw a revolver, from which he removed all the bullets and then smacked Smalls again.

"Now, we're going to have a little talk about you, Tuscarora, and black-mailing my dad," Michael said. "And by the way, this one's for Middleburg and my reelection."

Michael pulled Smalls off the floor and threw him in a chair. He then pistol-whipped Smalls across the jaw. Smalls, sobbing and trembling, seemed very much surprised at being beaten up by a clergyman. He had certainly bet the wrong way when he made the latest threatening calls.

"I know you ran Martin's Foundation, and I know you were one that threatened me back in 2005 over the Middleburg deal. But since I stopped your boss and cost him millions and have just given you the country ass-whipping of a lifetime, I'll let that issue drop. I'm here to ascertain what you know about my father and Tuscarora."

"N-n-n-nothing!" said a thoroughly defeated Smalls. "Mr. Martin told me to call you and say all of that."

"Martin has been dead since March. You'll have to do better than that."

"I can't say anymore. Martin told me to do it."

"What did Martin have to do with anything?" scolded Brandon.

"I don't know, and I can't say. Please. Leave my office now," said a terrified James Smalls.

"My family has deep roots and even deeper pockets. If you say anything about Tuscarora, my father, or what happened here this evening, we will sue you out of house and home. Do you understand me, Smalls? I will ruin you. I will fucking destroy you. Stand down, or there won't be a James Smalls anymore. Got it?"

Brandon opened the front door, keeping his eyes on Smalls as he left in a hurry. Confident that Smalls was, for the moment, pacified, Michael nevertheless cooked up a story if Smalls should involve the police on the ride back to Alexandria.

Michael would admit to confronting the man based on the voice message he received. When Brandon got too close to Smalls, the latter went for a gun, and the priest went into self-defense mode. He would not remember the awful violence that took place after he grabbed the gun first. Who would believe a sleazy lawyer and political operator over a priest anyway? Not many. Probably not the police either.

It was still light outside, and Brandon could see his clerical collar quite clearly in the rear-view mirror of his truck. It would appear that the priest now had a rather urgent set of prayers to offer God, asking forgiveness for his clear-cut cruelty. He knew he should, but his first Sunday as presiding Canon Priest at the Cathedral would go by without his asking for absolution for this act, or for anything else.

Monday, June 20

Sunday had come and gone, and Brandon had tuned out Friday's unpleasantries with the coldness of a killer. He performed the Cathedral Liturgy with precision and grace, was greeted warmly by his fellow clergy, and the 200 plus parishioners shook his hand and treated him as if he were an old friend. In typical Brandon fashion, he would not watch the online video of the service for several days.

"When I know I did well, I like to leave it at that," Michael once told Bettina. "It is when I'm knocked on my ass that I get self-conscious and nick-pick."

Michael slept late into the morning, then exercised at the gym in his condominium. When he went back upstairs to the concierge to get his mail, something was wrong. No less than four police cars were hovering just outside the Lobby. As far as he could tell, there was one Alexandria Police and one Fairfax County Police vehicle, coupled with two unmarked SUVs, one he recognized immediately.

Brandon slipped up to his unit and showered quickly, put on a polo shirt and jeans, and waited for the inevitable. His hair not yet dry, there was a robust knock on his door. He opened it and stared right into the face of a police officer he figured would be Detective Grimes. Instead, two uniformed men identified him and escorted him downstairs where Julie Grimes was sitting in a chair in the lobby.

"You couldn't come up yourself?" said an agitated Brandon.

"Shhhh, don't give these guys the idea that we know each other well," cautioned Grimes. She then grew very official. "Mr. Brandon, these officers are with the Fairfax County Police. Detective Sergeant Pete Fitzgerald and I need to question you immediately at the station. Do you have your wallet and identification with you?"

"Yes, but question me about what?" Michael asked.

"Do you know a James Smalls, Fairfax Attorney and Republican Party official?"

"Yes, I know who he is, but—"

"He was found murdered in his office early this morning," said Detective Fitzgerald.

"Murdered," a bewildered Brandon muttered.

"You're coming with us," Grimes said. "You are not yet under arrest but will be answering questions for the rest of the afternoon, understood?"

Grimes took Michael's cell phone and said he would have his phone call when they got to the station. That phone call would be to his parents, who in turn would call the most expensive criminal defense lawyer in all of Northern Virginia.

CHAPTER II

Treachery can be hell for the perpetrators as well as for the victims. It can also be bliss for those who call upon its peculiar powers at the right time, for the right reason. Those who engage in acts of great subterfuge may fail, or they may succeed magnificently in defense of a vital and worthy cause. Those on the losing side may be consigned to a bitter life. Those on the winning side may experience justification, even momentary and extended jubilation. But even they are unlikely to live out their lives unscathed.

Brandon would beat the wrap, as they say. The police did, in fact, charge him with the murder of James Smalls. His lawyer instructed him to acquire amnesia concerning the violent episode. Yes, he did go to Smalls' office to confront him, only to snap under the extreme duress of the blackmailing of his father.

In a request for summary judgement (which is a motion for an immediate direct dismissal of charges from defense counsel by the judge), Attorney Frank Dunning played on the accumulated weight of Brandon's stress, victim status, and priestly occupation — not to mention the prominence of the Brandon family.

What about his fingerprints all over the gun? Detective Grimes thought to herself in the courtroom. The Fairfax Detective Fitzgerald was white as a sheet when a sixth sense of Brandon's impending acquittal began to envelop him.

"But the fingerprints on the murder weapon..." His mind was one with Grimes. The sense of dread that a police officer feels when much hard work to hold an offender accountable was fading into irrelevance was unshakable for Fitzgerald. A veteran detective with 20 years' experience, he was always most nervous in courtrooms. It is in the courtroom where justice is so often ill served.

And yet, there were Brandon's fingerprints. Surely the judge would require a weighty explanation of the damning evidence.

"Your honor, the defense stipulates that these are, in fact, Reverend Brandon's fingerprints on the revolver which killed Mr. Smalls," said a confident Mr. Dunning. "He has never denied grabbing the gun, holding it, and hitting the deceased with it twice. But the CSI report showed no fingerprints on the trigger, the trigger guard, or the hammer of the gun. And the defendant's clothes worn that day have no trace of powder residue. The autopsy confirmed that James Smalls died of a gunshot wound to the head. Therefore, your honor, not only is there no evidence that my client fired the gun, but also the evidence clearly shows that he could not have fired it. And since a bullet from the gun in question is unmistakably what killed the victim, Mr. Brandon could not possibly have been the cause of his death."

Judge Maxwell Kent looked at his copy of the motion, removed his spectacles, and glanced at the defense attorney. Then he glanced at the police, the prosecutor, the defendant, and finally the defense attorney again. He then placed his spectacles back on, signed a summary judgment order, and declared, "There is no way Mr. Brandon could have committed this murder. All charges are hereby dismissed."

Bettina Brandon, who had rushed back to Alexandria the minute she learned of his legal danger, ran up to the row where Michael was seated and cried with relief, embracing her husband. Congressman and Patricia Brandon thanked and congratulated Frank Dunning on a spectacular defense.

The detectives were speechless. Nobody had even thought to differentiate exactly where on the gun Brandon's fingerprints were, for they were all over it. He had admitted to the assault and to handling the gun. Grimes was certain Brandon had perjured himself when he claimed he did not remember the beating of Smalls. Detective Fitzgerald asked the Assistant Fairfax Prosecutor to re-arrest Brandon and try him for attempted murder, or least malicious wounding.

"You saw what just happened," said the prosecutor. "That lawyer got Mr. Brandon off without even going to trial. The victim is dead. I think I prefer to use my energy finding out who actually killed him."

"But the man was nearly beaten to death," said Julie Grimes.

"Count me out, detectives. We all just got our asses handed to us."

The opposite of love would be indifference, and Grimes had harbored love and lust toward Brandon. But now he had become entangled with three homicides. Grimes's fellow detective, Fitzgerald, had told her at length that Brandon possessed a highly manipulative nature. In fact, outright devious. He had also resented Brandon's privilege and overpowering sense of entitlement. Although Michael had many very fine qualities, he was no white knight, as Julie Grimes realized during this brief but consequential legal proceeding. She also got a very real taste of the power of old family money and its connections — case in point, a five-star defense lawyer wreaking havoc on a police investigation and prosecution.

Grimes accepted the evidence that clinched the acquittal, but she was sure that Brandon had committed perjury when he claimed he could not remember the savage beating he had given James Smalls. Her hunch was correct.

* * *

The Hunter could not believe his good luck, and yet on some level, wasn't surprised by the opportunity provided by Brandon's rage. He had planned to kill James Smalls that Friday evening. He was stalking Smalls from a secluded parking lot across the street. Surprised by the arrival of the last-minute guest, he walked quietly over to a clump of trees and spied through his binoculars.

Brandon pulling the shade on the front door and window thwarted the Hunter's surveillance, so he waited for the commotion to end and took photographs of Brandon as he left Smalls' office. The Hunter then went quietly through the unlocked front door of the office and heard water running in the bathroom. He reached for his pistol when he saw Smalls' gun and the six bullets on the floor. Picking them up, he also noticed blood and several teeth on the floor.

Without a second's hesitation or questioning, the Hunter pieced together that Brandon had plastered Smalls to the floor and that Smalls had staggered into the bathroom to clean himself up. The Hunter loaded Smalls' revolver. As the victim emerged from the bathroom, startled, the Hunter ordered him at gunpoint to lie down in the position where Brandon had left him. In a state of shock, poor Smalls did not question why he was being told to lie down, but he did. And the Hunter shot him once in the forehead.

Dropping the gun, the Hunter left his third victim, but this time with the murder evidence pointing toward another man. And now, thanks to the superb timing, the police would have a hard suspect and not spend time and resources looking for the real killer of three men in Northern Virginia within a three-month period. He removed his gloves and drove away inconspicuously.

Brandon's problems did not all end at his acquittal. He had lost much of the trust, affection, and respect of Detective Grimes. He now had little if any control over her moves regarding the investigation. Now, a third victim who could be tied to either one or both of the others, just might prompt Federal involvement into these matters. Dean Stoneham and the senior clergy of Washington National Cathedral followed the incident and case closely.

They told Brandon in a letter that they were relieved he was acquitted of the murder charge, but they could not in good, prayerful conscience allow Michael to continue his pastoral job with them, since it was clear that he violently beat a man. Michael was terminated immediately.

Brandon began to suspect that everyone around him was looking at him a little differently. It was almost paranoia, the source obviously being his own internal conflict. He thought he had changed since he entered seminary. He was more spiritual and less attached to wealth, power, and prestige. Though imperfect, his conduct toward women had taken an honorable turn. He had become resolutely a one-woman man since he and Bettina had gotten serious. And the only infraction was the Julie Grimes affair, which happened primarily because he needed to control the murder investigation.

And this was where the rubber hit the road. Priest or not, he was a Brandon. His family's well-being and honor were threatened. And he was simply not capable of handling this adversity in a humble or resigned fashion. Lies, violence, and sexual impropriety were the tools at his disposal, and he used them to superb effect. But he was not happy with himself or the circumstances which compelled his regrettable behavior. He wanted seminary and the priesthood. He wanted the Cathedral job, in the worst way. But he could not condemn himself for his actions because he felt morally entitled to judge and to punish those who were harming him and his parents.

At such an insurmountable spiritual impasse, Brandon felt the need for a real confessor. He told Rector James Thompson of Christ Church everything, even about Julie Grimes.

"I'm not surprised, Michael," Rector Thompson said. "I saw you get into her car and take off your clerical collar. Your flirtatious body language toward the detective was noticeable from the beginning."

"Was it that obvious?" Michael asked.

"Yes, quite!"

"But Reverend, I never intended to do anything with her. I love Bettina more than I can say. I just felt I had to get myself into her business... the case, that is."

"Michael, you've done a superb job here during your internship," Rector Thompson said. "I meant what I said to the folks at the Cathedral that you were the most gifted parish priest and preacher I have ever worked with. But you have to decide seriously whether or not you really want to be a Minister of the Gospel. You just graduated and started your first job, and already you're savagely beating a man and seducing the lead detective in a murder case, where one of the victims was killed in our church."

"The way you put it, I should be looking for the Diocese to retract my credentials, or at least suspend me," said the troubled Brandon.

"I've taken care of that for now. You will stay here at Christ Church. The Cathedral people don't know you like I do, and they are publicity sensitive due to their official Washington status, and overly so. Everyone here at the parish knows you were rightly acquitted and that you got into a nasty fight with someone you believed was harming your family. What the Bishop and the Diocesan Committee will not tolerate is any discernible pattern of bad behavior. You know exactly what I mean when I say to clean up your act. You get one more chance, that's all. Understood?"

"Yes, sir, understood," Michael said.

"Now, I'm offering you an Associate Rector position here at Christ

Church, with one stipulation. You take a week off. Talk with your wife, talk with your parents, and pray. Pray earnestly for God to guide you during this trying period. And in a week's time, report back to me as to whether you truly want to be a priest in the Episcopal Church...and all the goes with it!"

"I will, Reverend, and thank you for such a magnanimous offer," said a grateful Brandon.

Michael had an idea what his parents would tell him, and he didn't really care at the moment. But he would talk to Bettina at length. Thankfully, he was allowed to make a lengthy confession to Rector Thompson and got the Julie Grimes guilt partially off his chest. For someone who had always delighted in getting away with things, Brandon was for once glad to be caught, especially by an authority figure who had his best interests at heart. It was choice time once again, and Brandon was leaning in the direction of honesty, minus telling Bettina about Detective Grimes.

Tuesday, June 28

"What about this John Gauge?" inquired the Deputy Chief to his squad of detectives. "Grimes?"

"We've been watching him ever since he interested us, Chief. Nothing new on him," Julie replied.

"And you think the judge was right for dismissing Reverend Brandon?"

"Brandon became the ideal suspect after the Smalls killing," Julie said. "He was connected to all three victims."

A uniformed officer entered the room and whispered something in the Deputy Chief's ear.

"Excuse me, detectives, I have another urgent matter to attend to," the Chief said. "We'll continue this meeting tomorrow, same time."

As he left the room, one of the junior detectives said out loud what every cop in the building was thinking: "Two low-life politicians and a prime sleaze bag businessman who funded them. We ought to pin a medal on Brandon's chest."

"Here, here."

"Damn straight."

"Guys!" shouted Julie Grimes. "Brandon didn't do the Smalls murder."

"That's what the judge says, anyway," said one of the detectives. "Brandon could have returned any time before early Monday morning and finished the job."

"Not a chance," said Grimes. "CSI said Smalls was beaten but got up shortly after. There were traces of his blood to and from the waiting room to the bathroom, and this is all moot. His charges have been dismissed. Let's put the heat on Mr. Gauge. He's older than Brandon and not as physically imposing, but he is a trained security man and a bodyguard. Diplomatic Security level at that. Which means he's a trained killer, especially with firearms. Let's pay him another visit."

Grimes was both frustrated and relieved to focus on other suspects than Michael. He hadn't played it straight with her and she resented it. He had committed a felony assault, perjured himself, and gotten away with it all. She was also disturbed by the apparent incongruities in Brandon's character. A loving and compassionate priest and family man who had no problem using violence and deception whenever he thought it was justified.

Grimes then retreated into deep and private thought. The individual who committed these three crimes, if indeed it was just one individual, was of a supreme quality. A true professional. A cold assassin. It made sense for Grimes to think so. It made sense for Grimes to continue investigating Gauge. But had she been at the Brandon farm in Charlottesville those several days Michael practiced his superior marksmanship, she just might have been chilled to the bone.

CHAPTER 12

Bettina Brandon held her sad and confused husband tightly on the family room sofa. She stroked his hair and kissed his forehead. Michael knew he was in good hands. Still on family medical leave from her job, Bettina would spend many hours that week with her husband, consoling him and helping him figure out his next moves. Brandon knew he could count on his wife. She had never let him down. She would be there for him that week too.

Many a young American man would happily change places with Brandon. Did he not have it all? Literally? He was unusually handsome and charming. His mind was sharp and his body fit. He naturally excelled at all the things he tried: hunting and the shooting sports, physical fitness and self-defense, football, and baseball. He was a superb writer, and his speaking skills were tremendous. He had an adoring wife and loving parents with a fortune to spend on their only child. And yet his insecurities were eating away at him.

His loss of opportunity at the Cathedral hit him harder than the murder charge. Brandon had conjured up in his mind that he could have all of his privileges and still live life as a self-made man. Distinguishing himself there would have spoken for itself. His dismissal from that job removed a certain tonic, an elixir which had dulled his past disappointments.

And there had been just enough distance between his Alexandria life and the prestigious Washington job he'd hoped to have for as long as he liked. Distance where he could begin anew. Now, his choices were to quit the priesthood, or resume his career under the caring but watchful eyes of the Rector from Christ Church. Either way, he could not escape Alexandria or his past. The Cathedral job had provided him just such an escape, but it was no more.

Circumstance had other plans for him. The pesky circumstances of life had gotten in his way again. And they hit him where it hurt. Brandon was a wounded puppy that night in his wife's arms. He could not shake the assault on his pride and dignity. When Bettina mentioned the associate position at Christ Church, he could only signal intellectually his appreciation for what a break it was. But he could not feel it. It could take weeks before he settled in resolutely to the new job. And still in Alexandria, not Washington.

The question he would ask himself, and his wife, was whether or not he chose the ecclesiastical profession for the right reasons. At the beginning of seminary and all the way through, he thought that he had. But he also reveled in the reversal of fortune, the brilliant chessboard move he had made — a move that wiped out his previous failures and cured his spotty reputation in the greater community. Everyone in town who was anyone either knew the Brandons or knew who they were. His father was wealthy and a colossal success in the legal and political worlds. His mother was a matron of the arts, an educator who radiated old money status. What was Michael before the seminary and the priesthood? A failed politician with next to no professional or financial success. Despite his exquisite gifts, he was the quintessential idle rich boy. And a spoiled one at that. And everyone knew it.

"Why do you love me?" a pitiful Brandon asked his bride.

"Do you have to ask?" Bettina said.

"Yes, I do."

"You don't have to make a billion dollars, or become president, or orbit the earth for me to completely respect you, darling," she said.

"Completely? You respect me completely, right now?"

"Of course, silly. Despite how you're always playing games, I know you're the smartest and most passionate man out there. You can do anything you want to do."

"But I...I nearly ruined my whole career," Brandon said. "Three years of seminary and all the fine people who helped me along in this career change."

Bettina abruptly cupped his face in her hands and gave him an adoring look. "I know why you beat that man up; it was for your family. I can't help but feel secure and warm inside knowing you would have done the same for me."

"It's all relative," Brandon chuckled darkly. "Had Smalls done anything like that to you, I *would* have killed him. And I'd be in jail and you'd...probably be back in Florida, which is where we both know you want us to end up."

They both laughed for several minutes.

"Seriously," Michael said, "why don't you tell me what you want me to do, and then we'll call it a day?"

"Oh no, Reverend Brandon," Bettina said seductively. "I'm helping you, but you're making the decision. Now, mister, it's late, so come to bed with me, and we'll pick up tomorrow."

Brandon poured himself a double brandy while Bettina was showering and getting ready for bed. He stepped out onto the balcony, where he looked at the river, the far-off monuments in Washington, and most of the Alexandrian historic district. A devilish grin appeared suddenly on his face, a grin that lunged in the direction of his whole hometown. He then pointed his finger toward the center of his city, and with contempt, gave his hometown a scolding.

"Whatever has happened to me, my fault or not, I am a priest in the Episcopal Church, and a dammed good one at that," Michael said out loud. "I graduated with honors from the largest Anglican seminary in the world. People come to *me* to confess and get bloody spiritual advice. Why? Because my sermons move people. I write the damn poetry myself."

As depression and sadness began to give way to arrogance and spite, his voice indignantly rose. "What's more, I married the best woman on earth. Me! I got her all by myself. There isn't one critic or one detractor, not one of you out there that isn't giving me the grudging salute."

Michael shook his fist and continued, "I'm speaking to you, Alexandria, Virginia. I win! I beat you. You and your pitiful political offices. You and your petty business elite with your insignificant pissant deals. You're all wet. You're all fucking wet because Reverend Michael Joseph Brandon II whipped your fucking ass!"

Thanks to a good supply of brandy, Brandon assumed the attitude of Lord of the Manor, wrongly slighted on that balcony. Despite the legal terrors, being fired from the Cathedral, and being saved from ecclesiastical ruin only by his parents' name and the good graces of Rector James Thompson, he achieved what he set out to do. Michael was an indignant man. He had been so since before embarking on his priestly vocation. Like so many of the extremely gifted, he possessed a kind of dualism in his inner psyche. The default position in his character was to make friends and be kind to people. But he tended to deal with conflict in the opposite manner. If somebody mistreated him or his family, or he thought somebody was out to get them, then kindness was replaced with fire and vengeance. He was a Christian, no doubt, but a Christian who didn't take any shit, as he told his friends.

"I just can't get my mind and spirit around this turn-the-other-cheek thing," he had once confided to Bettina.

His fiendish smile widened as he looked inside and caught a glimpse of Bettina. Marrying his wife was a "hole in one" move, in golf parlance. Now, he resolved that he would rack up success after success, accomplishment after accomplishment.

"I deserve another," he said, eyeing the brandy bottle. He would have three more while his wife dozed off to sleep. After he finished two of them, he went back out onto the balcony, raised a final glass towards the town, and in a low, sarcastic tone proclaimed, "Michael Brandon is an unqualified success, and anyone who says otherwise can go straight to hell."

He called his father, who knew right away how drunk Michael was.

"Tell Mom that her son is a winner, in the extreme!" Michael slurred. "This town has thrown the kitchen sink at me for years. Not only am I still standing; I won. Tell everyone, Pop, your boy could never be a loser. I'm a priest, the new associate at Christ Church now. And I have Bettina! I'm a winner, and all critics are loser pieces of shit. I'm a Brandon, and every Brandon should be damn proud of me."

"We are, son," the Congressman finally interrupted. "Me and your mother both. Now, get some sleep. Goodnight, son."

"Goodnight, Pop," said Michael. Brandon made up his mind to take the job Rector Thompson offered, and to remain a priest in the Virginia Diocese. It was the right decision, but was it the right motivation? Maybe and maybe not. He changed for bed and looked at himself in the mirror.

He pointed at himself and said, "Winner!"

He then climbed into bed and held and spooned his wife until morning.

By the way, Michael had far fewer critics than he imagined, the biggest critic of course being himself. His father had gently placated him over the phone because he knew the score. Liquor made Michael feel very good, but it also made him mean and amplified his paranoia over his reputation and self-esteem. He usually just slept it off and returned to normal the next morning. Bettina and his parents, however, had noted a sharp uptick in his imbibing.

Friday, July 1

"I'm taking the job with Rector Thompson, sweetheart," Michael said.

"Good morning to you too!" Bettina smiled. "I think that's the right choice, baby."

"Stay in bed, Bettina. I'm doing breakfast this morning."

Bettina smiled and hugged her pillow, enjoying a very rare occurrence. She did almost all of the cooking. She was very good. And he was lazy. "Michael, are you sure? We have some time to talk more if you want."

"You were right last night, baby. The Christ Church offer is a definite blessing. I will do very well there."

As Michael cooked breakfast, his mind wandered to the entire issue of Julie Grimes and the investigation. The closer he became with Bettina, the sicker inside he felt about screwing around with Grimes. He still considered himself justified, but he felt terrible. No one need ever find out. His father and Rector Thompson knew some of it. They were not only forgiving toward Brandon, but also, they resolved to protect him. And Michael endeavored to protect himself and his marriage.

He would never again lay a lustful hand on the detective. But the problem remained. How could he gain back at least some control, some inside knowledge, of the investigation that could damage his parents? The answer to that question would reside in a most unlikely place.

Michael called into the church about noon, apologizing for not meeting the Rector at 10 a.m. Water, what little breakfast he could eat, a shower, and what seemed like a gallon of coffee had repaired his drunken binge from the previous night. He got in his truck to make the 10-minute drive to the church, deep in thought about who he was and what he wanted to do.

Brandon was a political conservative and a theological liberal. This was an oddity among modern Episcopalian clergy, who were also politically liberal. What most Episcopalians shared in common was a staunch conservatism concerning their worship. The Anglican Book of Common Prayer reigned, second only to the Bible. And even then, Holy Scripture was interpreted through the Anglican lens of its liturgy. Episcopalians, who are the Church of England members in the United States, are Anglo-Catholic in their worship.

The Episcopal Holy Eucharist Service is far closer to the Roman Catholic Mass than it is to any Protestant Service. Factually, the least Protestant of all Protestant denominations, the only thing which keeps Episcopalians from being Roman Catholics, is the Church of England breaking with Roman authority in the 16th Century under King Henry VIII.

This long and grand tradition of conformity of worship is the glue which holds together Episcopal Dioceses, clergy, and parishioners of varying walks of life, in different parts of the country. And it is very powerful. One such traditionalist in all things ecclesiastical was the good Reverend James Thompson, Rector of Christ Church.

At 69, Thompson had three years to go until mandatory retirement. Many retired clergy take active jobs in parishes. But one must cease to be in the regular rotation of leadership. Rector Thompson had taken a liking to Brandon from the beginning. He was Michael's mentor in the church and helped him develop his sermons, leading worship and the sacraments, as well as pastoral counseling. Thompson was also conservative politically but was diplomatic in the extreme.

Nothing divides a church more than politics, and due primarily to the extremism of the dominant liberal wing of the church nationally, Episcopalians were losing thousands of members a year. What had been a body of over 3 million in the early 1960s had now dwindled to less than 2 million. And the receding showed no sign of abatement. Brandon had shown the Rector that he could be forceful and forthright in his theological and social proclamations and still leave parishioners across the ideological spectrum feeling inspired and comforted. To Thompson, Michael was just the kind of priest who might turn those dismal congregational numbers around. And Alexandria was a good place to start.

"Hello, Michael, come on in," the Rector said. "Shut the door."

Brandon sat down opposite the Rector in the latter's office. "I'll get right to it, Rector. I want the associate job, and I'm grateful to you for offering it to me."

"I'm delighted to hear it," Thompson said. "I thought you might accept."

"How many sermons a month do I get?" Michael asked.

Thompson laughed slightly. *This boy does love to hear himself talk*, he thought.

"I'll give you charge of the 5 p.m. service to begin with," Thompson said. "That's a sermon a week. Within the year, I'll work you into the Sunday morning services. If membership and donations increase enough, I'll ask the diocese for another associate. Then he or she can do the 5 p.m., and you can do prime time. Is that to your liking?"

"It's everything I want."

"Are you cleaning up your act?" the Rector asked.

"Yes," Brandon said. "No more pretty detectives for me."

The Rector laughed along with Brandon, then suddenly gave him an imperious look.

"You won't regret this, sir," Brandon assured. "Not a lick of trouble from me."

The Rector then got up and went over to an antique sideboard, opened the large door, and removed a bottle of Remy Martin XO Cognac with two snifter glasses. As he poured, Michael's eyes nearly popped out of his head.

"That's a mighty expensive cognac for two priests," he said.

"We have a splendid thing to toast, my boy," Thompson said. The Rector then sipped his cognac and spent the better part of the next hour telling Michael about his college days at the University of Richmond, as a personal friend of his parents. Michael sat up at once, looked the Rector straight in the eye, and began chugging his drink.

"Why did neither you nor my folks tell me about this, for the past two years?" Michael asked. "I mean...I knew that you were longtime friends in your capacity as a priest, and my mom and dad as parishioners and contributors."

"It's a little more serious than that. Richmond is a very expensive school. I got in with a fully funded scholarship. But your parents had the money to go, especially your mother. Well, they were two years ahead of me, but we all bonded due to our membership in a very conservative campus club. We raised hell back then, stealing financial records from the school, trying to determine if it supported any communist groups, and all that."

Brandon was stunned, almost paralyzed with curiosity. He took another cognac, then another. Unable to speak, he motioned for the Rector to continue.

"I fell in love with your mother from the start," Thompson said. "I don't have to tell you what considerable charms she possesses, even now. She returned my affections to a point, but nothing became of it because her family and your father's family got together, and then...well, you know how things happened in that high society."

Brandon tried to interject, but the Rector continued, "Your parents loved each other when they got married, I'm certain of it. We didn't tell your father anything at the time, so the friendship between us endured. But I was so heartbroken that the experience helped lead me to the priesthood."

"Did you and my mom...?"

"No, Michael, we did not," the Rector said. "But I still love her to this day. Oh, yes, my wife, Kerry...God bless her soul! I loved her and was faithful to her until the day she died. We never had children, so I guess that ever since you entered Virginia Seminary, I've kept a close watch on you. You're the closest thing I'll ever have to a son."

Brandon, floored with how much history was being imparted so quickly, struggled to respond. He knew he had to say something meaningful within the next few seconds.

"I want to thank you again for everything...the internship, and now the job," Brandon said.

"It has been my pleasure to help you in becoming what I know you will be, an exceptional priest," Thompson said. "One more thing I need to tell you. Put this murder investigation out of your mind."

"How can I?"

"Because I spoke with the Chief of Police last week. We convinced him that this a local matter, and that the church did not need outside forces like, say, the FBI giving it undo or harmful attention. The Chief agreed, but he doubled down on us to cooperate all we can."

Brandon, again, was aghast. Not 24 hours ago, he had been tormented by the prospect of the Feds looking into his family dealings. But how did the Rector know to sideline FBI cooperation? Then, a moment of clarity overtook him. His mother and father must have confided in Thompson. They had never been particularly close to any of the priests at St. Paul's. It all made sense. Rector Thompson knew about his father's legal exposure from deals gone by and was ready and willing to protect them all, especially his mother. Of this, Michael was now certain, but he did not broach the subject with the Rector that day.

"One more glass, Michael?" Thompson asked.

"Yes, sir, quite a perk to be drinking like this during the day."

"Study the lectionary for Sunday and tailor your sermon around the gospel passage."

"You got it!" Michael said. "And thanks again, Rector."

Brandon left the church to go home and work on his sermon and the 5 p.m. service for that Sunday. Omitting only the part about his infidelity with Julie Grimes, Michael told Bettina everything he knew, everything about the day's revelations from Rector Thompson. Now, Bettina needed a drink.

Brandon poured them both a brandy and they talked all evening. She was mystified by the old-world Virginian way of doing things, though she thought no less of her in-laws for it.

"You've got a guardian angel, sweetheart," she said.

"Yes, I do," Brandon implored. "It's you. The Rector certainly has been a great friend, though. How do I repay his kindness?"

"By doing a good job for him, and for the church, honey."

"You're absolutely right, my dear," said Michael as he and Bettina toasted and drank some more.

If Brandon's fortunes had turned for the better, Julie Grimes was not following suit in this regard.

She had sided with the Fairfax County authorities, or at least let them have their way in charging the young priest. Passion being what it is, Grimes's reduced opinion of Brandon's character had not yet had the intended effect of extinguishing the sexual and romantic feelings she still harbored for him. Ever since the dismissal of charges, Grimes dialed Michael's number more than a dozen times, only to hang up before he could answer.

Now, for the first time, she began to wonder what she actually was to him. Though she cared for him from the day they met, her self-esteem had not been in any way part of the equation. At that moment, it was. The thought of Brandon holding her in contempt, of not thinking well of her, of no longer finding her attractive and appealing, was intolerable. A slight reversal from the weeks before when she told herself she had lost all respect for the priest, but passion is what it is.

Unfortunately for Grimes, her professional esteem wasn't faring any better. All she and her team had now was John Gauge, a man who claimed to be Robert Martin's bodyguard and quit the case minutes before Martin was shot. If his story were true, he could not have been the shooter. There was no evidence suggesting Gauge was lying, but maybe there could be.

"Gauge is all we have at the moment," said Grimes to her detectives. "Get a warrant to search his home and car and call him back for more questioning."

Sunday, July 2

That evening at Christ Church, Reverend Brandon led the service, and after opening prayers and hymns, took the pulpit with a sanctuary full of congregants. His words were poignant, as usual:

"It is customary, dear friends, to mix the church and the flag during the 4th of July season. God bless America! It is a phrase I regularly use, and one for which I continually pray. As Christians, we are rightfully proud of our American nation and heritage, particularly our God-given rights, such as the right to worship freely according to the dictates of our consciences. We keep an American flag here in the sanctuary as a continual reminder that our country is special in human history. There are places in the world, unfortunately, where preaching the gospel is not safe. We therefore need to be ever mindful and vigilant to do honor to and safeguard our nation's founding principles.

"The church, on the other hand, is also a global body, composed of the faithful from nearly every nation around the world. In that character, we pray for, serve, and care about people beyond our borders and community. These two things are not mutually exclusive. We do our patriotic duty to our country as Americans, to the Commonwealth of Virginia as citizens, and for most of us here in this church, to the City of Alexandria. I remind you all that George Washington worshipped right here in this chapel.

"And as members of the body of Christ, we look also to people all around the world for the purposes of mission and ministry. The church is not the flag, and the flag is not the church. The state has no ecclesiastical authority, nor has the church the police powers of the state. And so should it ever be. The Christian faith and the Declaration of Independence share this essential truth; that Almighty God cared enough, thought enough of each one of us, that He gave us all rights and dignities which no government may never deny or molest.

"So, imbibe on this 4th of July holiday. Savor it. Rejoice and pray for our country and its communities. And make room in your hearts to pray for our Christian brothers and sisters around the world, and for peace in all of God's good earth. Amen."

Brandon completed the service with a recitation of the creeds, the passing of the peace, prayers of the people, and then the Holy Eucharist. Upon dismissal, he walked down the nave and out to the narthex (an old word which describes the lobby or gathering point between the sanctuary and the outside of the church). He shook hands with more than 100 parishioners and guests, not one who didn't offer a smile, a gesture of satisfaction and praise for his message, or admiration for his authoritative and attractive presence as their clerical leader.

Knowing he had done well that day, Michael was glowing with pride and basking with energy in the affirmation of his parishioners. A few more services of that kind would make the Cathedral disappointment fade into distant memory. As he greeted and exchanged words with the remaining congregants, he was experiencing a humble victory.

Then, to his great surprise, a large man in his late forties, dressed in a business suit, approached Michael and whispered that he wanted a one-on-one meeting of a spiritual nature.

"Here's my card," the man said as he walked away abruptly. "Please call me tomorrow."

Brandon glanced at the business card, which read, *William Garrison, Deputy Chief of Police, Alexandria, Virginia.*

Julie Grimes's boss, Brandon thought. *The investigation that seems to go nowhere but won't go away. How quickly the mood can change these days!*

Brandon had been feeling very good about the service — very peaceful and serene. With each Sunday success, he further established and entrenched himself in the Church. Now, what to make of this brief, new, and completely unpredictable encounter?

Monday, July 3

"Hello, Deputy Chief," Michael introduced himself. "It's Michael Brandon."

"Good morning, Reverend. Nice service yesterday. Call me Bill."

"Will do," Michael said. "I'm just following up with you from yesterday. You said you wanted to speak with me regarding a personal matter?"

"Yes," said Garrison in a low voice. "As soon as possible."

"I normally have Mondays off, and tomorrow is the 4th of July. Could we do this some time on Wednesday?"

"I can be at your church at 4 p.m.," Garrison said. "Will we be alone?"

"The Rector and the secretary leave by four o'clock," Michael said. "I can't account for the choir director or the organist coming by. But meet me at 4:30. We should have plenty of privacy."

"That works," Garrison said. "See you Wednesday. And thank you, Reverend."

"Goodbye."

"Did I hear you making a pastoral counseling meeting?" Bettina said as she sat in Michael's lap and kissed him. "So exciting! I wonder if he'll confess to something heinous."

"Bettina!" Michael cried. "This is serious stuff. A man I've never seen before came to church yesterday and handed me his card, said he needed help with a spiritual matter. The same thing happened with that Gauge fellow. Remember me telling you about that?"

"Oh yeah, he was connected with that shooting, right?"

"Something like that," Brandon said, vaguely sarcastic.

"Look, if you don't want me to be part of your professional life, just say so," Bettina said.

"Hush, sweetheart. I'm fine telling you these things. I'm just a little frustrated. I can't make sense of all the crazy stuff that's been happening to me. It's unsettling!"

"I know, right?" exclaimed Bettina. "Something bad happens, and then something surprisingly good, or the reverse."

"That's exactly the way I was thinking about it," Michael agreed. "But I'm tired of the bad. I'd just like to keep things like this for a while." He grabbed his wife gently around the neck. "To hell with change! I just want us to stay young and me to do my job with success and satisfaction. And every day, you and I can eat, drink, and fuck until we're dizzy."

"Reverend Michael J. Brandon, you have a potty mouth!" Bettina exclaimed.

"Only with you, baby, and my boys from the hood."

"I never heard of a silver spoon hood before."

Brandon laughed and tickled Bettina mercilessly, then they visited the bedroom.

After a little while, Bettina's phone rang, and she asked Michael to answer it.

"Hello?"

"Hi, stud muffin! Is my sister there?"

"Hello, Miss Nora. Yes. Is everything okay with your folks?"

"Oh yeah, I just want to talk to Bettina about me."

"Your love life? We don't have all night," Michael joked.

"Now you're a comedian too," Nora laughed.

"Kidding, sweetie, I'll go get her," Michael said. "Honey, it's Nora."

Bettina took the phone, and Michael told her he was going to his parents' house for a couple of hours. "I'll bring back some Chinese food for us."

"Great, baby," said Bettina.

"What a surprise," Patricia Brandon said as she opened the front door. "Come in, darling."

"Hey, Pop," said Brandon as he kissed his mother.

"Want a drink, Junior?"

"You know it. I notice I drink more now that I'm a priest," Michael said.

"Goes with the territory, son," the Congressman said. "The more experience and success you amass, the more this stuff does the trick. Worked for me anyway."

"Oh, Joe, if you're going to fill the boy with ideas, let them be good ones," Patricia groaned.

"It is a great idea! I think Aristotle said it."

Laughter engulfed the room as Michael's mother sipped some wine, and the Congressman and he knocked back four highballs a piece.

"Well, I can forget about that workout I was going to do tonight," Michael said.

"Exercise is overrated," the Congressman said. "Stick to the hunting and drinking, and of course, your smoking hot wife!"

Michael laughed, and his mother just stared at Congressman Brandon with a look of pious contempt. As if she was annoyed to have to replay the formulation of thoughts to which she had grown accustomed. *How did this man ever convince me to marry him?* she thought. *And how did he ever get elected to office, let alone remain there?*

The Congressman had always been one of those men who say and do off-color things and get away with it. Get away with what other people could not. In fact, nobody in all of Alexandria possessed the talent to that degree...except for one. His son.

On his way out the door, Michael's mother reminded him of their July 4th party.

"You and Bettina be here by 3 p.m.," Patricia said.

"I invited a couple of pals and their wives," Michael said. "See you tomorrow. Goodnight, Mom. Night, Pop!"

CHAPTER 13

Tuesday, July 4

The 4th of July is celebrated in most communities with fun and frolic. The point of the holiday is not lost on regular Americans, but it is not the driving force that it most certainly is for America's prominent families. Particularly those families with a conservative intellectual bent, like the Brandons.

What drives Patricia Brandon and her husband, the Congressman, is a sense of destiny in the directing of a state and a nation. Wealth for its own sake is always desirable, but for the Brandons and others like them, it is used to perpetuate their power and position in the country they consider the greatest political and societal experiment of all time. For Mrs. Brandon, Western Civilization is the crowning achievement of the human race, and the United States of America is the quintessential Western nation. The Virginian way of life is of nearly equal importance to the fine families of the Commonwealth. Education, the humanities, tradition, nobility, civility, and manners, mixed with the rural landscape and culture of country gentlemen and gentle ladies is a way of life that defines for them the very cardinal virtues of philosophy: beauty, goodness, and truth.

This helps to explain, in part, why the southern states seceded from and went to war with the United States during the Civil War. There was more to the story than just states' rights and the slave economy; the people of sensibility felt the exquisiteness of their culture threatened. This turned out to be a false fear, for after the war ended, the families of wealth, industry, and high culture in both the North and South found that they shared a great many of the same values.

In Fauquier County, as in much of the Virginia Piedmont, northern elite families such as the Mellons, DuPonts, and others from New York and New England bought property, did business, and fox hunted along with the older established Virginian families. The Virginia Piedmont country of the present day is still very much an intersection of northern and southern gentility, old money, and high culture. The history of this place can be felt in the air one breathes. Like a gothic novel, it emits a presence so refined and mystical, it is indeed hallowed ground. This ground and the society which occupies it will be defended with the utmost passion and precision against all threats, be they from politicians, businessmen, or activists of the wrong kind. Those defending the Piedmont will do so successfully, with a polite but unshakable sense of entitlement to stand in the way of change and destroy the progressive visions of their adversaries.

As for this 4th of July, our very prominent family, the Brandons, will host some old Virginian charm and hospitality at their farm outside Middleburg, in this this very hallowed county of Fauquier.

The Brandon family events are different from what one might think. They are not the F. Scott Fitzgerald "Jazz Age" extravaganzas one finds in Washington or New York. They are simple, quaint, and do not go on past 8 p.m. Guests are showered with reserved affection and served appetizers of game meat and fresh fruit. Drinks are beer, wine, and cocktails made with bourbon.

Michael snuck up behind his mother with some company.

"Mom, you remember Pete Chapman, my best high school pal?"

"Oh, yes, and is this your wife?" Patricia asked.

"Yes, ma'am, this is Brenda," Pete said. "We've been together since college."

"Oh, I just couldn't forget such a beauty. Let me take Brenda from you and have a Mint Julep," said Mrs. Brandon.

As the two walked outside to the drink table, Pete put his two cents in regarding Brandon's good fortune. "Where is that ridiculously luscious wife of yours?"

Michael blushed as he struggled to reply, for in his direct company was not only Pete, but also his childhood buddies Tom Henderson and Jamie Banks. Both men were doctors with pretty wives and children and had practices at the renowned Fairfax Hospital.

Banks had a general practice, and Henderson was a Vascular Surgeon. Both admitted to having fantasies and actual dreams about Bettina Brandon. As Dr. Henderson put it, "How did the clergyman in our gang wind up with the hottest woman any of us have ever seen?"

Of course, the two doctors were there stag at the party. Brandon suddenly smiled and very pleasingly retorted, "You guys could have gone to seminary too."

Much laughter bellowed from the four friends as they backslapped and went straight for the fine Kentucky Bourbon.

"Bettina is on her way," Michael said. "By the way, you need to check out her sister, Nora."

Brandon played a short modeling video of Nora Vasquez on his phone. It had its intended effect, and the boys were back in junior high school for a moment.

Brandon's friends were tall and athletic like himself and had enjoyed their share of female attention throughout the years, but all married early in life. A part of each of them lived vicariously through Michael and his antics over the years. Chapman was the technocrat of the four, owning an engineering company with the heavy framed spectacles to accommodate this image.

Henderson was an incurable fashion-plate playboy and somehow made an impossibly difficult profession seem easy.

Banks was more shy and retiring, a family man who occasionally indulged in naughty encounters with nurses. Unless one knew these men closely, these facts would surprise. It was Dr. Henderson who would be thought to cheat on his wife, more so than Dr. Banks.

Pete Chapman was a faithful family man too, but when these fellows got together, things happened. The last time was when Brandon was in mid-year of seminary, and the others still couldn't believe he was serious about becoming a cleric. Drinking and daring and recklessness overtook them one evening, and they wound up at Washington's premiere strip club called Easy's. One can go there today during the week and find congressmen and lobbyists enjoying the dirty martini lunch.

Banks still had photographs in his phone camera of six dancing girls sitting in Brandon's lap — stroking, groping, hugging, and kissing him until the manager broke up the fiesta. The four men got physical with the manager, and the bouncer and two Washington, D.C., police officers hit the scene and escorted the ruffians outside. The only thing that prevented their arrest was Brandon name-dropping his father, with whom the veteran policemen were acquainted. They hailed a taxicab back to his parents' house and passed out to Mrs. Brandon's displeasure and the Congressman's amusement.

Chapman was more than content to leave his wife with Patricia Brandon, and he, Michael, and the two doctors put away four Mint Juleps in less than 30 minutes. Well into their conversation, Bettina walked out to the veranda from inside the house. Predictably, Michael's three buddies stood transfixed with their mouths agape as the young Mrs. Brandon made her entrance.

Now, understand that these three friends were handsome, privileged, and gentile just like Michael; not to mention more professionally accomplished. But they all knew, just as everyone else in high-society Alexandria knew, that it was Brandon who had that special mysterious touch with people, particularly women. Not that they were jealous of him, for they all were secure in themselves. But Brandon never ceased to be the source of amazement for them, and when they saw Bettina, though they had all met before numerous times, the amazement was palpable. For there was something about this stunning couple that would set them apart in any society. That afternoon, Bettina Brandon walked right out of the pages of the best romance novel and levied her charms on her husband's friends.

"Excuse me for interrupting the frat chat," Bettina teased. "I have a habit of dropping in on Michael when he doesn't expect it. That way, I know what Mischief Man is up to."

"She's got your number, dude," joked Henderson.

Chapman's wife and Patricia walked up to Bettina, and the women hugged each other, and Bettina was given a glass of wine. Banks and Chapman each imagined how their friend's wife might get their number as well. As the drinks settled in, everyone's comfort level reached a crescendo, and the Brandons and all their guests were as content as people who could not imagine anything in life, so much as that everything would always go this well for them. Indulging in the company of this family was a privilege in itself, but the icing on the cake was being in an atmosphere of the good life being enjoyed, and with no end in sight.

Late that night, Patricia Brandon quietly left her bed, her husband sleeping soundly, and went downstairs to the den and shut the doors. Despite all the family fun with close friends, something was missing in her life on this most solemn of holidays. Fortunately and unfortunately for Mrs. Brandon, her remedy was a phone call away. She unlocked a drawer to the enormous desk in that room, took out an extra cell phone, and dialed.

"Hello, darling, it's me," she said. "I missed you today especially. I know how important the 4ᵗʰ of July is to you, and I wish you could have been with us."

A slow, pregnant pause ensued, and then, "Hello, mother, it's nice to hear your voice."

"I'm so sorry that I'm a part-time mom to you, that it's always been the case," Patricia said.

"Don't feel bad. Part-time is better than no time," said the man.

"You we're always so understanding, weren't you?"

"You have your husband and son, and I've made my choices in life," the man replied.

"I hear Joe waking up. I will call in a few days, I promise," said Patricia.

"Not to worry. Happy Fourth, Mom."

"Bye, darling."

The man hung up and went immediately to his wall safe behind a painting. He took out a framed photograph of his parents, a photograph of when they were young and in love, and together. Patricia's beauty and elegance was striking. The man she was with was handsome, refined, and had a twinkle in his eyes suggesting an unusual insight in, and compassion for, the human condition.

The picture was accurate. The Reverend James Thompson, Rector of Christ Church, is such a man to this day. The man stared at the picture for nearly an hour, then returned it to the safe with great care.

Wednesday, July 5

Reverend Brandon pulled up to Christ Church, parked his car, and looked puzzled as he got out. There were no other cars in the church lot.

There could be people in the church who parked on the street or took some other form of transportation. But all the lights were out, and it was only 2 p.m.

Oh well, he thought as he let himself into the church, where he first checked his mail and went into his office, sat down, and chose the liturgy and Bible readings for the Sunday services. When the choir director gave him the final decisions on hymns and choral pieces, he would put them and everything else in the church bulletin and make 300 copies. That should occur that very afternoon. He then began working on his sermon for the 5 p.m. service. Due to the warm weather and late sunsets of July, the 5 p.m. was enjoying a bump in attendance, with the last four services exceeding 120 congregants each.

At about 4:15 p.m., Brandon went to the small kitchen, put on a pot of coffee, and waited for his guest in the lobby. Deputy Chief Garrison was right on time.

"Hello, Bill," said Brandon.

"Afternoon, Reverend."

"Call me Michael. Coffee?"

"Yes, please. It's been a long day."

Brandon came back from the kitchen and handed the Chief a mug as the two walked into his office.

"I'll get right to the point," Garrison said. "Detective Julie Grimes has been a tad bit aggressive with this murder case, especially where you're concerned."

Brandon, taken by surprise, looked silently at the Chief for a few seconds. "As I nearly went to jail on her account, I would have to agree," he said.

"You can thank me for how it turned out later, and for what I'm about to do for you now," said the Chief.

"Wait a minute. I was charged and went to court in Fairfax. You're

Alexandria Police."

"My reach is farther than you think, Michael. After the judge dismissed your murder charge, the people I work for made certain that you weren't charged for felony assault, or anything else."

"That's funny, I thought it was my lawyer who performed the magic act," said a puzzled Brandon.

"He works with us too. He's the best in town, but friends in high places are your real guardian angels," said the Chief.

"I see," Brandon said. "What is it that you're about to do for me now, Bill?"

"I'm going to do what I have done all along — keep Grimes on as head of the murder investigations and control her."

"You mean control the investigation?"

The Chief nodded in the affirmative.

"What about James Smalls?" Michael asked. "He was killed in Fairfax."

"That's covered as well. You know, Grimes turned out to be cleverer than I had thought, so I'm reigning her in. And none of us expected you to go and beat the hell out of Smalls. We all had to rearrange our plans around those mistakes, Michael."

"Why are you telling me all this? I thought you were here on a spiritual matter."

"I'll get to that in a second," said the Chief. "Anyway, I wanted you to know that you have friends, Michael. Friends who have the power and the desire to protect you."

"Protect me from what?" Michael asked.

"From yourself, for starters. I know you tuned up Smalls to protect your family from blackmailers. And I know all about you and my detective. Everything."

"That too, huh? Who told you?"

"Give me some credit. I've been a cop for almost 30 years. Let me close out this discussion by calming your fears. I have been instructed to tell you to focus on your job and ministry, and not to worry about Julie Grimes, the Feds investigating your parents, or anything else. You and they are protected."

"That's comforting, Bill. Protected by who?"

"This is all you need to know for the moment," Garrison said. "Now, as to that spiritual matter. Is there a Hell?"

The policeman introduced a tension in the room that neither Brandon nor the Chief could quite control. He had come to the church on two simultaneous missions. The first he completed without hesitation, a true professional. The second concerned his own inner peace, which was not altogether safe. The Chief was a man of duty and rules, but he was asking, almost begging the young Reverend, for relief, as if he had now broken some fair-sized rules that might demand attention from the Almighty.

Michael was now in a state of reserved shock. He recited several of the Psalms in his head to slowly regain his composure. When his mind made the shift from self-absorbed operator to priest, he answered the Chief's question.

"The church has historically taught that those who persist in evil and in rejecting God face the possibility of an unpleasant afterlife, which is taken to mean an eternal separation from God," Brandon explained. "I personally struggle with this matter, but I do believe that God loves you and is ready to forgive anything that may be troubling you. Even the best of us fail to live up to God's standards now and again. Any of this make sense?"

An obviously troubled Chief sat back in his chair, eager to hear more that Brandon might have to say.

"Let me end this for today with these thoughts," Michael said. "Concentrate on being in a right relationship with God. The church is the right vehicle, but we clergy are not God. The holy books are not God either. We just do our best to point you in His direction. I believe He wants what is best for you and for all of us. I do not believe in an angry or punishing God. Allow yourself some peace in this regard. Is there anything you wish to confess?"

"Maybe this is all I need for today, Reverend," the Chief said, relieved. "Thank you. We will talk some more about this."

"Thank you for coming by, Bill. It would be a privilege for me if you start attending church services here."

"Perhaps," said the Chief. "And you take to heart what I told you, Michael. You have friends. Just do the job that you obviously do so well and let your friends handle the unpleasantries."

"Thank you. I would like nothing better," said Brandon.

The men shook hands, and the Deputy Chief left the church and disappeared into his black SUV. Brandon went straight to the bathroom and splashed his face. He looked into the mirror briefly and breathed heavily for two more minutes. He thought about the conversation that just happened and who it was with. He thought about the confessional meeting he'd had with John Gauge, the mysterious bodyguard of one of the murder victims. Then, he sat down at his desk and dialed his cell phone.

"Hi, baby, can you come to the church and we can walk across the street and get some dinner?"

"Sure, honey. Everything okay?" Bettina asked.

"I'm good, but you won't believe the conversation I've just had," Michael breathed. "I need to tell you about it, and I would rather drink than drive right now."

"I'll be there in 30 minutes," Bettina said.

Brandon put his phone down and reflected on how he'd been told he had friends who would protect him. He didn't have an inkling yet as to what that meant. But he did know who his best friend was — his wife.

Despite his secretive and devious streak, he was as honest with Bettina as he could allow himself to be with anyone. He would tell her things he could never tell anyone else. She was not only his passion, but his truest comfort in this world. Nothing could ever take her place. And nothing ever would. Brandon's emotions were a mixed bag at the moment.

On one hand, he had done a good pastoral deed for the Deputy Chief. And if this man was to be trusted, then he didn't have to worry about Detective Grimes or any murder investigation harming his parents. But despite the fact that his family was rich and powerful, who were those friends in high places? What's more, how could he explain the Deputy Chief of Police approaching him in the manner he did? Michael's first confessor, John Gauge, asked for him out of the blue.

These events, combined with his murder charge and dismissal as well as the Cathedral job he'd had and lost and his new job at Christ Church, all happened within a couple months of each other. It was most puzzling, to say the least. Brandon, despite this unbelievable turbulence, had the presence of mind to ask himself the right questions.

He called Rector Thompson and asked for a meeting the next day. The Rector was quite accommodating. Just as Michael logged the 4 p.m. appointment in his phone and began jotting down notes, Bettina knocked at the front door.

This couple, in more than one way, fit the conventional model of what a man and a woman desire and need in a relationship. While it is clear that Michael and Bettina were very warm, passionate, and sexually driven towards each other, Michael was content to have his wife be his main source of comfort and affirmation; while Bettina, though all of the above were important, derived her key source of fulfillment in being immersed in her husband's life.

She would never miss an opportunity to share something with him or to discover something new about him. To her, that was true intimacy. So, it is not surprising that when Michael called her and asked her to meet him for dinner and listen to him tell her all about an interesting and emotional experience that he just had, she naturally dropped everything she was doing or thinking about and rushed over to be with him.

It was just that wonderfully easy — almost.

CHAPTER 14

"How's that for an afternoon's work?" Brandon said after he relayed his rollercoaster of a meeting in its entirety.

When he mentioned Detective Grimes in passing, his knees shook under the table at the little café two blocks from the church. Brandon still was not happy about his ongoing deception in this regard, but the alternative was unthinkable.

"Unbelievable, sweetheart," Bettina said. "I'm so sorry. You look overwhelmed."

"Thanks, baby, but strangely enough I think I can handle this. At least I'm doing a yeoman's work as a priest. I actually calmed two troubled men spiritually. I could feel it so acutely, both times. I actually helped those gentlemen."

"I'm proud of you, honey," Bettina said. "I know you care. I know you want this to be your life's work. I just wish I didn't have to tell you what I'm about to tell you."

Michael's eyes suddenly grew wide, and he shook at the knees again as he gulped his wine. His thoughts raced. Did she not like being the wife of a clergyman? Was all this mystery and turmoil too much for her? Julie Grimes? What could it be?

"I can't have children, honey, at least not the natural way," she said. "I found out for sure this morning."

Bettina began to cry, and the big brown eyes that could slay an army of men were filled with tears that began to run down her cheeks like a flood. Brandon immediately came to the rescue. He pulled his chair next to hers, grabbed her hand, and cupped her face with his other hand.

"I know we've been talking about this for some time," Michael said. "I haven't changed my mind or my resolve. If you can't, you can't. We will adopt, and if you don't want that then we won't."

He looked seriously into his wife's eyes, and with an authenticity and sincerity of emotion as palpable as Bettina had ever felt from him, Brandon said these words: "You are the single most important, significant, and indispensable person in my life. You're the only one I can't live without. And we're going to be together and be happy, kids or no kids."

"But your parents, Michael. The Brandon family name. You're an only child."

"Doesn't matter!" Michael said. "What matters is you and me, and our beautiful life together."

"Michael Brandon, how do you always know exactly what to say?" Bettina said. "I mean, I'm a mess here, and you're—"

"Don't. Don't think about it anymore tonight. We can talk about options later, okay?"

Bettina took a few minutes to collect herself. She was not upset just for Michael; she had always wanted to be a mother and to give her parents grandchildren. But she had a sister who, at some point, would settle down. That, and Brandon's love and magnanimity toward her that night, had relieved the pressure she had been feeling for a while. But she would continue to carry some sadness with her. When she returned to the table from the powder room, Bettina asked Brandon again if he was sure he could handle everything that happened with the two visitors to his church.

He replied in the affirmative: "I'm meeting with the Rector tomorrow.

If anyone can navigate this craziness, he can. Don't worry for another minute."

Thursday, July 6

Julie Grimes was now operating under a false sense of command, with Deputy Chief Garrison quietly directing her steps. When she asked for some limited help from the Federal authorities, Garrison would say something colloquial like, "I've never trusted the Feds. They don't just assist local law enforcement; they take over the case. I trust you, Julie, to handle this with the resources at our disposal."

What could she say in response? Nothing. Her boss couched his refusal of Federal help in a manner that spiked her professional esteem, solidifying her loyalty to him and the department. But it did have the added effect of making the detective more determined than ever to solve these cases.

* * *

The Hunter enjoyed that particular Thursday off. A day off is always good. But when everyone else is working, it is particularly delicious. He woke up late in the morning next to a woman he'd been dating for a few months. The woman got out of bed and with only her skim, black panties on headed to the kitchen to make coffee and a late breakfast for the pair.

He grabbed her arm as she tried to exit the room and swung her back into the bed.

"Good morning, miss. I'm sorry, what was your name again?" said the Hunter.

The two laughed and snuggled as he planted a deep kiss into her mouth. The woman pulled away playfully and said, "Gargle and brush your teeth now, nasty boy."

"Why?" retorted the assassin.

"Because you licked me half the night, and I'm fairly certain you had your tongue in my ass."

"Fairly certain?"

"We did drink quite a bit," the woman exclaimed.

"You see, that's the difference between us, my dear. I notice everything, every little detail — drink or no drink. And I'm one hundred percent sure I put my tongue in your ass."

With that, the woman smiled and blushed, and the two tickled and teased each other for a while.

The Hunter and Michael Brandon were classic alpha males. And such men tend to emerge from the womb with sexual drive overload. The Hunter did not possess Brandon's level of charm and powers of persuasion, but his list of romantic accomplishments was impressive by any standards. The key difference was that Brandon's libido had regularly knocked him off balance, causing him to make mistakes throughout his life. Julie Grimes, case in point.

The Hunter had that rare gift of total control, even when indulging sexually. His natural and developed self-control had a wicked quality to it. No matter what circumstance threw at him, he reacted with brutal efficiency every time. Like Brandon, he tended to get what he was after. But he always got away with it. Trouble seemed to roll off this man like Teflon. It wasn't that he cared for nothing or nobody. He did. But what and who he cared about were governed entirely by his will and design. And these things were few.

The Hunter had met his lady friend under the most unlikely of circumstances. Miss Allison Peters was a law student at Georgetown University in Washington. She lived in Alexandria, where she had grown up. Her parents, both lawyers themselves, had just the one child. The father was white and Anglo-Saxon, and the mother was a light-skinned black woman from the Bahamas.

This all contributed to Miss Peters being outrageously beautiful and sexy. She was also very smart and dedicated to her studies. Several months before, the young woman had exited the elevator from Alexandria's King Street subway station after her classes. It was a foggy day with troubling visibility. Just then, a man with a Georgetown football jacket approached her, and she stopped. The two argued for several minutes, and when the coast was clear of any noticeable bystanders, the man tried to force Miss Peters into his car parked on King Street.

This man was not privy to the fact that another man in a trench coat, who had witnessed the entire incident from behind the elevator wall, was right on top of the two young people. He separated Miss Peters from the young man, who then swung hard at him. The man in the trench coat blocked, then kicked out the young man's knee. When he fell to the ground, his left ear was crushed by three lightning-fast palm strikes from the trench coat wearer's right hand.

The young man rolled into the street with his hand on his ear and limped away into the traffic and pedestrians a block away. The Hunter gently grabbed Miss Peters' arm, and they hurried away passed the subway toward his truck.

"Where do you live?" asked the Hunter.

Stunned and afraid, the young woman lied at first. But the Hunter's facial expression became immediately disarming.

"I'm sorry to have startled you, but I saw that man acting belligerently at you and try to force you into his car. I'm a Judo Instructor and a former cop. I'm trained to react quickly in these situations."

"I'm grateful that you did, sir," Allison said. "But that was my ex-boyfriend. He's been trying to get back together with me. He's obnoxious, but I was not in any danger. I was actually going to let him take me home."

The two stared at each other for quite a while.

"Well, I guess I beat that guy up for nothing," the Hunter said.

The woman laughed and told the Hunter her ex needed a good butt-kicking. The Hunter laughed and gave her the false name of Steve Wilson. She shook his hand and insisted he call her Allison.

"May I call you a cab, Allison?"

Allison by now was feeling very safe in the company of a tall, handsome, ex-cop and martial artist. She was, after all, a witness to his handiwork.

"No," she said. "But let me buy you a drink across the street at Murphy's."

The Hunter accepted, and since then, not three or four days would go by without him seeing her. They would spend nights together at his place, due to the fact that she still lived with her parents. Nearly twenty years her senior, the Hunter enjoyed his latest conquest. Allison was intellectually and emotionally mature, greatly paring the two up.

At the bar, Allison inquired about the Hunter's history. He told her a story that was as least partially true. He had been a police detective in Richmond, Virginia during the 1990s. At the time, several city crime families controlled the heroin distribution from Baltimore to Atlanta. He was city police for the first several years before joining a Federal Task Force, during which he was dangerously undercover, foiled numerous drug deals, and shot and killed four senior members of two of the families.

He linked the Richmond operatives to a Mafia connection in Philadelphia, which led to the arrests of some high-profile Mafia gangsters. For this, he said he had to leave the Feds and change his name. "I ended up here in Alexandria because we are close to D.C. There is next to no organized crime in this town, except for the government."

The two laughed heartily as Allison was mesmerized. Her intrigue and attraction toward the Hunter grew exponentially.

"In law school, we are always taught to hero worship the legal greats — Clarence Darrow, Thurgood Marshall, and the public figures who move our legal and political cultures forward," Allison said. "But you are a real hero."

"Stop...I did my job, that's all," he said.

"You are. You keep the rest of us safe." Allison swallowed her fourth wine, looked around the bar for any friends or acquaintances, and kissed the man she now defined as her knight in shining armor.

The Hunter did intervene that day on her behalf. He was in Old Town near the subway visiting his accountant and could very easily have minded his own business. He was a Federal Agent with the FBI and performed some harrowing duties in the 1990s, including killing some bad guys. But he was never a local cop, not in Richmond, not anywhere else. So, to consider him a white night would be partially correct. But that designation is easily offset by the other things.

Allison called in sick for classes that Thursday morning. She would spend all day and night with the man she was sure she was getting to know. The Hunter had already predetermined what she would discover about him. She was having her fun; he was having his.

* * *

Brandon had arisen late again, much to Bettina's chagrin, for she was an early riser. By the time he got up after 10 a.m., Bettina had done her yoga class and workout downstairs at Marina Towers' gym. She showered, dressed, and kissed her husband good morning as she went to her new office.

With the continual improvement of her mother's health, Bettina had taken a position as Vice President for Government Affairs for the

American Cancer Society. Her mom's near-death experience with a tumor that could have easily been malignant gave Bettina a new perspective on what it is important. She would use her skills and Washington connections to raise awareness and money from the Federal Government for cancer research and treatment. Interestingly, the office was just blocks away from Christ Church, a fact that had not escaped her leisurely husband.

For Brandon, it was very nice to have his wife close by, and not in Washington. But as much as he valued her, there still existed inside him that young boy who didn't want anyone checking up on him. He was still the teenage boy whose parents would often go out of town and leave him to his own devices, and plenty of money. The good Reverend was perfectly content to be the theologian and spiritual advisor, and to have his wife be the adult with a disproportionate amount of the practical responsibility of daily life.

Brandon arrived at Christ Church at 3 p.m. to check his mail and return any messages. The 5 p.m. service was already planned and published in the bulletin. He made some fresh coffee and waited for Rector Thompson to return. The Rector had been at lunch with the new Bishop, who had come up from Richmond to meet with several Northern Virginia clergy. Michael was in a jovial and nonchalant mood, but underneath that veneer loomed an anxiety about the meeting with the Deputy Chief of Police.

The Rector came in a few minutes before 4 p.m., and Brandon wasted no time intercepting him to commence their conversation. That particular conversation would have to wait.

"Shut the door, Michael," the Rector softly commanded.

"Rector, I have to get off my chest what happened to me yesterday," Michael said. "Coupled with the John Gauge meeting some weeks ago—"

"Michael, I hate to interrupt, but we have a slight problem with the powers that be."

Brandon could sense impending doom. "You mean *I* have a slight problem with the powers that be."

"Yes," the Rector said. "But I'm on your side. Let me just state it briefly. As you know, the Diocese just elected that new Bishop from New Jersey, Alice Burroughs. She is about as flaming a liberal as the church in Virginia will allow. To put it bluntly, she followed your assault case closely and even spoke with some of your former colleagues at the Cathedral. This is very unfair, Michael." The Rector looked visibly angry. "She and at least three members of the Diocesan Committee want to strip you of your priest credentials."

"I see," said Brandon, whose emotions immediately went cold and defensive. "Let me guess. I got into a physical altercation, I'm a vocal hunter and sportsman, and I refuse to preach the church wide talking points on gun control. Apparently, I have too much testosterone to be an Episcopal clergyman these days."

"That's just about spot on, my boy," said the Rector. "I'm afraid they just might succeed in getting rid of you. Bishop Burroughs is close with the Presiding Bishop, the National Cathedral, the Seminary, and many liberal clergy and congregants."

Brandon developed a look of contempt on his face that was common among his wealthy and conservative class.

"Not to be uncharitable, Rector, but this is not about the Gospel of Jesus Christ. It's pure, unadulterated politics. They don't care that my sermons and my counseling have increased the positive activity and growth in this church. They care about their left-wing progressive ideology. And they're demanding conformity. Well, I think on Sunday I'm going to use my sermon to extol the virtues of self-defense from the old-school times back in Virginia."

"Calm yourself. You'll do no such thing," retorted the Rector. "You do that, and they'll have your head on a platter."

"I can't take any of more this," said the troubled young priest. "I'm way past my stress tolerance because of these confession meetings, and now this. Rector Thompson, if they took the vote on me, say, next week, could I survive?"

"No," the Rector said.

Brandon leapt from his chair and grabbed his clerical collar with his right hand and stared at Rector Thompson. The elder clergyman motioned for Michael to sit down.

"There will not be a vote next week, or next month. September would be the earliest that proceedings would begin."

"Do you have a plan, Rector?" Michael asked.

"As a matter of fact, I do," the Rector said.

"Please don't tell me it involves my parents. I'm 40 years old."

"Any power play that I make in the Episcopal Church in this state would involve your parents. Stop being so casually independent, Michael. You need people in your corner. I have a plan to keep you in the priesthood and at my church. Would you like me to begin executing it?"

"Yes, sir," said a placated Brandon.

"For now, stick to the lectionary when you preach," Thompson said. "Maintain all decorum and tradition at the worship service. You said over the phone that the Deputy Chief of Police came to you on a spiritual matter? How did it go?"

"He asked about sin and the afterlife, then he told me I had friends in high places."

"I will reach out to him myself," the Rector said. "From today going forward, do your job and nothing more. If anyone asks to meet with clergy, I will meet with them. We have been dealt a rather nasty hand, and we must play it well."

"I'm grateful to you, sir," Brandon said. "Why are you sticking your neck out for me?"

"Reasons enough, Michael. Reasons enough. By the time I'm finished with this, your career will be safe, and that lefty bishop will be back up north where she belongs." The old Rector got up from his chair and winked at Brandon as he put his hand on his shoulder. "The liberals aren't the only ones who can play politics, my boy."

Brandon returned to the condo, where he saw Bettina undressing in the bedroom. As she put on her leisure clothes, she informed him that they had been summoned to a Brandon family meeting that Saturday.

"Damn...Rector Thompson works quickly, doesn't he?" said Michael under his breath. "A real, honest to goodness family meeting? I can't imagine what's in store for us, Bettina. Surely, some deep and dark secrets will present themselves, and in the most mild-mannered, chivalrous, and gothic fashion, I'll wager."

"You're such a poet, darling," Bettina laughed, "and your flare for the dramatic tells me you missed your true calling."

"And what would that be?"

"A Shakespearean actor, silly," Bettina said.

"I may need those skills come Saturday. I have a feeling that the elder Brandons are contemplating a move."

"A move?"

"Yes, the kind of move that tends to make the ground shake."

Saturday, July 8

Just four days after their annual 4th of July party at their Fauquier County farm, the elder Brandons hosted an even more intimate gathering at their house in Alexandria. The purpose of this day's dinner and drinks was not a celebration of country or tradition. Rather, it was a purposeful meeting of the minds.

When 4 p.m. arrived, so did Michael and Bettina. The house smelled of Beef Wellington and fresh crabs for salad. The bar at the far wall of the drawing room sported bottles of red and white wine that no longer existed — private French vintage from friends of Congressman Brandon. The younger Brandons greeted the elder ones, with one special guest.

"Rector, nice to see you in a social setting," said Michael to Rector Thompson. "I believe you know my wife, Bettina."

"Yes, delightful to see you again," the Rector said.

Bettina had her long hair teased and held by a comb to fall over her left shoulder. Her dress was lowcut and summer white, and she sported red pumps and a wide red belt. Her presence was more than enough to make two elderly gentlemen break into a cold sweat, which they did.

"Mmm, I've never tasted wine this good in my life," Bettina said.

"Enjoy that glass and one more," the Congressman said. "That's the last drop of the red in existence. Same with the two bottles of white."

Bettina sipped her wine and gave Michael a glance, then rolled her eyes. He knew what that look was all about. She was the child of immigrants, and he was a pedigreed rich kid whose advantages never ceased to amaze her. But she was grateful and gracious toward her in-laws, whom she loved and respected. When it came to Brandon's advantages, Bettina would always renounce judgment in favor of enjoyment.

As dinner commenced, Patricia Brandon got right down to business.

"This situation with the new bishop will not do," she politely but haughtily said. "Generations of my family have supported the Episcopal Church in Virginia in ways which apparently escape this new breed of clergy."

She looked straight at Rector Thompson, gave a gentle wave of her left hand, and said the following: "My son has earned his position in the church. He has earned it through his grades at seminary. He has earned it through his hard work and exceptional skills as a parish priest, albeit a very short time. Now, some liberal dandy female is elected head of this diocese, and all of a sudden, my boy is in danger of being defrocked. Not while I am alive. We are not leaving this dining room table until we all come up with a plan to thwart this contemptible nonsense."

"Well, the lad did bring this last round on himself, what with the beating of that terrible fellow, Smalls," the Congressman chimed in.

"Quiet, dear," said Patricia Brandon as she waved off her husband with her right hand. Mrs. Brandon, at this point, sat back in her chair and looked at all who were present at the table. She commanded the room with the strength and panache of a New York Mafia Don. The softer her voice, the more frightening she was.

At this point, the Rector came up with the solution. "When I was a young priest serving on the diocesan committee, Joe and I did a little deal. I urged the bishop at the time, and the committee, to buy the land that Christ Church now sits on. As you well know, the Brandon Trust stills owns the note on the ground and the building."

"That's the way I had the contract written...ground and building," said the Congressman.

The Rector continued, "The conservative breakaway Anglicans in Virginia and Pennsylvania left the Episcopal Church and tried to take their church buildings with them. The courts ruled against them, arguing that the Episcopal dioceses owned the building and grounds by virtue of canon law. But the Christ Church situation is slightly different."

"How do you mean?" Patricia asked.

"Those other churches had been on their sites for over a hundred years. And paid for in full. As Joe will certainly tell you, the deed to the Christ Church property is still in the Trust's name. It doesn't revert to the diocese for another eight years. So, theoretically, I could persuade the Vestry, and the congregation could take a quick vote at our behest..."

"Then, Christ Church could leave the diocese, join the Anglicans, and take all the property with us," said a cunning Michael Brandon.

"Brilliant as usual, James," said the Congressman.

"Hold on," Patricia said. "As much as I despise the liberals, I'm not sure I want to leave the Episcopal Church. There is too much history, too much tradition at stake."

"We don't have to leave, Patricia," said a confident Rector Thompson. "Just the threat of one of their most valued and elite churches privately threatening to leave and having the law firmly on their side should humble the bishop and make her stand down regarding Michael. I should go see the bishop immediately and have this conversation before she has more time to think and act."

The Congressman, Michael, and Patricia agreed at once. Patricia now looked at Bettina and said, "You are our daughter now, dear. Your opinion is quite important. What do you think?"

"I'm more knowledgeable about regular politics than church politics," Bettina replied. "But this plan sounds very intelligent."

Bettina was feeling unusually privileged herself, being included in a Brandon family scheme for the first time.

"Alright, you gentlemen get this done," Patricia directed.

Something had suddenly changed inside Michael Brandon. He had left the political world for the church. And now the church was being politicized by the new bishop, and against himself. No more did Brandon feel the need to distance himself from his parents' money and power. Rector Thompson was right. He needed friends in high places. He needed his powerful family. Like Bettina, he had been mightily impressed by the swift and efficient way his parents and the Rector launched an ingenious plan of attack on his behalf. And he was grateful.

On the ride home, and into the night while they both lay in bed, Brandon and his wife would marvel at just how treacherous this sneak attack on the bishop and the other liberals who were out to get Brandon was, and how much Michael deserved to defeat them, no matter the means.

Thus, we have come full circle in the character of this young priest. On the one hand, he was still a godly, compassionate, and committed clergyman. On the other hand, the old Brandon was back too. The one who was taught how to win and believed that he deserved to win. Not just this time, but every time.

CHAPTER 15

Thursday, July 13

Brandon went to his office at Christ Church. Besides the Secretary, he was alone. Rector Thompson had gone to see the bishop in Richmond. Almost precisely at high noon, Brandon's cell phone rang. He recognized the number and answered immediately.

"Yes, Rector. Okay. I thought it might. Does that end it? That's right... We have only eight more years to play this one. Thanks again, I'm very grateful."

Michael put his phone down and slumped back in the chair. The threat had worked. According to Rector Thompson, he and the bishop met alone without the committee members. She didn't even wish to consult an attorney.

"Wow," Michael said to himself. "The Rector really had her over a barrel. And that tells me another thing. Money and politics speak very loudly in the church. And ironically, they speak louder with the liberal progressive types."

He stood up and looked into the mirror on his office wall. He straightened his clerical collar and smiled at himself with attitude. He was to remain an Episcopal Priest, and he was a Brandon through and through. He was proud of both. It was a good day to be himself. That night, Brandon and his wife ate dinner and watched movies until late in the evening.

Friday, July 14

Brandon and the Rector enjoyed a well-deserved double martini lunch. They congratulated each other and toasted the reduction in power of a very liberal bishop. The toast was not entirely a self-serving or a self-congratulatory action. The progressive worldview was simply out of place with Virginia tradition.

Despite the explosive population growth and diverse migration to the Washington suburbs, Virginia's political and religious character were not ready for change. With this victory, the world made sense again to Michael, in a way he hadn't felt for years.

"We have work to do, Michael," the Rector said. "And now we can do it unobstructed by the busybodies in Richmond."

"What's on our plate, Rector Thompson, aside from our usual worship and sermons?"

"Michael, I want Christ Church to be a place where the disaffected Episcopalians feel they can return. When the conservatives broke away, most of them followed their parishes into the new Anglican Communion in the United States. They now have their own Bishop. But a great many began worshipping at Roman Catholic, Greek Orthodox, and in some cases, conservative Baptist Churches. I want you to do two things. First, attend the interfaith community meetings, where you can network with Catholic, Orthodox, and traditionally minded Protestants. Let them get to know you and understand that Christ Church is a traditional Episcopal parish that reveres Christian Orthodoxy in worship, faith, and morals. Don't try and steal parishioners away from these churches. Not yet!"

"What's the second thing?" asked a hyper-curious Brandon.

"The second thing is to steal parishioners back from the Anglicans. The Episcopal Church will always be recognized as *the* Anglican Church in the United States, under the Archbishop of Canterbury. The breakaway parishes will never by recognized by the Church of England and the Communion. Let these people understand that they now have a spiritual home which is still part of the old church, but which teaches the inspiration of Holy Scripture and traditional family values."

"How do you want me to go about this, Rector?" Michael asked.

"Connect with the clergy from the six Anglican breakaway churches in the area," Thompson said. "Connect with the clergy of the Orthodox, Baptist, and Catholic Churches in the area, and build relationships. You'll know that opportunity is knocking should they invite you to speak or preach. Then, just do what you do best."

Brandon liked what he was hearing. He understood that America and most of the Western countries were in a culture war. A war that was overtaking the mainline Christian denominations, including his. Now, he was second in command behind a world class Clergyman who knew power and how to use it. He would pay close attention to Rector Thompson, extra special close attention in the coming months, that he too might become an expert in wielding power — for Brandon had recently had his conversion.

As a seminary student, Brandon left power games behind in favor of the spiritual vocation. But with all that had recently happened to him, all of the threats to his family and everything he loved made him keenly aware that these power games between people, between institutions, will always be with us in this life. They are unavoidable, a permanent fixture of the human condition. And as such, Brandon was willing and eager to put his talents to work on behalf of his family, his church, and his worldview. He would now re-embrace power and politics and exploit them to his advantage.

"Count me in, Rector, count me in a thousand times over," Brandon said with the confidence of a young priest who now understood how the world works. "What happens if we get a tidal wave of supporters from these efforts?"

"Then, your parents and I will initiate the second phase of this plan," the Rector said. "We will stack the Diocesan Committee and force out the current Bishop. She will be replaced with an acceptable Bishop. We are at this moment buying land from the small and vulnerable parishes who cannot afford the upkeep. As we gain control over the properties, we will slowly gain control of the machinery in Richmond. The Bishop and all the committees will begin to do our bidding."

"Is that legal?" Brandon asked.

"Certainly," said the Rector. "Except nobody will be able to discover that the Brandon Family Trust is behind it. For now, just use powers of persuasion and build these relationships; and of course, maintain the highest standards as a priest of this parish."

That night, Brandon told his wife everything he and the Rector discussed. "Can you believe it? I'm actually a political operative again, in addition to being a priest."

"Are you sure this is what you want, sweetheart?" Bettina asked. "You did become rather disgusted with the whole political scene once before."

"I know, but it's different this time. I'm not some flunky chasing a public office. I am the Associate Rector of a vitally important Church, who gets to assist the great Rector James Thompson in a fight for the soul of our culture. It's quite thrilling, you see. I don't think I will be able to sleep tonight, I'm so excited."

Bettina, ever the supportive wife, saw right through his pontifications. "I know you believe what you're telling me, but deep down you still need to prove you're somebody, don't you?"

Brandon, caught off guard by this inconvenient truth, embraced his wife warmly and dodged the question. "Let's just say I do things for a variety of reasons."

Rector Thompson, still in his church office, stared at a photograph identical to the one possessed by the mysterious man who had spoken with Patricia Brandon the night of July 4.

"Where did we go wrong, Patricia?" he said to himself. "Why couldn't Michael be my son? And why did we allow our son to grow up without real parents?"

The Rector and Patricia Brandon had an illegitimate son. Congressman Brandon knew about it, but Michael did not. He had never met his half-brother, though his brother knew about him. But now, the two had more in common than ever. Michael was just beginning to understand the true Brandon family interests, and to labor on their behalf. The brother had been serving those interests for many years.

How would Michael and his brother receive one another when circumstances threw them together? What would Michael think of his parents, and of the Rector? Why was this young man, until very recently, shielded from an ill designing conspiracy that had begun to take shape and would unfold like a Shakespearean tragedy or comedy, perhaps a little of both?

For now, Brandon had his mission. It was pure political salesmanship. But it was clean. Rector Thompson made sure to give him the clean work. But there would be dirty work as well. Other people would do that.

Meanwhile, Congressman Brandon, whose senior age had not depleted any of his legal prowess, had been busy using the family trust to do a leveraged buyout of Robert Martin's Open Door Development Corporation, for pennies on the dollar. He had recently acquired controlling interest, as Martin's wife and son were no match for the Congressman's skills and spite. Martin's business deals had wrecked the rural character of several of Virginia's most important counties, and he blamed Martin for ruining Michael's political career.

But what drove the Congressman's spite more than anything was that Martin and everything he stood for was an affront to Patricia. Blood sport and payback were front and center in the Congressman's mind as he initiated the first phase immediately. He sold his controlling interest in the corporation to the Episcopal Diocese of Virginia, again for pennies on the dollar. The stipulations were twofold. First, Rector James Thompson would be the sole legal trustee of all property and assets for ten years, having autocratic control over any business decisions. Under the terms of this contract, all of the high-density development projects were terminated. Secondly, the zoning commissioners and Supervisors in the Piedmont rural counties would be pressured not to up zone any of their land, since nearly all of the property that was desirable for urban development was owned by Open Door Development.

When the Episcopal Church would assume total ownership of the broken-up company, the Western part of Loudoun County and the counties of Clarke, Fauquier, Orange, Madison, Greene, Culpeper, and Albemarle would be safe from any high-density projects and would be completely out of reach to the schemes of urban planners in Washington, D.C., and Richmond. The progressive projects of liberal social planners and their commercial allies were entirely thwarted by several strokes of the pen, and all their hopes and dreams for a changing society and culture was dealt a two-generation setback.

In the Brandons' world, this was what total victory looked like. Enemies vanquished, money made, control over the Episcopal Church, and dictatorial power over the future of their beloved state. Empire might be a better word. The most beautiful, historic, and desirable counties in all Northern Virginia were now under Brandon supervision. The Virginia Piedmont was their realm. The icing on the cake was Loudoun County, where Open Door was headquartered and owned massive tracks of rural land, was also under Brandon control. The same county where the Congressman did his infamous Tuscarora deal would yield a tidy sum to the family trust. And if and when the state and local authorities finally pieced together the shady deals of the Congressman and his associates, the Episcopal Church would own much of the land in question, and the statute of limitations on bribery and graft would long since run out.

As Congressman Brandon drank in the evening, he would laugh heartily at the misery he was causing the progressive community in Loudoun County and elsewhere. He and his wife were now the saviors of Virginian tradition and the chief benefactors of their church. Their son was now a burgeoning priest in that very church.

"Enough of leaving things to chance with our son," said Patricia Brandon to her husband. "Michael will be a Bishop of the Church before I depart this world. You and I have nearly failed our little boy. We gave him no direction. It was a stroke of luck that he chose to go to seminary and into the church."

"Enough of the recriminations, Patricia. The poor boy never took anything seriously his whole life. Like you, I've always loved him and would do anything for him. I even got him elected to office. But until he met Bettina and chose his clerical vocation, he was not a safe investment. I've been waiting for this day for a long time. Michael now understands how the world around here works. He understands his family's place in it, and he understands his own place in it. He's proven his loyalty, worth, and good sense these last few months. Now that we're in position, we can give him the whole store. Michael will be Bishop. He will inherit untold millions in cash and land. Virginia and the church will be safe from undesirable change and encroachment. He doesn't know it yet, but our son will be the most influential member of an old society which will be around long after the buzzards have finished with the carcasses of the liberals."

"To the Bishop, then," Patricia said with her wine glass raised.

"To our boy," said the Congressman.

CHAPTER 16

Michael was not entirely prepared for what his parents now had in store for him. He drank too much, and he talked when he should listen. Had he not been married to Bettina, his colossally sized libido would have overtaken him and defeated his every attempt at reform. And though he was blossoming brilliantly as a parish priest, he still had the business sense of a prep-school boy with a prodigious allowance. Thankfully, Bettina Brandon was very conservative and educated in financial matters.

The couple would remain together for life and would outlive Michael's parents. It would be the younger Mrs. Brandon who would steward the thriving upper-class life they would inherit. Of course, they would have plenty of help from the terms of the Trust. The Congressman had made certain of it.

Monday, July 17

Bettina was showing off her business and political capabilities at the American Cancer Society. She was well liked but did not make friends as easily as her husband. After several weeks there, she could only count one person as someone she might get close to, someone she might trust and befriend.

After spending all morning in a fairly useless meeting and making dozens of fundraising calls, Bettina walked to the other side of the office with two cups of coffee in her hand.

"Coffee, Allison?" she asked. As she peered into the accounting office, a lovely young woman stood up from her desk, delighted to take a break from the monotony of her job.

The two ladies walked into an empty conference room, sat down, and sipped their coffee.

"How's law school treating you?" Bettina asked.

"Oh, just fine," said Allison. "I just wish I could do it full-time. I hate night classes."

"I don't mean to pry, but didn't you say your family was wealthy?"

"Well-off, but not loaded," Allison replied. "Anyway, accounting is great practice for me. I want to specialize in tax law."

Bettina wanted desperately to joke about her in-laws and tell her friend she could work for the Brandon family, developing creative ways to dodge taxes. But she didn't.

"I'm glad you work here, Allison. I must be 10 years older than you, but I feel like we have a nice connection."

"Aww, Bettina, that's so sweet. I feel the same way. You're so earnest and sincere, not to mention elegant and drop dead gorgeous!"

Bettina blushed, for she hadn't expected such praise from Allison so soon. "You're the gorgeous one in this office, honey. Every guy here has his mouth agape when you walk by."

Allison smiled and blushed as she drank her coffee.

"What are you doing Friday night?" Bettina asked.

"I'm sure I'll be with my boyfriend...Wait a second, I forgot. He told me this morning he would be gone Friday and Saturday," said Allison.

"Wonderful. I would love for you to come to dinner. I am somewhat of a cook, and I want you to meet my husband, Michael."

"Oh, I would love to, thank you so much! May I bring anything?" Allison asked.

"Just your sweet, lovely self. Is 7 p.m. okay?"

"Perfect. I think we're going to be great friends, Bettina." Allison kissed Bettina on the cheek.

The two women gave each other a hug. It was as if these exceptional ladies felt they lacked close female companionship and had just found it with one another. Bettina returned to her office with a giddy smile on her face and called Michael.

"Hi, stud boy, how's your day? Good, mine is going well too. Be home Friday evening. I've invited a coworker to dinner. I think I'll make Carne Asada. Yes, I know you love that dish. And you're going to like my friend. Allison Peters."

Rector Thompson would be busy that week, firing the opening salvo in the battle to make Michael Brandon a Bishop according to his mother's wishes. It's curious that neither he nor his parents consulted Michael about this latest ambition. Michael had zero interest in high office within the church. He had his own plans, which were to succeed Rector Thompson as the Rector of Christ Church, and to write novels and enjoy the literary life. He had secretly desired to become a writer soon after he entered seminary. But life had been busy and distracted him. The literary passions began to consume him, and fortunately he had an outlet — his sermons. Once he became established as Rector, he could then devote himself to writing books as well. The last thing Michael wanted was to be on the track to Bishop, which would require back-breaking travel and extra administrative duties he did not care to perform.

This would necessarily add some tension within the Brandon family.

* * *

The Hunter was busy that week — busy doing a disappearing act. He literally disappeared from his condo with all of his possessions, leaving a furnished apartment behind. A computer-typed printout saying, "Thanks for everything and have a great life," was all his lady friend of the last few months received from him.

The Hunter had one more job to do. He had decided to do the fourth job before he got out for good. His decision was to pay off, for he received a sum of money from his employer on which anyone could properly retire. Upon the final killing, the Hunter's account would be stuffed with the bonus for agreeing to do the fourth hit, plus another larger bonus for doing the jobs so well.

As his employer told him over the phone, he had exceeded expectations in his precision, follow-through, and ability to throw so much confusion to the scenes that no police detectives would be able to piece them all together. In addition, the Hunter had in his possession three phantom credit cards with false names, from three different Wall Street banks. Each card had a $100,000 charge limit and 6% interest rate. He could live off those cards luxuriously for two to three years before the accounts were frozen. The genius of this particular crime lay in the virus planted into the banks' central files that automatically approved a charge from the credit card, as if it were a corporate officer using a legitimate expense account. If the Hunter was cautious and spread out his charges, he would never call attention to what he was doing. The cyber security people would never notice because they would not know to look for anything.

Adding genius on top of genius, the Hunter also hacked into the Credit Bureau and constructed a phantom profile with credit history and a nearly perfect score. He had two banks with whom he did business and obtained two legitimate credit cards based upon these phony credit scores. He could deposit, withdraw, or borrow at will anywhere in the United States and many places in the world. And if the authorities or any bank security officers were ever onto him, the ingenious virus would notify him through a secure email. Thus, with over $5 million in cash payments, phony corporate credit cards, and a false credit profile, the Hunter could choose his place of repose and live safely, and large.

Wednesday, July 19

Julie Grimes walked into the station just minutes before her briefing with Deputy Chief Garrison. She saw two of her detectives in the break room getting coffee, and she helped herself to some. The colleagues exchanged the usual pleasantries and went into the chief's office, not knowing exactly what would unfold. For Grimes, this meeting would signal the end of her sense of reign over the most mysterious, unique, and potentially sinister string of murders ever to hit Alexandria. She had been laboring for weeks trying to find hard evidence that the killings of Robert Martin and Harry Penrose in Alexandria, and of James Smalls in Fairfax, were linked. She entered the afternoon's meeting with the assumption that her efforts were supported at the highest level. She was wrong.

"Grimes, it's time for a housecleaning — a new strategy with this whole mess," said Garrison.

"What do you have in mind, Chief?" asked Grimes nervously.

The Deputy Chief paused as he made eye contact with all of the officers in the room. "Everyone except Grimes, get out. Go do something useful with the rest of the day," he said.

"Yes, Chief," muttered the other detectives as they exited his office expeditiously.

Julie got up and closed the door upon the Chief's motioning. She sat back down, sweating with a sense of impending doom and waited for the bomb to drop.

"Julie, you can relax. I'm not backtracking on you. You're still the lead detective, and you still have my confidence."

Grimes began to breathe a little more easily, but her confusion was not assuaged. "Thanks, Chief, we've been working this thing as hard as it can be."

"I know you have, and I'm going to make it easier on you," the Chief said. "On all of us actually. I'm going to give you your new orders, and then you will give those same orders to the other detectives. As of right now, this investigation will cease to be about patterns and linkage between the three murders."

"How do you mean?" interjected Grimes, sweating again and feeling her heart pounding uncontrollably.

"Just listen," Garrison said. "I called Fitzgerald over in Fairfax and told him our department is no longer involved in the Smalls case. It's their jurisdiction. They need to investigate it as a simple homicide. There is no more cooperative investigation with Fairfax County and us. If you and your team stumble on evidence or leads of obvious relevance, share them. Otherwise, they do their thing and we do ours. As for the two Alexandria cases, I want you to direct all your time and resources to the Penrose murder."

"Why Penrose? Martin was the first and the highest profile."

"I'm getting to that, Julie," said Garrison, who motioned through the window for his secretary to bring in more coffee.

Grimes reluctantly accepted the coffee. She did not need the extra caffeine as she was becoming nervous. She had operated these last weeks on the idea that there was one killer and three victims. She was given a green light to steer the investigation anyway she saw fit. Now, the man at the top was telling her how it was. She might be lead investigator, but he would be pulling the strings moving forward.

When the Chief finished with his orders, Grimes would be tugged in a direction she did not care to go.

"Ah, excellent coffee for a cop station, wouldn't you say, Grimes?" Garrison remarked.

"Yes, excellent coffee, sir," Julie said.

"Let me wrap this up now, Grimes. Nobody cares about a sleazy, greedy slumlord like Martin. State police kicked the case over to us because they couldn't find anything. As of this morning, I officially kicked it back to them. Now, Penrose was assassinated in the most popular church in one of our best neighborhoods. This is the one we need to solve. So, any witnesses or other persons of interest in the other two cases need to be dropped from your itinerary and your radar. Focus everything on Penrose."

"But Chief—" pleaded Grimes.

"This is not a request, Julie. If I find out you're actively working either of the other cases, I'll have no choice but to remove you from all cases. If you want to remain a detective in this department, you follow my directive. Understood?"

"Yes, Chief," Grimes said.

"Dismissed."

Garrison had informed Michael Brandon during their meeting at his church that he had friends in high places. By keeping Julie Grimes on as lead detective but under orders to look into only one case out of the three, the Deputy Chief reduced the scope of the investigation to such a small denominator that the media, state, and federal authorities would lose even the smallest amount of interest they had in what could have become a massively high profile set of circumstances for the greater Alexandria community. The lower the profile, the better for all of the Brandons.

Incidentally, Fairfax police detective Fitzgerald had been given a similar set of instructions from his boss.

Detective Grimes gathered her team and gave them the new instructions. She added the caveat that they investigate any evidence, come what may. It was her covert way of leaving the door open for linkages to the other cases that all of her instincts told her existed.

Friday, July 21

Poor Allison Peters, sad and bewildered, pulled the Hunter's note out of her purse and just stared. She looked out of her office window, then stared back at the cold and brief note from the man with whom she had been intimate for months.

She looked outside the door and saw Bettina Brandon, a warm new friend she made and the very person who might give her some comfort that night at dinner. She then stared again at the note. As she ran through the litany of her emotions concerning the Hunter, she could not decide whether she was simply enthralled with the man or in love with him. All she knew for sure was that she was in pain. Why would he run away without a reason, or without saying goodbye in person?

The accountant and law student was puzzled, and analytical types tend to not tolerate being puzzled for long. Allison had worked through every scenario that made sense to her over the previous two days. She concluded that he never talked to her about his work, not since that initial conversation the day they met. She had seen him fight on that day, and they worked out together numerous times. He was very cerebral and quick-witted, very physically able, and very opaque. He described his police experience fighting organized crime and his having to assume a new identity with such confidence and precision. Her conclusion was that he was a secret government operative who should never have gotten into a relationship with her or anyone else. He was obviously called away to another city to do other duties and could tell no one.

The fact that he could just as easily have been an enemy agent, a jewel thief, or a hired killer never crossed Allison's mind. He was good, brave, and noble. Her strong gentleman protector. In the weeks to come, Allison's curiosity would overtake her. But for the moment, she needed the compassion and sympathy of a friend. As she would tightly cling to Bettina Brandon, the two women would share feelings that, for the moment, were undefinable. Allison left work early to go home and get ready for her evening with the Brandons.

Michael left the church and got home around 4:30 p.m. He instantly smelled the early stages of Bettina's gourmet meal. In his mind, he had two choices — change and go work out in the gym downstairs, or just settle in and drink and nibble at the food as it was being cooked, and at his wife. He chose the latter.

"I'm hitting the shower now and will be out here to help you," said Brandon as he kissed his wife.

"You mean help yourself," Bettina replied with a grin.

"That too, of course," he said.

Brandon readied himself for company, and promptly at 5:30, fixed himself the first of many drinks. He hadn't lifted a finger to help his wife with the meal. Fortunately, his assistance was unnecessary. Mrs. Brandon had it all covered. The evening was hot and sticky humid. The kind of summer day where the air did not move but hovered over everything like a thick, wet blanket. The scores of little creeks and streams that comprised the tributaries to the Potomac River smelled of the stagnant water of deep southern swamps. The air conditioning in the building was old and despite recent maintenance was producing not half the cold air desirable.

Add the heat from the kitchen, and the Brandons and their guest would smolder until sundown. Michael was on the sofa reading a leather-bound complete works of Robert Louis Stevenson, the author of *Treasure Island*, *Kidnapped*, and *Dr. Jekyll and Mr. Hyde*. The 19th Century Scottish author was not renown for writing in elevated Jamesian prose, but as Brandon put it, "He sure could tell a story." This was a quality he always placed as paramount to the preaching profession.

Bettina soon emerged from her labors, and as she headed for the shower told her husband to head down to the lobby and meet Allison at 6:45 p.m.

"She's always early, sweetheart," Bettina said. "Please go down before she gets here."

It was 6:15 when Brandon decided to make his move downstairs, taking a fresh Gin Rickey and his book. For 30 minutes, the front desk man buzzed in visitors, but Michael was so ensconced in his reading that he didn't even notice the never-ending train of beautiful young women entering his lobby. When he finally paused at the end of a chapter, it was just before 7 p.m., and he heard a soft, sweet voice say, "I'm here to see the Brandons in 201."

Michael got up and greeted Allison Peters. "It's delightful to meet you, Allison. Welcome to Marina Towers."

"So nice to meet you, Reverend. Bettina never stops talking about you," she said as she shook Brandon's hand. Were it not for the heat of the day, both of them would have been embarrassed at their sweaty palms. As they took the elevator for the short ride, Brandon couldn't help but catch a glimpse of Miss Peter's stunning figure wrapped up in a tight blue and white sundress, as well as her moist cappuccino-colored skin. Allison was oblivious to the brief stare, for she had not dressed for him.

The two walked into the condo, and Michael poured Allison a glass of Sauvignon Blanc, then gave her a brief tour of the unit and the stunning view of D.C. from the balcony. Then, Bettina walked out into the living room, looking ravishing as ever. Brandon sipped his gin and winked at his wife, who sported a very short pink cocktail dress. Allison put down her wine, and despite the intense heat and humidity, threw her arms around Bettina, kissing both of her cheeks. The women clasped each other's hands as Bettina welcomed Allison to their home. Allison hugged Bettina again. Brandon's mind was swimming with a variety of pleasant thoughts at that moment as he made another drink, poured wine for his wife and guest, and the three sat down for delicious food and engaging conversation. And they sweated.

Bettina was delirious with glee all through the evening, as if in addition to her already dreamy life, she may have found the woman who would be her best friend. Allison felt the same emotions as Bettina and was positively giddy about having this big sister figure to love and comfort her through her current travails. As for Brandon, his foremost thought was directed at the permanent mental picture he had of these two excessively attractive women hugging and kissing each other.

It was after 9 p.m. when the sun set, and a mild breeze began to blow. Since the kitchen heat was still palpable, the three retired out onto the balcony, where the conversation soon shifted to the Hunter. Allison told the couple all about the day they had met and about his likely work situation.

"You should go to the police and file a report," Bettina offered. "Missing person or something. Maybe they can help locate him."

"Doubtful," said Brandon as Bettina shot him a sharp glance. "My recent experience with parishioners who are in similar lines of work is that they come and go in the blink of an eye. Either they don't want to be found, or they cannot allow themselves to be found. Most of these guys I've talked with seem lonely, but they've chosen this lonely life and perhaps prefer it that way. What makes your guy seem different is that he began a serious relationship that he probably shouldn't have. He's probably hurting like you are, but it's the life he chose."

Bettina had her friend's interest at heart, and she wanted to argue with Michael. Persuade him to tell Allison something more comforting. But she suspected he was right, so she let him keep talking.

"I can imagine how mindboggling and hurtful this is for you, Allison. But based on my pastoral and personal experience, you need to begin the process of letting this go. You are young and beautiful, with your whole life ahead of you. Don't spend any more time chasing a mystery that does not wish to be solved. Well, I'm off duty until Sunday," said a chuckling Brandon, trying to lighten the mood.

After a big smile came over Allison's face, he thought he had. Then she started to cry. Bettina motioned for Brandon to go back inside and leave them. She pulled her chair close to Allison's and held the younger woman to her breast. The ladies remained in that position for over an hour. Bettina comforted and caressed Allison as she sobbed.

Distraught, exhausted, and with too much wine in her, Allison acquiesced later to Bettina's demand that she spend the night. She thanked Bettina and passed out on the balcony chair. Brandon, who saw what happened, went outside, picked up Allison, and carried her into the spare bedroom. He removed her shoes and tucked her into bed. Wide awake and amorous, Michael couldn't wait to get into bed with his wife.

That evening had been important for Bettina. All these years in D.C. had produced short careers, a husband, and many friends who could better be called associates. She did not have a friend on the scale of her sister, Nora, or one of her many cousins in Florida who she adored. She and Allison had only just met weeks earlier on Bettina's first day at the Cancer Society. Allison was much younger, yet she was mature, intellectually stimulating, fashionable, and strikingly pretty. Just like herself.

"Thank you for being so nice and gallant toward my friend," Bettina said.

"You're welcome," Brandon said. "I like her. She's very spirited. She is irresistibly vulnerable but emits a spark of strength as well. I bet she'll be alright, and fairly quick."

CHAPTER 17

Everyone in the high Virginia society of the Brandons believed in capitalism. It was, after all, the only economic system whereby one can make a fortune. But few practiced it in its pure ethical form. The Hunter's first victim, developer Robert Martin, had talked a good game whenever he gave a speech, touting his love for entrepreneurship, working the hardest for the lowest return and other self-serving bullshit.

He was the kind of capitalist that would make Adam Smith turn over in his grave; a political hack, a classic bottom-feeder. Every town and county he developed was less beautiful, less peaceful, and less socially harmonious after he was done. He literally built the cheapest, most dense housing and the worst looking strip malls on some of the most hallowed, historical, and breathtaking landscape in the region. And the Brandons had quite enough. When Martin tried to use a zoning variance to build on the cheap near Middleburg, young Michael put a stop to it.

Twenty years earlier, the Governor of Virginia struck a deal with the Disney Company to build a theme park on some of that hallowed ground. It was Mrs. Patricia Brandon who mobilized her wealthy friends, Civil War Historians, and conservationists into action. The result was the legislature killed the proposal with extreme prejudice. No developer or politician has since proposed anything of that kind.

"Don't fuck with the Brandons," became a familiar cry behind the scenes in Virginia's corridors of power. Three self-described players on that scene did not heed the warning, and all came to a bad end.

Congressman Joe Brandon was a player, perhaps the J.R. Ewing of Northern Virginia. As the head of the family, he ruthlessly defended its interests. He would use his superb legal and operative mind to manipulate the law, manipulate public officials, and amass favors on a grand scale, only to call them in at the right time. One of the principal pillars of the free-market system is competition. When it came time to cast a vote dealing with business and the economy, though, the Congressman was more interested in suppressing competition than defending it. Yes indeed, the Brandons and the other blue bloods oozed principles from their pores when it came to the land, tradition, and cultural values. However, when matters of family wealth and power were in play, the elder Brandon was no different than the rest of his class. In that area, all of them felt they did not have the luxury of principles.

But the Congressman was not a killer. Nor was his son, Michael, though he took after his father as a fighter. But young Brandon excelled more in fighting with his passion, and sometimes his hands and feet, than with treachery. The father and son were different in other ways. The Congressman couldn't care less if he was popular, an interesting trait for a politician. No, he used politics to gain for himself and for his family and friends. Michael, on the other hand, truly wished to be liked and admired. He was the natural salesman, the natural politician of the family. And yet he could succeed in neither over the long haul. What does that say about the state of affairs in business and politics? Draw your own conclusions, dear reader. The elder Brandons were now actively plotting to secure their son's ultimate political success: high office within the Episcopal Church.

Wednesday, July 26

Allison Peters was feeling better and better as the previous few days passed. She adored her new best friend, Bettina Brandon. She also felt very safe with her friend's husband, the Reverend. With her parents, her new friends, job, and law school, she realized how full her life was and how promising was her future. She had left some framed pictures of herself at the Hunter's condo and decided she was strong enough to let herself in and retrieve them. She was too late. The owner had changed the locks and called the maid service.

Allison, hearing the vacuum cleaners inside, knocked on the door. One of the maids opened the door. She did not speak English, but Allison used some broken Spanish to communicate who she was to the previous occupant.

"Ay," said the maid. "Un momentito."

The maid came back to the door 30 seconds later and gave Allison a shell casing. The maids had found it while cleaning the unit. Allison knew nothing about guns, but even she saw this for what it was. Seeing that her pictures were gone, she left the condo looking at the shell. She looked at the bottom of the shell in a glare of sunlight from the lobby windows. *7mm Magnum*, it read.

She might have been completely ignorant of firearms, assassins, and criminal masterminds. But there was one area where Miss Allison Peters was not deficient. And that was with tedious, in-depth research. She went home to her computer and put her legal training and prowess to work. It would take every night that week and half of that Saturday, pulling up news articles and police reports and statements. When she was done, she was convinced her ex-boyfriend was involved in the nefarious activity in Alexandria. But who to tell? Where to take the evidence and her assumptions? Based on his actions and her recent discoveries, she was certain his real name was not Steve Wilson.

They say hitmen always make a mistake, which often leads to their capture and arrest. Could this be the Hunter's one mistake? If so, it's a major one. How could such a professional not have disposed of this kind of evidence?

Saturday, July 29

Brandon was practicing his sermon at home. The condo was hot with steam from the shower that he and Bettina had taken together some minutes before. Michael had been feeling particularly amorous. He had worked out that morning, and at Bettina's suggesting, gotten a very expensive and luxurious massage from a friend of hers.

Ashley was from the Philippines originally and had come to the Washington area back in the 1990s. She and her husband owned one of the premier salons in Old Town Alexandria. They did not advertise doing massages because they didn't want the creepy element coming in off the street. But by word of mouth, a man or woman could get up to two hours of relaxation and therapy from Ashley's soft and gentle petite but strong hands. Brandon had gotten several of Ashley's massages before, and he was quite taken with her charms. It was all very innocent, but this exceptionally lovely woman, who gave such tender loving care to her preferred clients and friends, had told Bettina, "It was a pleasure to meet Michael the other day. What a beautiful man! And such a gentleman. Devastatingly handsome."

Bettina relayed the compliments to her husband, who loved what he heard. He loved it so much he could barely speak. Now, Ashley was married and so was he, happily.

But like some of his literary heroes, Brandon secretly fantasized about being both a faithful husband and a ladies' man, too. How would that work? Simple. He would be everything to Bettina that she wanted him to be. And he would continue to take excellent care of himself. He would never miss an opportunity to be pleasing to the opposite sex. He would store up compliments and flirtations from other women like squirrels store acorns in the winter.

Ashley from the Philippines was gorgeous and elegant. She had a gift for making others feel special. Michael had been borderline obsessed with impressing her. When his wife informed him that he had, the adrenaline flowed like a river, and Brandon enjoyed yet again what seemed like uninterrupted affirmation of his ultimate desirability as a man. This is what Brandon meant when he considered himself to be a blissful married man, and a lady killer. When he got home from his massage that day, he was flying high, and Bettina was the prime beneficiary.

Hearing his landline ring, he saw that it was the front desk.

"Brandon," he answered. "Sure, let her come up. Honey, it's Allison. She's on her way up here." Michael opened their front door.

"Okay, I'm almost done. Be right out," Bettina said.

"Hey, guys," said Allison as she walked in.

Bettina greeted her, and Brandon got up to leave the room. "I'll just finish my work. You two have the run of the place."

"Actually, Michael, it's you that I came to see," Allison began. "I have a problem that I think a conversation with you might help. Would you mind terribly?"

Bettina knew the drill. This was a plea for her husband, the priest, to counsel with Allison on a private matter.

"I need to go to the store," said Bettina. "You two stay here and talk." She kissed Michael and hugged her friend.

"Now, Miss Allison, what can I do for you?" Michael asked.

"I think I've been sleeping with a hitman," Allison exclaimed.

Michael, surprised and not knowing quite how to respond, turned to humor.

"Do you love him?" Brandon half-joked.

"Seriously, I didn't come here for judgment," Allison said.

"You obviously came here for spiritual advice of some kind."

"No, not really."

Brandon looked puzzled. "Why are you here?"

"Because I love Bettina so much, and I know she wouldn't have married you if you weren't sincere and trustworthy. I'm not that religious, but I feel like you're somebody who cares about people and wants to help them."

"That is my job, Allison, and I'm ready to help you. What's this all about? Why would you think your ex is an assassin?"

With that, Allison pulled the rifle shell casing from her purse and handed it to Brandon. Owning the same caliber of rifle himself, he instantly knew what he was holding.

"The maids found this in Steve's condo when they cleaned for the new tenants," Allison explained. "At first, I freaked and wanted to go to the police. But then I realized they would not believe or understand anything I told them. I more or less lived with this guy for five months. I don't know his real name, but it is definitely not Steve Wilson. He beat up an old boyfriend of mine easily, with one hand. He told me stories of his days as a cop and a federal agent. And when he disappeared, I thought he was on a mission of some kind. But after the new evidence and researching I did all week, I think he may have been involved in the murders back in the winter."

"Why did you get involved with this man in the first place?" Brandon asked.

"He was gallant, well-dressed, a gentleman," Allison said. "Better than that, he was a gentleman protector. I felt safe with him. To tell you the truth, I'm bisexual. I've always preferred being with women, but I've usually had a boyfriend in my life to feel safe and normal. Oh, please! Please, Michael, don't tell Bettina. I need her friendship so very badly."

"Calm yourself, Allison," Brandon assured her. "This conversation is strictly between us. But Bettina is very compassionate and understanding. If I were you, I would pick the right time and tell her yourself. I am confident she wouldn't think any less of you."

"Oh, I just couldn't. I'd be so frightened to lose her affection."

Brandon placed his hand on Allison's trembling hands and looked tenderly into her eyes. "Are you in love with my wife, Allison?"

Her voice cracked as she replied, "I don't know, maybe. I mean I love her to pieces as a friend, and she's so, so hot! But I know I can be happy with just her friendship."

"I tell you what," Brandon said. "Leave this shell casing with me, and I will give it to a friend who will handle this properly."

Brandon took Allison's hands and leaned in to whisper a prayer. "Amen."

Allison wiped away tears and threw her arms around Michael, clutching him tightly. As they rose from the sofa, Michael offered her a drink.

"Bettina is going to cook up something tasty when she returns. Stick around for dinner?"

"Okay, but I'm a mess, Michael," Allison said.

"That's what the drink is for," he said.

"You have got to be the coolest priest who ever lived," Allison said.

"Careful, that kind of rumor could get me defrocked."

The two laughed and drank. Bettina later joined them. They ate and drank more. That evening, three people felt very, very good. And Brandon instructed Allison to tell no one about the shell casing, not even Bettina.

He had also made it clear to Allison that if she wanted to hear more about faith and God's peace, she could come to his 5 p.m. service the next day at Christ Church. Allison said she might. Later, after Allison left, Bettina, ever protective, admonished Brandon to go lightly on religious matters concerning her friend.

"Not before she's ready, honey. Don't push."

"Nobody's pushing, sweetheart. She came to me, remember? Go to bed...I have a few minutes more of work, and then I will join you."

Brandon went out onto the balcony, shut the door, and called a police cell phone. It was not Julie Grimes.

"Yes, it concerns one of your cases. I have something to give you. Can you meet me at the church tomorrow at 4 p.m. Your office? No. It's better you come and see me."

Sunday, July 30

Rector Thompson had finished with the morning services and asked Michael to come to the church early for a chat. It was 2 p.m., and the talk would be brief since Brandon had to prepare for evening service at 5 p.m.

"I assume your parents have told you what I'm up to right now," said the Rector.

"You mean the ecumenical stuff you assigned me last week?" Michael asked.

"No, the plan to get you positioned for Assistant Bishop. I would have thought they'd tell you by now."

"That's news to me," Brandon said. "I don't want to be a bishop, assistant or otherwise. I want to be Rector of this church when you retire."

"Well, that puts an interesting take on things," said a puzzled Rector Thompson. "Why don't you just do the things we talked about, and I will revisit this other thing with your folks? Don't say anything to them about this yet."

"Whatever you say," said Brandon. Michael was confused, but also content to let his mentor handle most anything concerning his career. He walked down the street and got a large coffee and a cinnamon roll. He waited to eat and drink until he got back to the church, then went over the sermon and service bulletin one more time. Shortly afterwards, Deputy Chief of Police Garrison walked into the church. Michael got right down to business, pulling out the 7mm Magnum rifle shell casing.

"It's got my fingerprints on it, of course, and the fingerprints of Allison Peters, a friend of my wife's who had a romantic relationship with a mysterious man," Michael said. "She said the maids found this casing in his condo while cleaning after he suddenly moved out and disappeared."

"Have you or she told anyone else about this?" asked the Chief.

"No. The maids there didn't speak any English and, according to Miss Peters, didn't seem to know or care about its significance."

"Ask your friend what company the maids work for," Garrison said. "I might need to interview them."

"Sure," said Brandon. "You know that I turned in my 7mm Magnum Rifle to Detective Grimes?"

"Yes, I know," said the Chief. "I see no reason not to give you back all of your guns now. Come to the station tomorrow morning and I'll have them for you."

"Thanks! Glad to know I'm out of the woods," Brandon said.

"You were never in the woods, Reverend," said the Chief as he left the church.

Brandon was ready to perform when the first parishioners arrived at 4:30. This early crowd was demanding simply by their over accented punctuality. But Michael appreciated them, both as committed congregants and a guaranteed audience for his sermons. These sermons were becoming more and more his dominant passion and art form. The beauty and aptness of his words and the skill with which he delivered them were the reason the 5 p.m. service was becoming an institution, both at Christ Church and throughout the faith community in Alexandria. He welcomed more than 100 church members and gave the altar boy and altar girl the proper instructions for beginning the service. There was no choir at the 5 p.m., but the organist was there, and he piped the service through the introit and into the processional hymn. After the Gospel reading, Reverend Brandon took the pulpit.

"In this latest series of messages I have delivered, the main theme has been the unconditional and everlasting love God has for each one of us," Michael began. "The proof of this astonishing love is borne out in the three pillars which comprise our Episcopal theology: the Bible, Church Tradition, and Reason. Our beloved brothers and sisters down the street at the Methodist Church added a fourth — Experience. Last week, I spoke about how God's love shone brightly in our holy scriptures. Today, I wish to say something about tradition. Tradition is out of fashion, it seems, in this scientific, hi-tech progressive society. Everyone looks for the latest invention. If one's cell phone is over six months old, one feels left behind."

The congregation laughed, then Brandon continued, "In his masterful comedy, *The Tempest*, Shakespeare reminds us, 'What is past is prologue.'"

Brandon sermonized for over 30 minutes, an unusually long time for an Episcopalian service. He regaled the parishioners with his literary chops, quoting from authors William Faulkner and Henry James and poets such as T.S. Eliot, who serve as reminders that we are all heirs to a tradition, to a store of knowledge and ideas which transcend time. And he finished with more on the Bible, quoting Ecclesiastes: "There is nothing new under the sun."

"What is the Bible if not literature?" Brandon asked. "It is our sacred literature, but literature none the same. And tradition is ever present.

The new prophets quote the old prophets, and Jesus places himself in that prophetic tradition."

Brandon closed out his sermon by reminding everyone that the world does not begin today. Trying to separate a church, society, or culture from its past is anti-historical, anti-intellectual, and culturally suicidal. Progress and change occur, but conservation and preservation of what is timeless and classical is paramount.

His message was well received. Rector Thompson had stayed for it and gave Brandon the thumbs up. The diverse congregation was again wooed by the charm and eloquence of the young priest and praised him for his wise insights. In baseball terminology, this was a grand slam home run.

In the back pew, almost out of sight, sat Allison Peters, looking both at home and uncomfortable at the same time inside a church. She greeted Brandon in the line of parishioners at the end of the service and quickly left to go to her car, as if she needed to be seen there by Michael, but also to get away as soon as possible.

CHAPTER 18

Two Months Later

As late September approached, the Congressman's health began a rapid decline. The expensive medication he had been taking prevented major life-threatening strokes, but it did little in battling those mini strokes which cumulatively reduced him to a wheelchair and slurred his speech. His mind was occasionally lucid, but his vitality was a pitiful shell of its former self.

Patricia Brandon had gotten power of attorney and was now making all Brandon family decisions unilaterally. The couple sold their Alexandria estate for nearly $10 million and moved out to their Fauquier County farm near Middleburg, hiring a full-time, live-in nurse to care for Congressman Brandon around the clock. Friends were supportive and sympathetic, dropping by the farm to check up on their compatriot, often times unannounced. This kind of un-southern conduct miffed Patricia, but she was grateful, nonetheless, for their kindness and concern.

Michael and Bettina were always cheerful during their visits, though a cloud of sadness would descend on them always during the long drive home, with Michael taking it especially hard seeing his father so reduced. But it was Patricia Brandon who surprised. Her emotions concerning her husband's tenuous health were met not so much with heartbreak, but with rage. And she knew exactly where to place it.

Mrs. Brandon recently had a chat with her priest. She confessed privately how much she loathed the men who were killed months before, how Martin, Penrose, and Smalls had blackmailed her husband, causing him sufficient distress to ultimately destroy his health.

"Reverend, I hate those men," she said.

"I see," said the priest. "And how do you feel about these murders?"

"I not only approve, but I celebrate them daily, privately in my heart," Patricia said. "It is so much easier to blame and to hate than it is to resign oneself to circumstances of misery. Anyway, I came here for prayers and blessings for my poor husband. I really do love him so. We were always faithful to each other, even though a cross word was said now and then."

"Of course, Patricia, let's go into the sanctuary," said the priest with compassion.

After 30 minutes or so of prayers, Patricia thanked the priest and was almost out the door when he told her that all that hate would eventually burn her up if she didn't do something to arrest it.

"Oh, my dear Reverend, it's the only thing that warms me on a cold night," Patricia replied.

The priest retired to his office, confident he had properly ministered to his parishioner, but Patricia's last comment chilled him to the bone.

Mrs. Brandon arrived at the farm around noon that day. She poured herself a glass of wine and sat on the front porch, surveying the vast front section of her property. The Congressman was sleeping, and she needed a distraction from her woes. Ever the lover of irony, Mrs. Brandon smiled as she contemplated her present living conditions. She had wanted to leave Alexandria for years but stayed to make life convenient for her son. Had he stayed married to his first wife and been firmly entrenched in a profession, she would have insisted that she and her husband make the move. But she was determined that Michael amount to something more noble than a crafty, dealmaking politician. And when he chose seminary and the priesthood, Patricia endeavored to ensure his success.

The irony, of course, was that Michael was succeeding, despite the reckless parts of his character, and Patricia was enjoying life on hundreds of acres within 50 miles of downtown Washington, D.C. Her county of Fauquier and most of the others that spanned the magnificent Piedmont region had drawn battle lines years ago to keep out the masses of migrants, both within the United States and without, from pouring into their counties.

It was 2009, and literally millions of people were clamoring to live in the Washington region for the job and educational opportunities. The Virginia Blue Bloods were determined to keep them out. Under no circumstances would Piedmont society allow their pastoral paradise to be compromised. And Patricia Brandon was the self-appointed Empress of the Piedmont.

A literary insight into this train of thought was made manifest by Michael's reading of Ernest Hemingway's novels and stories. Not long ago, Michael, Bettina, and Patricia were discussing Hemingway over tea. Michael impressed his two favorite ladies with his clear observations and memory of the Hemingway hunting stories. Hemingway had written with beauty and poignance about the African landscape and country.

"I had always loved country," Hemingway said. "I loved country more than the people. I could only care about people a very few at a time."

Hemingway might not have realized it, but he echoed the Virginian rural society with a startling clarity. Thomas Jefferson would have taken notice of that quote, for it was he among all the nations' founders who viewed cities as dens of iniquity, evil and destruction of all that was good. And although the Brandons and their class would benefit financially from the progressive elements of America's commercial society, they would never give up their Jeffersonian sensibilities. To the true Virginians, people accepted "a very few at a time" was standard orthodoxy. And an influx of masses and masses of strangers was out of the question.

Friday, September 22

All of Virginia was geared up for the November 7 elections. The Governor, Lieutenant Governor, and the Attorney General were on the ballot, as was the lower House of the General Assembly. Despite the mass influx of non-Virginians into the Northern Virginia region, who tended to vote en masse for the Democrats, the Republicans were outperforming their opposition in both fundraising and messaging. If the polls were correct, and polls were always a dubious proposition, a Republican landslide was coming. That should normally be good news for the Brandons and their allies, save for one problem.

On the Republican side, the woman running for Attorney General, the man seeking the Lieutenant Governor's office, and most of the legislative candidates were in favor of keeping mass migration and development out of Virginia. But the man running for Governor was of the opposite take. He had amassed political power by sucking up to the commercial interests of Washington and New York. He was the worst kind of Republican, a poster child for why Americans at certain periods of history have hated Republicans. He was all about the money, only about the money. To Patricia Brandon, he was a barbarian, a man of low character and a threat to the values of the Blue Bloods.

She and the Congressman had seen this coming and could have spent much money drafting a primary opponent, but they decided to watch cannily from the sidelines to see what might unfold.

One very tight knit group of people watching this election were the

Hunter's employers. For reasons obviously not shared with him, he was on call to make one last execution should his employers decide to go forth. He had agreed to the arrangement back in the summer and was fronted a lofty sum to remain on call. The Hunter had moved out of Alexandria like a bat out of hell in order to escape notice for the three killings he had done, and to rest in solitude on a farm he rented near Charlottesville. At two hours driving distance, he was close enough to Alexandria in the north and Richmond to the southeast to spring into action. And he was secluded enough to be out of sight and to practice long distance shooting with his rifle.

Before he bolted from his apartment and his girlfriend, he was told that if he were ordered to kill again, the act would take place either in Richmond or Alexandria. His temporary Blue Ridge sanctuary would also allot the Hunter time to plan a brilliant exit strategy. For he now had more than enough money to retire handsomely and receive an additional bonus on top, should he perform a successful fourth assassination.

Meanwhile, Michael was on his way out to see his parents and check on his father. In the truck with him were Bettina and Allison Peters, who Michael had actually encouraged to spend time with his wife. She was not a third wheel to him. He liked her, especially her candor about who she was. He particularly liked her love and loyalty toward Bettina and understood that his wife needed a special friend like Allison.

Over the summer, Rector Thompson had put out the Brandons' flames over their desire to make Michael a Bishop. The Congressman was in no condition to be riled up over anything, and Patricia had resigned herself to have her son take over the Rectorship of Christ Church after Thompson's retirement. She was already so proud of him and, over the weeks, had thought it for the best for Michael to have more vocational and spiritual happiness and as little politics as possible in his future.

They arrived just after 2 p.m. that day, Allison remarking about the stunningly beautiful, quiet, and serene property. Being an Alexandria local, Allison had been to horse shows and Polo matches out in Hunt Country, but she had never had an intimate experience with one of the fine estates.

Michael greeted his mother and went directly upstairs to see his father, while Bettina cheerfully introduced her new friend to her mother-in-law. Patricia was normally quite formal when it came to meeting strangers, but she was remarkably warm toward Bettina's family and friends. Bettina would never forget the first time she met Mrs. Brandon. How thoroughly intimidated she was to meet this fine southern lady of incredible distinction. Despite her being Cuban and not of the Virginia old stock, Patricia immediately took a liking to her future daughter-in-law. She had, in fact, told Michael that very day to "hang on to this one." Patricia had sensed that Bettina was a person of values and loyalty. Her beauty and good manners won her over instantly.

"She is a true lady, Michael. Endeavor to treat her that way," Patricia had said.

Of course, Brandon told Bettina everything his mother said about her, and the two women loved each other very much ever since.

"Welcome to Dungannon, Miss Peters," said Patricia as she embraced Allison and put her hands on the latter's cheeks. "You have the face of an angel, darling."

Allison didn't know exactly what to think about the warmth being thrust upon her, but she liked it.

Upstairs, Michael was getting a fatherly lecture from a very reluctant invalid who had a sudden burst of energy that afternoon.

"It's fine with me if you want to stay a parish priest, my boy," the

Congressman was saying. "Truth be told, your mother wanted you to be Bishop more than I did. But don't fool yourself. There is politics inherent in all positions of power and distinction. Every time you give a sermon, there is politics. Some of your congregants will like it and some may not. Most of the naysayers will have the good manners not to tell you directly. But it takes on a life of its own. If you want to succeed Thompson as Rector of Christ Church, you have to resign yourself to master the politics of your profession."

"I prefer the term diplomacy," Michael replied.

"Diplomats are politicians too, my boy. Are you hearing me?"

"Yes, Dad. I hear you loud and clear. I'm prepared to do just that," said the priest. "Get some rest, and I'll check in after dinner."

Michael descended the stairs and found his mother in the kitchen and Bettina out in the fields with Allison. He and Patricia sat down and chatted over some iced tea. As the minutes elapsed, Michael couldn't help noticing that his wife and her friend had been holding hands the entire time they were outside. A slightly wicked grin on Michael's face brought inquiry from his mother.

"Now, what's got you so giggly this afternoon?"

"Oh, nothing, Mom," Michael said. "Just a passing bit of humor I was going to put in my sermon next week."

His mind was active that moment, but not on anything spiritual. Many men harbor a secret urge to be part of, or at least close in proximity to, lesbian encounters between desirable women. For Brandon, this was a pronounced and dominant sensual fantasy.

Several of his school friends had regaled him with passionate stories about making love with two women at once, even three. Brandon himself had never acted upon the fantasy, but he entertained it often. Ever since Allison's admission of her bisexuality and her intense feelings for Bettina, he had felt not so much a heightened pleasure in making love to his wife, but a delightful added ingredient to an already near perfect desire. What if Bettina was attracted to Allison in that way? Would he feel cheated? No, certainly not. That would be a completely different thing than if she wanted another man.

His mind began to wander to the time when one of Patricia's best friends used to visit when he was an adolescent. Kathryn Schaefer was an antique dealer and would buy and deliver beautiful and rare English and Early American pieces to Mrs. Brandon. At age 14, Michael developed a severe sexual crush on Kathryn, who at age 40 was an elegant and full-figured woman with short blonde hair and porcelain skin.

No matter what he was doing on a particular day, he made sure to be home when he knew that Kathryn the antique dealer was coming over to do business with Patricia. On one visit, Michael's teenaged ecstasy was realized. After an hour-long visit, Kathryn kissed Patricia goodbye, and seeing Michael right behind his mother, she held out her arms to him. Very shyly, he walked into a warm and snug embrace from his mother's friend. The hug lasted long enough for Michael to feel her body pressed against his, and he kissed her on her magnificently soft and creamy cheek. No chasing and hugging and kissing of girls his own age could even begin to dazzle his hormones like this innocent little encounter with the older woman.

Six years later, Michael was 20 years old and home from college for the summer. Patricia asked him to drive over to Kathryn's house to pick up some estate jewelry. The antique dealer was divorced and looking as delightful as ever. Brandon broke out in a cold sweat when she greeted him at the door with a kiss. He followed her upstairs where she kept the jewelry, and as she bent over slightly to open a drawer, her white sundress clung tightly to her thighs and hips. Brandon, operating on pure lust and instinct, put his arms around her and said, "This hug is from my mom," as he tightly embraced her.

Kathryn relaxed her arms, paused for a second, and then drew Michael into herself, kissing him on the forehead and his cheeks and neck. She stopped and forcibly held Michael's face in her hands and looked him as though she had committed a sin. The two stared at each other for a long minute, then Brandon hugged her around the waist and kissed her lips repeatedly. Then, with all the finesse of a 20-year-old, sat her on the bed and asked her to remove her dress.

Nervous beyond repair, Michael took off his shirt, and Kathryn removed her bra and panties along with the dress. As she lay back in her bed, the young man clumsily French-kissed the older beauty, and Kathryn directed him downward all over her breast and stomach. Then lower. He had done these things several times before, but never with someone he felt so incredibly lucky and undeserving to be with. Kathryn turned over, stood on her feet, and leaned forward on the bed with arms stretched out as Michael took her from behind. He did not last long and was happy that he had pleasured her prior to himself.

An hour later, he bid his hostess farewell and took his mother's jewelry into the car. She followed him out and whispered in his ear, "That was lovely to the extreme, dear boy, but it has to be our one-time little secret. Okay?"

"Okay," said Michael, wondering if he had died and gone to heaven. Despite his other difficulties and disappointments in life, he would continue to fulfill his most intense sexual fantasies like this one with storybook success.

Brandon had never since gone a day without indulging in memories of the spectacular encounter. The combination of surprise and of fulfilling a long-held powerful fantasy were overwhelming. Not only would he never forget it, but years later when he began dating Bettina, Michael took her to Kathryn's house to look at her massive antique collection. Kathryn still had the short blonde hair, her figure was fuller but still quite enticing, and her face and skin were still radiant and delicious. They stayed at her house, looking and talking for a couple of hours.

Kathryn made Bettina feel at home, taking a quick liking to her. Just before sunset that day, Kathryn showed the couple a rare Spanish table and four chairs. It was from the 17th Century. Bettina gasped when she saw the little table. Her parents had one just like it from about the same period. It was the pride and joy of their home décor, until one day, when little Bettina and her sister were playfully wrestling with each other in the living room, they both fell on the table and — fragile thing that it was — splintered beyond any hope of repair.

"You okay, Bettina?" a concerned Michael asked.

"My goodness, it's my parents table," she had said. "How much to buy this from you, Kathryn?"

Kathryn looked at Bettina with kind, motherly eyes and said, "Normally $3,500."

"Honey, you can't afford that. We can look for something else," Brandon said.

"This is the one regret I still have, honey," Bettina remarked. "I have never ceased to be devastated over breaking my parents' table. My parents would collapse with joy if I got this for them."

"Well, then, I will hit Mom and Dad up for an early Christmas present," Brandon said.

"No, sweetie. I couldn't let your folks buy this for me."

The couple argued gently back and forth for a moment, and then Kathryn came to the rescue. Taking Bettina by the hand, she informed her that she owed much of her business success to Patricia, and that she would gladly offer the table to Bettina as a token of undying friendship and gratitude. Bettina's eyes welled up with tears as she looked into Kathryn's face.

"You mean...?" Bettina said.

"Yes," Kathryn said. "It's yours."

Bettina threw her arms around the older woman's neck and shoulders as Kathryn placed her arms around Bettina and one hand on the back of her head. The embrace between the two got stronger by the second as a crying Bettina repeatedly said thank you to Kathryn. Rocking back and forth, with their bodies and cheeks pressed tightly against each other, the two women stood in the doorway hugging for several moments. Bettina had never been so elated by a piece of good fortune, and Brandon had never been so turned on by two women before.

Now, on this late September afternoon, Brandon's complicated passions were aroused in a very similar way. As his mother spoke with him concerning important matters, he just nodded in approval and stared lustfully as he watched Bettina and Allison sitting on a blanket watching the sunset. This time, Bettina was the older woman and young Allison was hugging on her, resting her head on Bettina's bosom. Bettina stroked Allison's hair and laid several gentle kisses on her cheeks and forehead. Brandon would never openly ask his wife if she had tendencies for women. Certainly, she could tell him if she wished, if it were the case. It would not change his feelings toward her for the worse if that were true.

No, Michael was quite content to leave things alone. He knew his wife was an unusually affectionate woman. He could look forward to her kissing and hugging other women for the rest of their lives.

"Mom, is your friend Kathryn Schaefer still around?" Michael asked suddenly.

"No, honey, she moved to Arizona last year. Why?"

"Oh, nothing, I was just remembering something interesting."

Michael, Patricia, Bettina, and Allison were each enjoying the day in their own respective ways. What they all had in common was the breathtaking property on which their delights commenced. The Brandon estate in Fauquier County was 875 acres of lush, pastoral land with thick woods behind the main house. The mansion itself was built in 1924, stone on three sides with a veranda, swimming pool, and guest cottage in the back. There were seven bedrooms in the two-story home, a formal dining room, two parlors, a kitchen, a family room, and a ballroom; all which gave the home a brilliant mixture of southern charm and early American, British, and French provincial tastes, a la Henry James.

The front lawn descended from the hilltop where the mansion set in a most gentle and gradual angle for nearly two hundred yards until it hit the elegant stone wall just before the old gravel county road. The entire property was walled and fenced, an ideal estate for horses to roam. But Patricia had developed rather severe allergies to horses, and the men in the family had to be content with a pack of hunting dogs who all lived in the out-building.

In the summer and early fall, the Piedmont countryside in Virginia could not be more picturesque. After a heavy rain, the landscape was as green as the patchwork of the English countryside. With no horses or cows, all the smells at the Brandon home that day were heavenly, with honeysuckles, fresh cut grass, and the dissipating morning dew permeating the fresh pastoral air.

"This is true paradise, Bettina," Allison said.

"It sure is. Why do you think I married Michael?" joked Bettina as she and Allison looked at each other, walking back up to the house. The two burst into laughter.

They were all ready to stay for dinner and spend the night. Allison had her own room just down the hall from her new best friend, and Michael, who had worked up the most intense passion earlier in the day, took his wife on a wild ride that left her pinned to the bed exhausted.

"I literally cannot move, mi amor," Bettina said. "What's gotten into you?"

"Can't a man just make love to his wife?" winked Brandon.

"Well, keep it up. I just might have to grow old with you."

The young priest laughed, proud of himself for satisfying his wife, even though he did so by indulging in a rather wide array of titillating thoughts of other women. Women in the arms of other women. Judgment of Michael in this matter is not necessary, for he knew precisely how blessed he was to have Bettina. She was his love and delight, and he could not imagine being married to anyone else. And with the exceptions of the Julie Grimes episodes, he would not lay a finger on another woman for as long as they lived.

Allison, overhearing some of the heated activity from their room, couldn't help but be a little jealous. But not so much. Just like Michael, as long as Bettina was with him, there was no problem. If Bettina ever took a liking to another woman, it would be a huge problem, perhaps. But Allison did feel a little like a third wheel that night as she went downstairs to get a glass of water. To Allison's surprise, Patricia was awake and sitting in the room off from the kitchen.

"Come in, dear, and have some wine with me," she said to Allison.

After an hour or so of drinking and talking, Patricia had convinced young Allison that her liberal politics needed adjustment. Her worldview and legal philosophy were now subject to reinterpretation. So subtly persuasive was Patricia Brandon that she could convince a diabetic that he needed more donuts. As Allison reentered her bedroom, armed with a copy of former senator Barry Goldwater's *Conscience of a Conservative*, she found herself immersed in a book that neither she, nor her family or friends, would ever have considered.

That night, while the Brandons and Allison enjoyed the Virginia Hunt Country good life and Michael delighted in his peculiar passions, a cell phone rang in Charlottesville.

A man left the restaurant to go outside and answer in code.

"November 8," said the voice on the other end. "The modified plan. Go ahead with it."

The Hunter answered in the affirmative, destroyed the cell phone, and went back inside to finish his dinner. The fourth hit was in motion.

Tuesday, September 26

Brandon's work week always resumed on Tuesday morning. Taking Monday off was normative, since Saturday was filled with preparations for the Sunday service and sermon, with Sunday being the actual day of performance.

To serve a large church in the capacity that Michael did was taxing. One had to be a counselor on call, a student of Scripture and Theology, and a bit of an expert on the human condition. He also had to produce a show every Sunday, and with the stamina of a stage actor. He would wonder from time to time if he hadn't missed his true calling, the stage. Michael certainly had the appearance, the presence, and voice to dazzle an audience. His mother's English teaching would have provided him with a very definite advantage had he shown any interest at a young age.

Be that as it may, he was delighted to be a late bloomer in the arts and humanities, and in poetry and literature, and to use that interest and knowledge to put a very exceptional polish upon his ecclesiastical profession. His only real challenge in making and maintaining a brilliant career was to heed his father's advice, and to understand and reckon with the practical politics of his job; politics being nothing more and nothing less than a one-word definition of organized human actions and human nature. The church has its own strange brand of politics, and no more tender than any of the other kinds. In fact, history has borne out that there is seldom anything crueler than church people who act aggressively against other church people because they are certain that they're doing God's will.

Brandon would soon tangle with the liberal Bishop in his Diocese. She would behave less than tenderly toward him in the name of a cause she deemed righteous, that of social justice and equity. The Old Testament Book of Proverbs cautions that the "wise man learns by counsel and the fool by experience." Would Brandon act the fool? Would he provoke, something that is not easy for him to resist? Or would he breathe deeply and think before speaking and acting, like his father always counseled, like his father always operated?

Astonishingly, he chose to be his father's son in this case. When it came to his attention that the Bishop was not in his corner for the eventual appointment to Christ Church, or any other appointment, he decided not to confront her, but to hold his tongue and let his seasoned family and friends take the reins. Rector Thompson had informed the Bishop that he would be taking early retirement at age 70. He would stay on part-time to serve as a pastor emeritus, primarily to finish mentoring Michael Brandon to become the Rector of the Church. Their phone conversation was unusually tense.

"I understand that Reverend Brandon is gifted and that parishioners in general take to him," said Bishop Burroughs. "But Alexandria as well as Virginia Seminary are becoming more ethnically and culturally diverse every day. Brandon is not only white, but he is the poster child for old money and white privilege."

The Bishop was forcefully interrupted by the elder Rector, saying, "Are you suggesting the best man for this job should not get the job?"

"I'm telling you that as long as I am Bishop, I intend to change the culture of this Diocese, and that especially includes Christ Church," said the Bishop. "And don't go thinking about using your friends, the

Brandons, to throw money around and make another thinly veiled threat like the last time. I've had it with all of you arch conservatives and your power plays."

"Is this your final word, Bishop?"

"Indeed, it is."

Rector Thompson would not inform Michael about the Bishop's plans just yet. Instead, he called Patricia.

"How unfortunate," she said. "Perhaps something should be done about this."

"I quite agree," said the Rector.

"This woman will ruin our church if she has a free hand. It is quite impossible for me to let that happen," said Patricia.

"Right, I'm on it," said the Rector, who hung up on Patricia and made another call.

CHAPTER 19

Friday, September 29

The Richmond Police descended on the Episcopal Diocese headquarters at 11 a.m. Two officers entered the lobby with a search warrant as the other two popped the trunk to the Bishop's official car.

They unscrewed the compartment where the spare tire was kept and then one of the policemen presented two kilograms of cocaine. The officers inspected the conference room and the Bishop's office, and to the horror of all of the staff members, declared that there was cocaine residue on the conference table and on the Bishop's desk. The staff were ordered to go home and to have no contact with Bishop Burroughs, lest they be charged as an accessory.

Meanwhile, the Bishop was at home working on her sermon as two detectives knocked at her door. As she let them in, she was dumbfounded to hear the words, "Alice Burroughs, you're under arrest for possession, use, and intended distribution of narcotics."

"Narcotics?" she repeated.

"A large amount, ma'am."

The officers briefly searched her personal car and her house.

"Please come with us," one said.

The Bishop, a product of upper-middle class parents who encouraged their daughter in education and in breaking down barriers for women in leadership, was stunned beyond reckoning. She had never even seen an illegal drug or been with friends who were doing them. How could she possibly face her parents, her fellow bishops in the church? She was single and without children; perhaps that was the only saving grace.

It was a short ride to the police station in a suburban part of Richmond. Bishop Burroughs was allowed her phone call, which she made to a lawyer friend, who advised her not to answer questions until she could arrive in one hour. That was all the time required for the plan to be set in motion. As she was left alone in the interrogation room with nothing but a nearly tasteless cup of coffee, a large man walked into the room.

"Bishop Burroughs, did the men who placed you under arrest read your rights, and do you understand them?" the man asked.

"Yes, to both questions," she said. "Now, why am I here? I am innocent."

"How long before your attorney arrives? I assume you called one."

"About an hour from now. I'm not supposed to answer any questions before she gets here."

"Miss Burroughs, I'm going to make this easy for you," said Deputy Chief Garrison, who just happened to be one hundred miles outside his jurisdiction. "You don't know it yet, but you have friends in high places."

The Bishop just stared at the policeman, bewildered.

"I'm going to have these impending charges dropped and all evidence will remain in my sole possession," Garrison continued. "As for the raid this morning, the police and the media will say it was a bomb threat and certain people were taken away for their own protection. Your staff will be informed that the cocaine found in your office and car was protein powder. No one will ever know about this."

"What friends do I have who could do that for me?" asked Burroughs.

"You will resign as Bishop of Virginia to be effective two weeks hence, citing personal health and stress reasons," Garrison said. "I suggest you return to New Jersey for your own recuperation and well-being. The day after your resignation is accepted and official, the sum of $100,000 cash will be in a briefcase in the trunk of your car. If you tell anyone, anyone at all about this arrangement, the evidence will suddenly resurface and chase you down wherever you are."

"What do I tell my lawyer?" the Bishop asked.

"Tell her you made a deal. Lawyer-client privilege will preclude her from saying anything," said the Chief. "Do we have a deal? You have exactly fifteen minutes to decide."

"Yes, yes!" said the distraught Bishop, now crying uncontrollably.

Garrison was smart to allow the Bishop to resign with her reputation intact. She could literally cook up any story she wanted. The cash was a definite salve for this crushing blow. She could start over with a career that might fulfill her. But she would remain devastated by the loss of her prominence, her ability to influence church and society. Her bishopric had been the fulfillment of her dreams since high school. But what could she do? Fight? Not hardly, not against this airtight conspiracy concocted coldly by a woman who would eat alive anyone who threatened her son.

When cocktail hour arrived at Dungannon, Patricia pushed the Congressman in his wheelchair out onto the front porch. Within 20 minutes of each other, Rector Thompson and Deputy Chief Garrison arrived.

"You'll stay the weekend, won't you, James?" Patricia asked the Rector.

"Naturally, Patricia, thank you. Think I'll get in a little fishing."

"And you, my good Deputy Chief, your reward is en route to your bank," said Patricia.

"Thank you, ma'am," said the Chief.

The sunset that evening was particularly beautiful, full and red-orange. The sun went down over the nearest mountain, leaving the pond of water glistening for minutes after it disappeared. Such were fall sunsets in Piedmont country. For Patricia, it was all the more delicious, for in a metaphorical sense, the sun was rapidly setting on her enemies, the enemies of her family, the enemies of her sharply manicured sensibilities. Yesterday, the Episcopal Bishop of Virginia had threatened the old order, and now she was gone.

"I still can't believe Michael doesn't want to be Bishop," Patricia told the others. "With the ease in which we dispatched Miss Burroughs, he could have walked right into the room and taken his seat."

"It will all work out," the Rector said. "I get to retire early, and Michael will take my place, no questions asked."

Congressman Brandon, too tired to speak, gave a thumbs up and smiled. Yes, this was a day of days for the mighty Brandons.

At the dinner table, the conversation shifted over to the elections. Enemies, friends, and useful tools among the various politicians were identified and catalogued. As the night grew long, one could marvel at the cold malice with which the participants plotted. The Deputy Chief might be excused for just doing what came naturally due to his profession, the same being said for the ex-Congressman. But to be a fly on the wall in the Brandon dining room that evening would have revealed the twisted irony of the Lady of the Manor and the Rector of the Church hatching the treacherous plot and instructing the policeman in every wicked detail which comprised it.

The night of September 26, 2009, at Dungannon would be as thoroughly Machiavellian as any date to ever occur in Virginian social and political society, save for another date in the very near future. If all went according to the Brandons' plan, everything that disturbed their peace would soon be eliminated. Michael was not invited to either the dinner or the plot. He would be kept in the dark for his own protection, as well as on the off chance that he might have a sudden attack of conscience that might jeopardize the carefully laid plans.

After Garrison left and the Congressman was safely tucked into bed,

Patricia and Rector Thompson shared a nightcap in the front parlor.

"Why did you name this estate Dungannon, Patricia?" the Rector asked.

"You don't remember anything, James," Patricia said gently. "I told you when we first met that my family came over from Ireland in the early 1700s. They lived on a farm outside the town of Dungannon."

"That's right," said the Rector. "The memory goes a bit at age 70."

"Well, mine is just Jim Dandy these days," said the elder lady.

"Were they poor?" asked Thompson.

"Who?"

"Your Irish ancestors."

"Yes, they were poor, hence their long journey to America," exhorted Mrs. Brandon.

Thompson sipped his brandy and chuckled as he glanced at Patricia.

"Now, just what is so altogether funny, James?"

"Forgive me, but you have always had the air of someone who never knew poverty existed, let alone experienced it. No, I'm quite confident that you could not have hailed from humble roots."

"We all hail from humble roots if you go far enough back, James. Some of us just get over it faster than others," declared the Lady of Dungannon.

"Humility is a prime Christian virtue, Patricia," said the Rector, seeking to pick a friendly fight.

"And haven't I given a son over to the church, not to mention spending considerable time and money supporting it? I believe I also pulled the strings to make you permanent Rector at Christ Church," Patricia replied, now irritated.

"My apologies, dear lady, you have indeed done your service to God."

Thompson could have continued the playful exchange by reminding Mrs. Brandon that Michael chose the ministry on his own accord. But deep down that wasn't quite true. No matter how the young man strayed from the narrow path, Patricia was always there, patiently steering her son where she wanted him to be. Unlike her husband who chastised their son for selling real estate and even more so for entering political office, she used a combination of motherly affection and the power of suggestion on Michael. She always used it to such affect that no matter how much time he wasted in his revelry, he always ended up where she wanted him.

Patricia wanted her son to be married to his first wife, and gently nudged him toward commitment. When Michael could no longer stand that marriage, she waited, and waited for him to find Bettina, then applied the gentle nudging again. The hundred or more affairs in between those marriages was just a cross for her to bear until he came round. For the Congressman, that part was a constant source of amusement and admiration. Michael's successful and extreme womanizing was the only area of life where father would live vicariously through son. In the end, Michael had two choices, though he didn't know at the time. Patricia would not have her beloved son remain a salesman of any kind. His vocation was to be either an Episcopal clergyman or a Professor of History or English.

Michael's spiritual quest came independent of Patricia's schemes, but when it did, she pounced like a mountain lion, securing his appointment to Christ Church, under Rector Thompson's tutelage. Using his sermons, in part, to show off his literary mastery and competence as a poet gave Patricia the reward of a lifetime. Michael's charm in the pulpit was the gift that kept on giving to the proud mother.

* * *

Detective Julie Grimes had nothing like the advantages of a Michael Brandon, familial or otherwise. Had she chosen another profession, she could have harnessed her sex appeal to her advantage. As a cop, however, she was still a woman in a man's profession. No matter how much rope Deputy Chief Garrison gave her in her current cases, she felt controlled. She knew that any moment she breathed could be her last as a detective were she to run afoul of Garrison. Strikingly, Julie Grimes would eventually close in on the murderous activity in Alexandria, Virginia and vicinity. But she would do it without the 7mm Magnum Rifle shell casing that Brandon had turned over to the Deputy Chief.

Even the best laid criminal schemes seem to produce either several minor mistakes which can amount to something, or one major mistake that can eventually get the perpetrators caught. Grimes was determined to find these mistakes out. With tedious precision and the determination of someone who literally had nothing else, she threw her every thought and desire into solving these murders. Absolutely convinced they were connected, she would not let up for a minute. And she was equally determined never again to be a victim. She had allowed men to take advantage of her. No more.

From now on, Julie would read her ex the riot act if he were one minute late returning their daughter Tina from his weekend with her. She would run the investigations as she saw fit, taking no crap from anyone except Garrison. She would play the kiss-ass game with Garrison in order to keep her position and would never again be used and romantically devastated by another Rev. Michael Brandon.

Brandon had played the detective like a fiddle, though he wasn't proud of it. A cruel necessity, more like, he thought. But although she knew she was being used, Grimes felt the certainty of Brandon's attraction as he caressed and kissed her. She knew how much he had enjoyed her body as he helped himself to it. That, after all, is what led to her obsession and to her lack of objectivity concerning anything to do with him. But when she saw firsthand how his rich parents and their lawyer removed

Michael from any and all legal accountability for his felonious assault of murder victim James Smalls, she slowly began to dislodge her obsessive crush on him.

Grimes was a police officer, a person of duty and sacrifice. Civilization must have rules, and she was a rule follower. All people must be held accountable for their actions. But the Brandon incident had showed her another side of society, and another side of the young and gallant priest. When family and self-preservation are at issue, people like the Brandons make up their own rules, and they play by them with crushing affect.

CHAPTER 20

November 8

Election Day

It was 10 p.m. as the Brandon family, Patricia, the Congressman, Michael, and Bettina watched the election returns on the television.

Rector Thompson was there, but nobody else outside the family. The Republican candidates for Governor, Lt. Governor, and Attorney General won handily. The Brandons were anxiously awaiting the news for the Virginia House of Delegates races. At 10:20 p.m., the press officially called a Republican majority, 61 to 39 seats.

"Much better than expected, Mom, don't you think?" Michael asked.

"A splendid evening," said Patricia as she raised her glass to toast the success. But everyone in the room knew that the man at the top, Governor-elect Matt Robinson, was not a friend. Republican or not, he might do serious damage to the Brandons' Virginia if not checked.

As Michael and Bettina ascended the stairs to their room at Dungannon, Bettina asked her husband why his parents and their friends didn't openly oppose Robinson during the primaries.

"I guess they figured he bows to pressure from the other politicians in the party," Michael said. "And I wouldn't put it past some of Mom and Pop's friends to offer him some healthy bribes. Idle speculation will just drive us crazy. Let's see how he operates as soon as the legislative session starts in January."

"I agree, but the curiosity can just kill you, honey. You know what I mean."

"That it can, my dear. Now, on to important matters," said a frisky Michael as he grabbed his wife by the butt, tossed her onto the bed, and shut the door.

Despite Bettina's pleas to wait until she took a shower, Brandon peeled her dress off and laid on top of her, squeezing and kissing her deeply. When he felt her more than wet enough, he penetrated her, slowly but ferociously. He climaxed within minutes and kept thrusting until Bettina climaxed. Before she could move, Brandon was tonguing her feet, working his way up the back of her legs.

"Let me go soak in the tub for a bit, baby," moaned Bettina, purring and laughing softly.

"Not finished yet," Michael said as he turned Bettina on her stomach and slightly spread her butt checks, spending the next few minutes kissing and biting them. He then licked her vagina, moving to her butt crack, where he rimmed her. Never quite sure how she liked this kinkiest piece, he turned her over again and ate her out, making long strokes on her labia, while at the same time isolating her clit between his lips.

The pleasure for Bettina was overwhelming. Her body twisted and convulsed so savagely she nearly fell off the side of the bed. After holding each other for several minutes afterward, Bettina was the first to speak, telling Brandon she couldn't say exactly how many orgasms she'd had, but she counted at least seven. Michael was pleased with his performance as his beautiful wife went to the bathroom to clean and pamper herself. Not so much pleased by the seven orgasms for which he was responsible, but more so by the fact that he experienced such a happy shock of ecstasy simply making love to his wife. Looking at his wife, touching his wife. No lesbian fantasies or other extra stimulus had been present or required this time; just the woman he loved.

This, coupled with his fixation with her not bathing beforehand. He wanted to taste Bettina's natural tastes. And smell her natural smells. No shower gel or body lotion, just her. The menu that night was Bettina Brandon in the raw. What a delicacy.

Downstairs, Patricia and the Rector were eerily thinking the same thoughts concerning Governor-elect Robinson. He just might be a candidate for the Brandon style of persuasion, perhaps the Bishop Burroughs treatment. The two looked at each other with devious upper-class smiles. The kind that showed no teeth but revealed much mischief.

Wednesday, November 9

Governor-elect Matt Robinson, Lieutenant Governor-elect John Bland, and Attorney General-elect Martha McLaughlin held a rally in Richmond at noon. The crowd was large and very excited, and the candidates were all smiles and high energy despite the grueling campaign. None of the three had slept a straight seven hours for over a week until the previous night. The Republican Party had wanted to show the public a proper demonstration of unity, though the candidates and their operatives secretly despised one another.

Bland and McLaughlin were conservatives in the style of the Brandons but were miffed at each other over peccadilloes. Bland had been the Virginia House of Delegates Majority Leader, McLaughlin a back bencher rookie. Bland supported her opponent in the primaries and caused unnecessary consternation by being a little too public about it. But both candidates detested Robinson, who they considered unprincipled in the extreme and a whore to out of state money interests. After the noon rally, Bland and McLaughlin were scheduled to travel to the Tidewater area, Norfolk, and Virginia Beach, and Robinson was to make several stops in Northern Virginia, the first being Alexandria.

At 2 p.m., the crowd was swelling in Old Town Alexandria. The impending rally took place at Lee Park in the north part of Old Town on the Potomac River. The park was named not after General Robert E. Lee, but after his father, Revolutionary War hero Light Horse Harry Lee. Lee had lived with his wife and young children in a townhouse in Alexandria, which still stands today on Oronoco Street. The park comprised several acres and was bracketed to the north and the south by very expensive colonial style townhouses, some new and some very old. To the north behind the several rows of homes was a single hotel and a single high rise apartment building. The hotel was almost a thousand yards away from the platform where Governor-elect Robinson would deliver his address. But the luxury apartment building was only about six-hundred yards away. A rooftop and six different apartment balconies faced the park. But the Virginia State Police, augmented by the Alexandria Police, were taking no chances.

The rooftops and the balconies at the apartment building and hotel were manned or heavily scrutinized. As the motorcade pulled up, out popped an excited Matt Robinson, with two bodyguards and several campaign aides behind him. The crowd roared as the Governor-elect took the podium with scores of police and security all around the perimeter. About ten minutes into the speech, a manhole cover slowly lifted from underneath the street, no more than a hundred yards away. The police had secured all of the manhole covers and storm drains on all the adjacent streets, except one. It was an abandoned work site, a street permanently closed in order to expand the park. Just to the right side of a condemned warehouse on the water was an extension of water main that city officials had ordered closed. It was not.

The Hunter slowly popped his head out, covered by a white hardhat worn by city workers, and a yellow shirt with the official insignia. He scanned the area in front of him with field glasses, as well as the sides and briefly to his back. All clear, he carefully lifted up his rifle and put the crosshairs of the scope on Robinson's head. At a hundred yards give or take, and next to no wind, his shot should be easy. As Robinson dropped his arms down to his waist, his head was completely exposed, and the Hunter engaged the trigger. As he began to squeeze, he suddenly felt a sharp agonizing cramp in his left bicep, causing him to flinch as he shot. A man went down, and people began to run and scream and dive for cover.

The scene was so chaotic that the Hunter dropped his field glasses and hat down beneath the street, and with his wetsuit and a snorkel, ran and dove into the river heading north with a rifle strapped on his back; all before he could ascertain whether or not his target was dead. But there was no time. Seconds after he hit the water, police were all over that closed off street with the abandoned warehouse.

The police officers guarding Governor-elect Matt Robinson had thrown him to the ground, then escorted him into a black SUV speeding off with two other security trucks and several motorcycle cops. An ambulance pulled up to the park, and paramedics ran the several yards to the podium to attend to a Virginia State policeman, shot in the head and being held in the crying arms of his ex-wife, Detective Julie Grimes.

Army Staff Sergeant Jamie Grimes had recently joined the Virginia State Police, and due to his combat and protective service experience, was immediately assigned to protect state public officials. This was his first assignment, and his last.

As night fell, the police were wrapping up their evidence gathering, and the Hunter, who had been snorkeling around the rocks in a small cove several hundred yards north of the incident, saw a boat headed his way. One man was driving, and he was alone in the boat; he was right on time. The Hunter jumped in, and the boat sped away to the south, where the shoreline would have already been canvassed by police.

The Hunter was dropped off just south of the Mt. Vernon mansion, in a slip adjacent to the Mt. Vernon Yacht Club. The assassin, seeing no bystanders, sprinted to his small single-family house he was using, thanks to his benefactors. He slipped inside, lit a fire in the fireplace, and burned the wetsuit. Briefly glancing at the TV newscast, he learned of his mistaken shot. He showered, made some coffee, and waited for the phone call he now began to dread. He would have to explain to his handlers why he shot the wrong man.

Also that night, Julie Grimes had the considerably harder duty of telling her little girl why she was never going to see her father again.

"My left arm cramped up, and at the worst time. I'm surprised I hit anything at all," the Hunter said to his benefactor.

"This raises the temperature considerably. I'd like for you to leave town until we can get a handle on this. Don't let anyone see you leave the house, inform us when you get out of sight, and await instructions."

"So, our affiliation is not yet over?" the Hunter confirmed.

"No, not for the moment. A police officer is dead by your hand, and the target is still alive. Your bonus and freedom depend on a fix of this problem."

"Very well," the Hunter said. "I'll reach out when I'm settled."

The assassin felt, for the first time in his life, the sting of failure. That uncontrollable disability which toppled a giant and sent him tumbling down the stairs into the realm of amateur. His most important kill shot disrupted, thwarted by his own extremity. He knew it, but it would take weeks for the Hunter to accept it. He had exercised too hard. He had taxed his arm muscles far beyond what any shooter should do. Approaching middle age is hard for men of great physical capability, and the killer was overcompensating by juicing up his workouts.

He ran like a schoolboy and lifted weights like a college linebacker. When the tendonitis had struck his left arm a month before, he had ignored it to his peril. The consummate professional, he would fix his mistake, for though he obsessed about retirement, he was unwilling to go out this way, the way of failure. Imagine for a moment this cold-blooded contract murderer as an artist. Killing a target who deserved to be killed, doing it in a way that few people on earth could do; and getting away with it. This was the Hunter's art, his makeup.

Yes, he had been more than ready to retire, but to retire in peace, to enjoy life and be able to live with himself. He was having a very hard time living with what had just happened. He required a chance for redemption. He would lay low and wait for his chance. In the coming weeks, the Hunter would cease all weightlifting, all exercise, save running. He would apply home remedies and arm stretches to his ailment. And he would very carefully apply muscle relaxers and pain medication to his very religious daily regimen of rifle shooting at his new temporary residence — a farm in rural Pennsylvania less than three hours from Virginia.

Thursday, November 10

Meanwhile, Brandon made frantic attempts to reach Detective Grimes on her cell phone, trying to ascertain her safety and that of her daughter, as well as her emotional state. Grimes called him back later in the day. Despite her recently diminished opinion of him, she accepted his offer to meet him Friday afternoon at his church. Michael had pastoral motives toward Julie Grimes that day, mixed in with a desire to redeem himself in her eyes as a person. He had used her, and now welcomed the opportunity to minister to her as a friend.

Not everyone in Virginia was in a state of ministerial good will. The Hunter's employers were downright frantic, their master plan having taken a beating from dumb circumstantial luck. They were scrambling to find the next opportunity to kill the Governor-elect before he could take office in January. At that point, his security apparatus would multiply. And just as the conspirators drank their scotch in the home of their ringleader, something happened that no one expected, or even could imagine. News reports from all of the major networks broadcast a 5 p.m. Thursday special report.

"Matt Robinson, Virginia's Governor-elect, set to announce his resignation for the office of Governor immediately," said the broadcast.

Robinson and his family were sufficiently shaken up by the attempt on his life, and he could not in good conscience put his family through four years of agonizing stress and worry. He would resign, and the Lieutenant Governor-elect John Bland would be sworn in as Governor of Virginia just after the New Year.

Joys unspeakable descended on the Piedmont and the rest of conservative rural Virginia. The unwelcome changes championed by Robinson and his outsider business and liberal allies would now be entirely thwarted by the new Governor, who just happened to be a friend of the Brandons. The conspirators looked at each other and drank a toast. A delicious toast, for they got what they wanted without taking on further risks and bearing the guilt of further evil in the process. Yes, even those who hire hitmen to kill people have consciences.

The question is always one of degree. How far is one willing to go? How much wickedness is too much? If the question is one of survival, the ethical bar gets lowered significantly. Thus, everyone involved in this conspiracy was the happier for the days' transpiring. That is, everyone except the Hunter, who received a message to stand down and wait for his bonus. His employers were not foolish. They knew that he was telling them the truth about his arm being injured at the moment of truth. They had to believe him because he had proven so flawlessly efficient in his other hits. So, they agreed to pay his bonus so he would have no hard feelings against them.

The conspirators didn't count on the Hunter's overpowering sense of professionalism, though. Bonus or not, he could not retire and fade into the mist a failure. The sniper who flinched and missed his most important target. As soon as he had gotten to safety, the Hunter felt the sting of defeat begin to eat away at his sense of worth. It was torture to him. He wanted his money and a secure and safe retirement. But he made a promise to himself that he would do another kill first. Not wanting to mess up the plans of his employers, he reached out to them for another target. One that needed killing, and a time and place of execution, well worthy of his skills. He would take his bonus and do the next hit for free, and go out with a bang, literally.

Brandon was whistling a happy tune when he exited his truck and entered his apartment building. He was happy about his opportunity to do something lovely for Julie Grimes. He still did not regret the tryst with her, or that he had technically cheated on his then fiancée. That was business, not personal. But he had always sensed that he hurt Julie, and very much welcomed the chance at a nice fix. But Michael would have to wait for that fix.

As he pushed open the door to his apartment, he found Bettina standing in the hallway with her cell phone to her ear. She fixed a stare at Michael and her eyes welled up with tears.

"It's your mom, sweetie," she said with a cracking voice.

Michael pulled his phone out and saw the battery was dead. Patricia had tried to reach him first, but being unsuccessful, she called Bettina, who said goodbye to her mother-in-law and walked hand in hand with

Michael over to the sofa.

"Your father died early this morning, honey. I'm so, so sorry. Your mom couldn't stay on the phone any longer. She wants us to go out to the farm tonight and stay the weekend. Oh, Michael, baby."

Bettina threw her arms around her husband. The couple stared at the river from the sliding glass door, tightly fixed in each other's embrace. Brandon was sad but not surprised. In his prayers and contemplation, he had been preparing for this moment.

Sunday, November 13

The weekend at Dungannon went as expected. Funeral arrangements were made, a memorial service and burial at Christ Church scheduled. The eulogy would be delivered by Rector Thompson, for Michael turned down flatly his mother's request that he do it. He wouldn't be able to do it without weeping. Patricia had also wanted her husband buried in the Episcopal cemetery near their farm, but the Congressman was very clear in his will. He greatly desired to be interred in Old Town Alexandria, the city that meant much to him. He had raised a son there, had empowered himself and his family there, both professionally and politically. And he owned the very ground on which he was to be buried ten years hence. This all created some friction, so Michael and Bettina left on Sunday afternoon to go back to Alexandria. It seems as though Patricia Brandon was not getting her way that weekend. And a tinge of discomfort felt by everyone usually followed such an occurrence.

On the drive back to Alexandria, Michael handed Bettina an unopened letter from his father addressed to him. Patricia gave it to him when they arrived Thursday night. He had been afraid to open it.

"Open the letter and read it to me, honey," said a wet-eyed Michael.

Bettina opened the letter and read, "I'm not much for this emotional crap between father and son. I'm confident you know that by now. I just wanted to say that I'm proud of you, Michael. I always have been. I guess it's because your mother spoiled you rotten that I felt I had to toughen you up. The world is an unforgiving place, and it pleases me that you understand that now. Stay close to those who love you. Your wife, your mother, and true friends like Rector Thompson. Don't place your full trust in anyone else. Keep on doing the wonderful job you were obviously born to do. One more thing. Watch out for a man named John Gauge. Do not trust him an inch. If he should approach you for money or favors, tell Deputy Chief of Police Garrison immediately. God watch out for you, son. I love you. Your Dad."

Bettina could hardly compose herself as she tried to speak clearly amidst her sobs. Michael almost missed the John Gauge warning entirely; he was so wrapped up in his father being proud of him.

"If he had just said that to me once or twice in my life, I think it might have made all the difference," Michael said.

"Maybe he was right in his own way, sweetie," Bettina said. "Maybe you turned out just like he would have hoped in the end."

"I need a drink now, sweetheart. Is there a bottle of scotch in the back?"

"Here, pull over," Bettina said. "Yes, there are two Glenlivets."

"You drive please, Bettina. I can't deal with this sober."

The two switched sides, and Michael safely imbibed on the contents of that rather expensive bottle while his wife drove the 90-minute commute back to their condo.

Whether it be 2009, or 1809, a young man needs his father's approval. It is a subconscious craving which if not met may produce disaster in the life of that young man. In this world of constant change, human nature remains fixed. No amount of forward-thinking or innovation can alter the state of facts in this case. We human beings are what we are, some having been privileged enough to experience life as a Brandon. And yet despite having everything that would green up his neighbors with envy — the perfect and adoring wife, the doting mother, a family fortune with a respected name — Michael had to wait until his father died to hear the words so many fathers say to their sons regularly: "I am proud of you."

No one knows just how large the void had been for Michael, how big the gaping hole in his chest. Would the day's news fill that void, and could it repair that gaping hole? How would our protagonist handle this contingency? Would it strengthen or embitter him?

"You know, it's yourself who you have to be proud of, Michael," said Bettina gently from the driver's seat.

"You're a real pain in the ass, honey, especially when you're right."

"I'm right about this one," Bettina said. "And coming from a bystander these last few years, it's obvious he was proud of you. He even told me so the night you skipped family dinner when Nora and I went."

"You never said anything about that," Michael said.

"I never thought it was an issue."

"Bettina." A now very drunk Brandon struggled for his next few words. "I'm just so glad to have you with me."

"Tonight?"

"Not just tonight. I mean all the time. I can't do without you."

"I know, me neither," Bettina said.

Brandon stared at his wife, then looked at the letter. Then he looked at Bettina again and began to cry. He cried the rest of the way home with his wife holding his hand. When they got inside, Bettina made Michael drink a substantial amount of water, helped him undress, and put him to bed. He went fast to sleep as she lay beside him and stroked his head.

In the coming weeks, Michael would use his emotional confusion in a surprisingly adult and emotionally intelligent way; he would harness his father's affirmation to be the best possible priest at his church and hopefully as its new Rector soon.

CHAPTER 21

Two Months Later
Monday, January 22

Rector Thompson had waited for less than what most people would call a proper amount of mourning time before he moved into Dungannon with Patricia. It was savory sweet, this once in a lifetime second chance to live in a perpetual state of bliss with a loved one, one the Rector had pined after his whole adult life.

The two would never marry, and the Rector would live on the farm with her but never ask to be on the deed. What he did have was money of his own, a net worth which dwarfed his retirement pay from the church. James Thompson had been a first-rate clergyman in every respect. He made the trains run on time, and he was a brilliant administrator and fundraiser. He was a superb preacher and teacher of the faith and had proven himself to be a mentor among mentors for Michael Brandon. Not a hint nor wink of dishonesty had ever been alleged, nor any accusations levied against him. He did, however, have benefactors. And as we saw in the Bishop Burroughs affair, Thompson had been willing to do the dirty work in order to defend his church, his conservative values, and his friends. And this work never went unrewarded.

Thus, in a lustrous career, Rector Thompson could look back with joy in how he advanced God's loving kindness toward all people he met, how his door was open to every man and woman in his church, and how he used his ability to turn potential adversaries into friends simply by being gracious. All these things were he, but that same record will also show a dedication to prioritizing the interests of his patron friends when push came to shove. He had especially served the Brandon family well — Patricia and the Congressman first, then the son.

Now, at age 70, he sat on the back porch on an unusually warm January evening, holding hands with Patricia Brandon, the two enjoying the silence as well as each other's company. They looked out over the horizon at the Blue Ridge Mountains. Life was good.

"You'll forgive me if I don't say the three little words just yet, James," said the Lady of the Manor.

"Leave me alone?" the Rector joked. The two exchanged a glance and abruptly laughed. They looked out at the Piedmont horizon, a daily and majestic scene enjoyed by American founders Thomas Jefferson of Albemarle County and James Madison of Orange County, each within a 90-minute drive from Dungannon.

Chief Justice John Marshall enjoyed his grand view from his estate in the very same Fauquier County which housed Dungannon.

The Brandons' daily visitors were every kind of wildlife from squirrels to deer to the occasional black bear. Birds of the most pleasant beauty and variety populated this pastoral paradise: cardinals and blue jays, mockingbirds and robins, yellow finches, sparrows, and starlings. Bald Eagles and Cooper's Hawks swooped over the meadows and streams, almost every day at dawn. In the fall, thousands of ducks and Canadian geese flew over the grounds, sometimes watering themselves in the large pond between the front of the manor house and the stone wall looking slightly downward at the narrow state road.

Thompson and Patricia were 70 and 71 years old respectively, but they both were unusually physically strong and healthy for their twilight years, and remarkably sound of mind. They knew what abundance they possessed and had every reason to speculate a very long and contented life together.

Mr. Jefferson and Mr. Madison would have been quite pleased with our machinations over the decades, thought Mrs. Brandon to herself.

At the same time, the Rector's mind was joyously preoccupied with his newfound fortune. *After all these years, I finally have my girl. And life here at Dungannon. Paradise in this life, who would have thought?*

The couple finished their thoughts almost simultaneously, and with a leisurely turn toward each other, locked eyes and gently squeezed each other's hand.

The next morning, Mrs. Brandon and the Rector were visited by the newly inaugurated Governor John Bland. They were expecting him, for they were to ride in the Governor's limousine from Fauquier to Alexandria, where Michael was to be formally called by the vestry of Christ Church to be their new Rector. This process was somewhat irregular. Normally, when a Rector retires from or leaves an Episcopal Church, an interim Rector is appointed while an extensive search is done for the new one, normally choosing someone else.

But Michael was universally loved by the congregation, and Rector Thompson's influence was almost total in that church, and those two facts on the ground made Michael's rapid ascendancy to the clerical leadership at Christ Church an unstoppable force.

As they left Dungannon, Governor Bland's motorcade sped toward Alexandria. Patricia and Rector Thompson rode in the limo with Bland. Not only was she a major contributor, but her family and the Congressman's family went very far back with the Blands, who were one of Virginia's First Families dating back to well before the Revolution.

After no more than 20 minutes of driving, our regal party found themselves assaulted by a mass of interminable traffic. Mrs. Brandon did not wish to be late to her son's big ceremony.

"Ah, John. What seems to be the trouble?" she asked.

"A lane closure due to work on a new bypass," said the driver to the Governor upon hearing Patricia's question.

"Perhaps you might tell them to stop work and let traffic commence," Patricia said.

"Well, as gratifying as that sounds, I really can't do that, Patricia," the Governor said.

"Oh, I thought you were the Governor, John."

He thought for a moment, and then Governor Bland grabbed his phone. "Shut the work down on Route 50. What? I don't care if it's vital or if the road work goes all the way to D.C. Shut it down and pick up the cones."

He then ordered the police cars and motorcycles to turn on lights and sirens and hit the right shoulder hard. They would make Alexandria in plenty of time. As the Governor winked at Patricia, she just laid back in her seat and smiled. It was the smile of landed gentry. The smile of a blue blood who had helped a politician, and that politician did exactly what he was supposed to do — her bidding.

Fixing the traffic to her expediency was the smallest favor Bland would do in the coming months. When any development, conservation, or culturally conservative issue would surface, the Governor would take Patricia's call personally, and in a most timely manner. Her agenda was his agenda. The counties in Northern Virginia were cash rich and usually did their own thing, but they ultimately needed and desired state approval, as well as state money for their big projects. During the reign of Governor Bland, these counties found themselves victims of subtle threats and other tactics from the state. Zoning officials and Boards of Supervisors were either voting no or stalling large dense housing and multi-use projects. The developers and their lobbyists couldn't grasp what was happening. They were used to getting their deals rubberstamped in Northern Virginia. Someone or some group was getting to these local public officials. And Patricia Brandon was winning her war against development in Virginia. It was a quite gratifying revenge.

At Christ Church, everything went off as it should. The vestry voted unanimously to call Reverend Michael Brandon to be the new and permanent Rector. All that remained was for the Bishop of Virginia to ratify the decision, which due to the diligent operations of Rector Thompson was a *fate accompli*. When he and the Brandons had gotten rid of the ultra-left Bishop Burroughs, they quickly followed up and spread their influence over the diocese, and a moderate Bishop was selected as interim. It was Thompson who selected the man, and it was Thompson who worked on enough committee members to solidify his choice.

Michael and Bettina were overjoyed at the dignity of the small and preliminary ceremony, especially having the Governor of Virginia escort his mother and Rector Thompson. Bettina took a hundred pictures or more of her husband with the Governor, Thompson, and Patricia. She looked proudly at her especially dignified husband, decked out in his robe, stole, and other partial vestments.

The rest of the honors would be bestowed in a grander ceremony when Bishop and Diocesan committee formally met in the spring to solidify Michael as the full and permanent Rector of the parish. It was a happy day for everyone. The leaders and congregants of Christ Church were thrilled to have the beautiful couple as Rector and wife, and a pastor who was popular and so clearly gifted. But the scene was unintentionally usurped by the presence of Virginia's top politician at a routine church event.

Such things were highly irregular, and it served only to further the mystique of the Brandon family's disproportionate power and prestige among the attendees. Patricia did not lord such position over her friends and neighbors, but she used the Governor's presence to please herself and as a gentle reminder to all that her son's career and new position had real power behind it.

For Michael, all the troubles of the last year were reduced to nothing compared with how he felt at the moment. He had stayed the course and given his career and his marriage his best. And it was paying off in spades. Though he missed his father greatly, he looked across the room at his life partner, beautiful and loyal Bettina Brandon, his loving mother, his mentor, and dozens of school mates and professors from seminary, not to mention Christ Church parishioners.

The young Rector would work long hours every day that week. He would take the Church secretary, the newly hired seminarian, and the sexton out for lunch to thank them for their service and offer his continued friendship and affection. He would have dinner with the vestry members, prepare his office in Thompson's former office, attend choir practice and any other significant meeting to show all he would be a very hands-on and accessible spiritual leader of this parish church. He prepared the order of services that week with the help of the organist, choirmaster, and secretary. And he put some extra diligence and panache into his sermon. Yes, Michael's first week as Rector would go well, as would his Sunday services and sermons.

But that particular span of time would not pass without some strikingly unexpected happenings.

* * *

After briefly watching a news report, the Hunter called his employer.

"I have my new target, my next and final kill," he said.

"Is this who I think it is?" said the employer. "I just watched the news. Interesting target, challenging hit."

"Since you gave me that nice bonus, I will do this one for free, and then I'm retired. I'll disappear to a place of my choosing. Nobody is to ever know my whereabouts. If anyone should come looking for me, it will mean an insurmountable problem for you."

"Understood," said the employer. "But I think we have proven loyal and trustworthy."

"You have indeed. I'm just giving you my standard speech, so there's no confusion. Will you approve my target?"

"Yes. No collateral damage, only the target. Agreed?"

"Agreed," the Hunter said.

The assassin went to work straight away, for he had until February 17 to be fully ready and in position to take out his final victim. To avoid a repeat of his last disaster, the man lifted no weights. He ran on his treadmill and did isometric exercises: push-ups, sit-ups, and others, which he took lightly. After studying the event on the 17th, the whereabouts of the target, size of the crowds around and near the meeting, as well as the position, itinerary, and movements of the target, he decided upon the place of shot, type of firearm, and caliber.

Due to the noise of the crowds and traffic in the streets, few if any people would hear the shot go off, and it would be a cake walk to get away this time. Still on the Pennsylvania farm his employers set up for him, the Hunter placed silhouette targets at various ranges and practiced with lethal affect. When he wasn't shooting, he was studying. When he was neither shooting nor studying, he was plotting and planning his escape. It would appear that this target would not stand a chance on February 17.

Friday, January 26

Detective Grimes had finally mustered the courage to come meet Brandon at Christ Church. He had, after all, showed genuine compassion upon the violent death of her ex-husband. She sensed some spiritual counseling might be of some help to her. She also thought a long, casual conversation with him might bring to light some new, tiny shred of evidence or even an infinitesimal lead that might point her in the right direction. Perhaps toward some links to the now four murders she and her department were dealing with.

Despite the conflicts with her boss and nearly all of her colleagues, Grimes was as dogged as ever in proving them wrong. She remained convinced, even despite her own occasional misgivings, that one person (or group of people) was behind everything. She entered Brandon's office at 4 p.m., where she was greeted with a tight, warm embrace from the priest that lasted nearly two minutes.

Julie shivered, and as they let go of each other to sit down, her eyes moistened.

"I'm sure the wound is still fresh, Julie," Michael said. "Again, I'm so sorry about Jamie. We never stop loving people with whom we were so close. I'm talking from personal experience, not just from pastoral textbooks—"

"Oh, Michael," interrupted Grimes. "Your wife is cheating on you."

"My wife?" Michael said. "Are you having her followed?" He struggled for words after this punch in the gut, but he was sure he had no idea what the detective could be talking about.

"It's not exactly what you think... I think she's having an affair with a woman."

Michael's calm and soothing disposition suddenly turned prickly. "What are you talking about, Julie?"

"The Deputy Chief ordered my team to follow a young woman named Allison Peters. One of my guys saw her at the waterfront last week holding hands and hugging with another woman. Is this your wife?"

The detective handed Brandon a photograph.

"Yes, indeed it is," Michael said.

Grimes knew the woman was Michael's wife but had never been introduced to Bettina, so she wished to remain coy.

"It's nothing at all," Michael exclaimed. "They're good friends and very affectionate with each other. I don't know why your boss told you to follow Miss Peters, but could you please leave Bettina out of whatever you have going on?"

"It wasn't my idea, believe me."

"Why don't we go inside the chapel, and we will pray together?" Michael said. "You will feel better, I guarantee."

Brandon and Julie walked together from his office and into the sanctuary. They prayed, Grimes departed with a nice, solemn blessing, and Brandon returned to his office quite flummoxed. He pulled a letter out of his desk drawer from Mr. John Gauge, which he almost gave to Detective Grimes after she had told him about Deputy Chief Garrison. Garrison had promised Brandon he would not tell Grimes or anyone else about Allison Peters, the rifle shell casing, and her cohabitation with a possible assassin.

Michael's letter from his father had counseled him to trust Garrison, and to alert him if a John Gauge approached him for money. Gauge had. The short letter in Michael's hand read as thus: *We need to meet, Reverend. I have information you will find vital. After I tell you, of course, you will wish to pay me $50,000.*

Michael talked to himself backwards and forwards. Who should he trust? Garrison went back on his word, but perhaps he had a good explanation. He trusted Julie Grimes, as far as a married man could trust a cop with whom he'd had an affair of sorts. She did alert him to activity concerning his wife, something she did not have to do. His father had directed him to reach out to the Deputy Chief if contacted by Gauge, and he trusted his father implicitly. *There!* He had the answer he needed.

Brandon decided to contact Garrison and tell him about the letter from Gauge. He was ambivalent as to whether or not to confront the Chief about putting a tail on Allison Peters.

Garrison walked into Brandon's office later that day. Michael handed him the letter.

"I suppose you already know what to do about that," he said.

"Of course, Reverend. I'll take care of it today," said the Chief as he turned to walk away.

"Why did you have Allison Peters followed?" Michael blurted out. "And my wife, Bettina, by default? I thought you told me Grimes would be left out, that you would take care of all issues regarding Allison yourself."

Garrison shut the door to Brandon's office and sat down. The mood grew immediately tense as the two glared at each other. "We've all tried to keep you out of this, Michael," said the Chief. "But you just keep stumbling into things."

"Stumbling into what? I have no idea..."

"Come to your mother's house Monday afternoon," said Garrison. "It's time you were clued in on some things. Four o'clock. See you there."

Garrison turned to exit the room.

"Don't tell Grimes I told you about Allison," pleaded Brandon. "And please don't discipline her. She was just looking out for me."

"Still sweet on her, I see. Don't worry. Detective Grimes is useful to me. She's safe. Remember, Monday at four."

Sunday, January 27

Brandon awoke early, for he had three services to perform at Christ Church. Bettina chased him down as he entered the kitchen to brew some coffee.

"What are you doing?" she asked.

"Getting some coffee. Go back to bed, honey."

As he turned away toward the counter, Bettina hugged him from behind, as if to signal that he would have a silent partner while he made his breakfast. The two had a very lovely time the night before, drinking wine, watching movies, and cuddling with each other on the balcony. It had turned cold later in the week, and the couple enjoyed spending time outside bundled up together in an electric blanket. Bettina normally slept in on Sundays and attended the later church service. But this Sunday morning was one where she did not want to let go of her husband.

To their friends and family, the Brandons had the ideal marriage. Some were happy for them, and others were privately envious. Bettina was on cloud 9 that day. Michael, however, was slightly grieved. The Allison thing, as he thought of it, was starting to bother him. He knew Bettina needed a best friend, but why did she need one badly enough not to tell him she had been out with Allison?

Having to hear of his wife's whereabouts and who she was with from a police officer was upsetting. But he didn't confront her for being secretive. We are all hypocrites, but Brandon's hypocrisy went only so far. He was not about to interrogate his wife over something this minor while he continued to conceal his prior liaisons with Julie Grimes. He thought about the gospels where Jesus commanded his disciples not to judge, but to first remove the "beam in your eye" before you pass judgment on the "speck in your neighbor's eye."

Brandon would suffer in silence for a while.

He preached the same sermon at all three services that day. It was both a treatise and an exhortation not to fall prey to the misleading debate over science and religion. Christ Church had members who worked for NASA and other government agencies. Other congregants were engineers. This was an audience tailor made for Brandon's message.

"Science can tell us how to produce a hydrogen bomb," Michael preached. "But it cannot tell us when, if ever, to use that bomb. Science, despite its increasing wonders, cannot begin to answer the moral questions of life."

This sermon ran twice the length of his normal sermons, due to what Michael felt was an urgent subject to impart. He ended with this:

"As long as there is death, there will be religion. It has always been so, and always will be. Humanity has tried the godless society. And we all know the result. The hope for a religionless humanity is the speculation of fools. And the idea that we human beings will ever be capable of explaining existence on our own also belongs to the realm of idiots and fools. Which people will you and I be? People who yield to the truth and to common sense, or the other kind?"

Michael and Bettina shook hands with the congregants at the 5 p.m. service, then retired to his office. Brandon was mentally exhausted from writing and delivering his lengthy sermon.

"I think most of the people today were stunned and challenged by your message, baby," Bettina said.

"I hope so. I couldn't help noticing some blank stares."

"Everyone was just trying to take it all in," Bettina promised.

"Well, I wouldn't be a very good priest if I simply told people what they want to hear all the time."

"You did beautifully, Michael. I'm so proud of you, as usual." Bettina kissed him.

"Sometimes I think I get too cerebral, too philosophical and literary, for some of my parishioners," Michael admitted.

"Don't change a thing, honey. Your church is full of educated people, and they expect as much."

"I know, but sometimes I think I take what should be a simple, straightforward message and dress it up so much that it loses its punch," Michael said. "I don't want to alienate anyone. Religion and spirituality are serious matters not to be toyed with."

"You'll alienate more people if you stop being erudite and cerebral," injected Bettina.

The couple relaxed in Brandon's office for a few more minutes, then walked down the street to one of their favorite dinner spots. All in all, it had been a good day.

Monday, January 28

Brandon was accustomed to being summoned to his parents' home with little notice to attend the proverbial cocktail hour, where pleasures were had and matters of great import discussed. But this day he was answering the summons of someone else. Somebody who was obviously in his mother's employ. Why else would a secret death bed letter from his father trouble itself to assert that Deputy Chief Garrison of the Alexandria Police Department was the man to call if Brandon should find himself threatened?

He would arrive there alone at 4 p.m. Not wanting to trouble Bettina with a family encounter towards which he had been feeling great unease, he played down its importance when he suggested she stay at home. He turned into Dungannon and drove up the long, winding driveway to the house. The day was clear and cold. With no leaves on the trees, one could see for miles down the meadows of the Piedmont farm and enjoy the breathtaking view of the Blue Ridge Mountains. Small flocks of ducks and Canadian Geese noisily exited the pond and flew over Brandon's truck and the house.

"Hi, Mom!" shouted Brandon as let himself inside.

Rector Thompson came to the foyer and greeted Michael. The two fixed themselves drinks at the wet bar and adjourned into the larger parlor on the left side of the house. Patricia kissed her son and bid him to sit down for a visit. Rector Thompson was in a bath robe and slippers, for he had just finished a swim in the indoor heated pool. Sitting in the large leather reclining chair was Deputy Chief Garrison.

"Give the lad another drink, Patricia," the Rector said. "It will come in handy."

Michael took the second drink from Patricia in a cloud of mystery. He couldn't ever remember his mother serving him a drink. That was his job, or his father's. Even stranger was Patricia remaining standing and offering a toast.

"Everyone, raise a glass to the Rector," directed Patricia. "To Rector Michael Joseph Brandon, my son."

"Thank you, Mom. But you didn't have me drive 50 miles for a toast."

"No, honey, I didn't. Michael," said Mrs. Brandon, pointing at chief Garrison, "I would like to introduce to you to your half-brother."

"Glad to finally make your acquaintance, little brother. In an open-door manner, that is," said Garrison as he shook Michael's hand firmly.

Michael sat back down in his chair and chugged his two drinks. He did not speak. He gazed across the room at the seemingly nonchalant and untroubled faces, as though this were just another routine revelation in the Brandon family's daily lives. It took less than two minutes for Michael to be overcome by silent rage and disbelief as he stood up and bid his mother and the gentlemen goodbye. His fast walk out of the room turned into a full sprint toward his truck. He could hear his mother calling after him.

"Michael, Michael! Go after him!" Patricia said.

He sped down the winding driveway, nearly hitting one of the pillars next to the flagstone wall where the driveway met the narrow state road. He did not look back, even in his rear-view mirror, until he turned onto the interstate. It was just after 5 p.m. when he called his wife.

"I'm on my way back," Michael told Bettina. "Dinner, you and me, Mt.

Vernon. Yes. You're driving, okay? And bring a gin and sprite with you, a double."

With total disregard for the speed limits, Brandon zoomed back to his condo, where Bettina was waiting in the lobby. As she came out to the truck, Michael switched over to the passenger seat and his wife climbed in and began to drive. As he grabbed her hand gently and kissed it, she passed him his drink. Not exactly in a temperate mood, Michael threw down the double gin in a flash as the couple drove the 12 miles down the parkway hugging the Potomac River.

Bettina could obviously sense that something was wrong but was too smart to ask questions while he was imbibing. She had properly deduced why he wanted the two to go to dinner at a small and out of the way restaurant where they have could privacy. She knew it had to be his family, for he was fine when he left for Dungannon earlier. They just spent the ride clasping each other's hands, Bettina giving off a tender reassurance that whatever is wrong will get better, and if it doesn't, they will deal with it together.

Michael and Bettina walked into the charming restaurant, which was all decked out in colonial furnishings, the rooms lighted by candles and the fireplace. A separate operation but on the Mt. Vernon Estate grounds, the wait staff dressed in 18th Century attire, and they even served a duck dish which George Washington had considered one of his favorites.

"Let's take our usual corner table, honey," said Brandon as he motioned to a waiter he knew to bring him a Gin Rickey and his wife a glass of Pinot Noir.

* * *

"I don't like the abrupt manner. This turned out all wrong," said Patricia Brandon to her other son and companion.

"It had to be this way," said Garrison. "He seems incapable of maintaining distance from our goings on. You wanted it that way, but it all started when he diddled one of my detectives. He got himself all tangled up with this mess. He had to be told."

"I don't appreciate your locker room language, Bill," said Patricia. "And I don't know why he would do such a thing when he has such a lovely wife as Bettina."

"He's just like his father, Patricia," chimed in Rector Thompson. "The smooth operator, only more reckless. Anyway, he needs to hear the details from you, his mother."

"He just stormed out of my house," Patricia said. "I've never seen him act this way."

"What did you expect?" asked the Rector. "We just cornered him. Bill, you get him back out here so he can spend time with his mother alone."

"Okay, Rector," Garrison said. "Or, Dad. What am I calling you both these days?"

"You call us whatever you'd like, son," said Patricia.

"I'll take care to smooth things over with your favored son," Garrison said.

"Now, not one more word of that kind, Bill. You know what our situation has been all these years."

"And I'm fine with everything, but you've spoiled that kid all his life," Garrison said. "Probably to make up for neglecting me."

"You haven't been neglected," Patricia said frustratedly. "You have our love and company, you're in my will, and I made certain you had the career and position you wanted. I will readily admit to spoiling you both and would have it no other way. Now, how are you going deal with this John Gauge fellow?"

"It's already taken care of, Mom."

"I need to tell you something, sweetheart," said Bettina to Michael back at the Mt. Vernon restaurant.

"Fire away, honey," barked an inebriated Brandon as he raised his gin glass.

"You're probably wondering why I've spent so much time with Allison."

Brandon briefly skated the edge of sobriety, as his wife began to serve up the answer to the question he had refused to ask her.

"I'm so happy with you and our life together, Michael," Bettina said. "I know Allison is bisexual and that she has strong feelings for me. I've never considered myself that way, but I have always needed women in my life I can be close to, affectionate with. Can you understand that, honey?"

Brandon just nodded in the affirmative, pleasantly baffled by his good luck.

"She wants to be intimate with me," Bettina continued. "I said no. Even if that's what I wanted, I'm married to you."

She grasped Michael's hand. He squeezed back, realizing that all the consuming fantasies about lesbian encounters and threesomes were unimportant compared to the monogamous intimacy he shared with his wife. Brandon would drink a little more that evening and would tell Bettina all about his newfound half-brother, his mother, and Rector Thompson.

Bettina would marvel for weeks to come at the soap opera nature of the lives of the rich and powerful. Southern eccentricities abound with the Virginia gentry, not least of all because they can afford them. So many secrets and lies underneath the veneer of tradition and propriety. Do not make the mistake that Bettina was cooling to her in-laws. She loved Patricia and enjoyed the unique charm of life at Dungannon. But she relished the straightforward simplicity of her background, and of her life with Michael.

Brandon went to bed that night with the unshakable belief that God had given Bettina to him as a precious gift. A gift for its own sake but also one without whom he stood no chance of serving as an effective priest. Michael tended to say his nightly prayers while lying awake in bed next to his wife. He prayed silently. And he made a vow to God that if He were to keep Bettina healthy and loving toward him always, then God would see him reformed. The young rector was serious about his character growth and purity of heart, really serious for the first time in his life.

However, as the Good Book says, "The spirit is willing, but the flesh is weak."

CHAPTER 22

Sunday, February 17

That Sunday morning, Governor John Bland took a short brisk walk from the Governor's Mansion to his office adjacent to the State Capitol Building. His police guards waited outside in the hallway while Bland closed the door to his office, sat down at his desk, and pulled out two documents from the top drawer. In his hands were official executive pardons, one for Mrs. Patricia Brandon, the other for Rector Emeritus James Thompson.

Under Virginia law, the Governor has the full power of pardon for the violation of any state laws. This power applies after a conviction or before, or simply to shut down any possibility of investigation. Negative political feedback is the usual check on that very acute power.

Michael had called his mother the prior evening to clear the air after two weeks of avoidance. "I'll deal with Garrison as my brother in my own time, but please tell me one thing. Did Dad know about this?"

"Yes," said Patricia without hesitation. "I realize that this is a difficult pill to swallow, but it's rather uncomplicated, sweetheart. James and I fell in love, perhaps we had always been so. Your father and I married shortly after William was born. It was our families' edict. But he and I grew to love each other very much. James married Kerry, and they were happy. We gave William to my cousin Elizabeth and her husband, who could not have children. That's how things operated in our world back then. Everyone did turn out quite well, honey."

"Don't worry, Mom, I'm not holding grudges," Michael said. "Just give me time to process all of this. Love you."

"Goodnight, dear."

Brandon said what he had to in order to keep the peace and not worry his mother. But he held sneaking suspicions, the foremost being that, but for circumstance, his mother probably would never have told him about Garrison. What other family secrets lurked in the background to which he might never be privy? Worst of all, for the first time, Michael felt like the outsider in his own family.

Before all this, it was just himself and his mother and father. Now, he had to deal with his mother, the Rector, and his half-brother. Too much change, and too fast. Perhaps things could remain as Brandon wished between himself and his mom; perhaps not.

* * *

The Hunter peered through the lenses in his binoculars. Old Town Alexandria was uncommonly inflamed that particular day. Adjacent to Lee Park was the new Washington office of a Wall Street Bank with considerable European Union connections. It was a first class multi-national, the kind which had enraged so many people in the Western World after the recent financial meltdown and government bailouts. The Chairman and CEO of the bank had barely avoided prison. Now he was in Alexandria with the Mayor and other dignitaries to dedicate the opening of the D.C. branch. Hundreds of protesters were in the park kept at bay by police.

With considerable ease, the Hunter had leased the old warehouse just yards from where he had taken the failed shot at Governor elect

Robinson and barely escaped. This time, his planning had been slower and more deliberate. It was as close to perfect as one gets. On this chilly afternoon, the killer was inside the warehouse, looking out of a make-shift window he had cut out of the concrete himself. It was approximately two feet across and two feet up and down. The distance from the front of the bank building was about 400 yards. His rifle would be a .300 Winchester Magnum, which packed a bigger punch than even the .7mm Magnum of his other shots.

Just one more successful squeeze of the trigger, and the killer would be off to his life of ease and anonymity. Just one more kill, and he would have his revenge over circumstance, which had denied him success just weeks before. He had chosen this particular target because the Hunter preferred to hit people who deserved it; people who make the world worse every day they go to work, and whose timely exit from the world would make it just a little bit better for the good people in it. The 2008 financial crash had affected millions of people, destroying the life savings and property values of thousands just in the United States. Men like the one coming into resolution in the crosshairs of the Hunter's scope had willfully engineered this collapse and spent their rotten profits on gold toilets and million-dollar rugs. Unsure of whether God existed, the Hunter was betting for divine approval with this kill.

The scene was gruesome! The Bank CEO walked up to cut the ribbon with the Mayor and was plunged head and shoulders into the brick wall of the bank. When he hit the pavement, blood and brains covered his face and head. He felt no pain. His final thoughts were surely about his continuing string of commercial successes. Then, he felt nothing and was no more.

The Hunter made ready for his usual lightning-fast retreat, but stopped to look at the scene once more to make sure it was the target, and only the target, who was down. Ascertaining the affirmative, he headed for the back door which led to a water main. Suddenly, a violent gas explosion rocked the warehouse and the ground beneath. Flames engulfed the inside. Minutes later, four police officers happened on the scene. They called the fire department, and two of the officers did a foolish thing.

They entered the flaming warehouse without proper backup from the firefighters. Barely escaping with their lives, the officers coughed up smoke and then signaled to approaching firemen that there was a man lying down inside. The firemen entered the warehouse and saw a man in a trench coat laying on the ground aflame. One fireman pulled him by the feet as the other firefighter doused the flames. They both noticed a high-powered rifle next to the man, and the fireman at the front of the body reached out with one hand and skimmed it along the floor, sending it almost to the door.

Chief Garrison and Detective Julie Grimes arrived just then. They got an intense and lengthy report from the police officers as more paramedics and more firefighters arrived. The man in the trench coat was pronounced dead at the scene by the paramedics. They sent him off to the medical examiner.

"My office, Grimes," ordered Garrison. "One hour, and bring your team."

"Is that the gun?" she asked.

"Yes, it was next to the dead man," said a police officer who doused the rifle with a fire extinguisher.

The Chief departed alone with the rifle while Julie Grimes directed the scene of inferno and assassination. Grimes was able to remain professional despite the visual horrors at the bank building and the warehouse. Her thoughts raced to the possible best-case scenario; the dead man was the killer of four men and the attempt on one more. Were that the case, then she would be vindicated as the lone proponent of linkage to all the violence of the previous year. Grimes had never wavered. She had done great honor to her convictions and her gut assumptions, assumptions based on first-rate police instinct, training, and skill.

Back at Marina Towers, Bettina and her friend, Allison, were glued to the television, as was much of the greater Washington, D.C. area. It was just after 4 p.m. when Michael got home. He had canceled the 5 p.m. church service due to the chaos less than two miles away. He had been steadily drinking more and more, beginning earlier in the day. He poured himself a double scotch, neat, and sat down beside his wife.

"I've lived here all my life," Allison said. "I can't imagine the year we have had. Assassinations?"

"Comes from being next door to the nation's capital...center of the universe," Brandon said.

Just then, the news crew at the warehouse reported that the body of the probable killer of the international banker today is currently with the medical examiner: "Police say there is a chance they may be able to close all four of the murder cases they now think are related."

None of the three people in the Brandon's condo could think about anything else. Bettina and Allison went to the kitchen to make dinner, while Michael drank and stared at the TV. During the course of an hour, he picked up his phone a dozen times, started to dial his mother, then hung up. He had spoken to her briefly when he was leaving the church to assure her that he and Bettina were fine. But questions of the most suspicious kind now permeated his mind. He had demons to confront but would instead tune them out. When they promptly returned, as they always seem to do, he drowned them with whiskey.

"Bettina, I hate drinking on an empty stomach," Michael said. "Is dinner coming?"

"Five minutes, okay?" Bettina said.

Allison, concerned for both her friends, asked Bettina if Michael was having problems.

"Too complicated for tonight, honey," said an ever-protective Bettina. "Thanks for your concern, but I've got him."

The couple and their guest ate dinner with eyes glued to the TV set. Michael passed out on the sofa while the ladies cleaned up and shared a bottle of wine.

When 10 p.m. rolled around, the news reports were high energy: "Police have identified the assassin from today's killing. DNA was found on a rifle in the warehouse next to the dead man. Ballistics confirm it was the gun used to kill the banker. The DNA from the rifle, as well as on the concrete window and of course the body, was matched to samples found at Christ Church, where a Mr. Harry Penrose was killed, at the law office of Fairfax attorney James Smalls who was found murdered there, at the man hole cover where former Governor-elect Matt Robinson was shot at, and at the condo across from the Hilton hotel where Real Estate magnate Robert Martin was shot and killed. Police now say they believe that the man who died in the fire this afternoon was most probably the triggerman in all cases pending. This man here, a Mr. John Gauge."

The news anchors spoke as a photo of Gauge appeared on the screen. Michael sobered up enough to feel the significance of what had just happened.

"That's the man who came to me months ago," Michael said to his wife. "The first confession I took. Look, it's him, baby. I talked with him, prayed with him, honey."

Bettina just stared at the screen and grabbed Michael's hand. Brandon's scotch binge gave way to crystal clear memory flashes which began to torment him. He had counseled a serial killer. And one who Rector Thompson had fixed him up with.

"What the hell has been going on the past year?" he asked himself silently, over and over.

The news anchors came back on and informed the viewers there would be a press conference at police headquarters in the morning. They discussed the issue for another 15 minutes, all the while leaving Gauge's picture on the screen.

Meanwhile, Allison had been on the balcony talking with her parents, who were vacationing in South America.

As she walked into the living room, an excitable Bettina said, "Looks like the police found your ex-boyfriend. They're saying that he was the one killed in the fire. They're saying he was responsible for all four murders. What a frightful thing you were involved with him."

Allison stared at the television, gulped, and said, "That's not him."

Brandon and Bettina gave Allison an intense stare, then they stared at each other. Everyone's mind went blank. It was all too much to process.

Monday, February 18

Michael drove Allison down to the police station to speak privately with his half-brother.

"That's not the man I was involved with," pleaded Allison to Deputy Chief Garrison. "I think he may still be out there. How do you explain the shell casing the maids found in his apartment?"

The Chief looked at both of his visitors with a calm and commanding disposition. "Would you like some coffee?"

Allison jumped up, agitated, but Michael sat her down and said, "Coffee would be great, thanks."

The Chief left his office momentarily.

"Be cool, Allison. Let's see what the police have pieced together, okay?" Michael asked.

"Okay," she replied.

"Here we go," said the Chief. "Two cups of rot gut coffee paid for by the taxpayers. Now, Miss Peters, about that shell casing. I and two of my colleagues interviewed the maids and their employer. Everyone said that a Mr. John Gauge was the owner of the condo they were cleaning. If you spent time with a man other than John Gauge, it had to have been his tenant."

"For curiosity's sake, did you find out the name of the tenant?" Michael asked.

"Builder's Trust," said the Chief. "A subsidiary of Open Door Development, Inc."

"Martin's company," whispered Brandon to himself. "So, Allison's boyfriend was having his rent paid by the first victim, Robert Martin, and his company?"

"It appears so. Maybe he was doing security for Martin in some form or fashion. Miss Peters, before you leave, would you sit with our computer sketch artists? We need a good photograph of your friend to keep on file. Although, there is little doubt in our ranks as to who the killer was."

"Gauge?" asked Michael.

"Yes, Gauge."

Allison complied, and she and Michael left.

"May I stay at your place until my parents come home next week?" Allison asked Michael. "I'm so freaked out right now, I don't want to be alone."

"Of course you can," said the priest. Michael was a bit freaked himself over the events of the last day. It just added to the stress and confusion on top of the Garrison familial revelation, his father's death, and letter mentioning Gauge, and all of the weird goings on over the past year. Apart from his wife and his rectorship, he had little stability in his life.

Later that night, Chief Garrison slipped back into his office and logged into a computer in the IT room. With latex gloves on, he logged into the central files of the police department, using a password from the IT section. Pulling up the sketch from Allison Peters, he altered the facial features of the man she described and had been living with. He then called a contact who worked at FBI headquarters.

"Is the DNA on Killer 1 gone?" Garrison asked.

"I deleted it six weeks ago," said the other voice.

"What exactly does that mean?" asked an anxious Garrison.

"It means that any DNA uncovered from anywhere your officers or Federal agents might discover would hit a black hole, were it to be run through the system in the FBI or Interpol. Killer 1 does not exist."

"Excellent work," said Garrison. "You'll have a proper bonus waiting for you shortly. Goodnight."

The Chief went home and called Dungannon. "It's done, all over with. Understand?"

"Understood," said a very satisfied Patricia Brandon. As she passed Rector Thompson a glass of sherry, she raised her glass and smiled the smile of success.

She uttered these words: "Things are just as they should be, finally."

Michael could not sleep and was looking for something to occupy himself with. Church business and sermons, perhaps? No. Read something interesting? Television? Another scotch or gin? Well, a drink, yes, but none of the usual distractions had any appeal.

He poured a drink and went to the study, turned on a dim light, and pulled out the letter from his father. He had read it a thousand times, but this time he just stared at the part warning him about John Gauge asking for money. Several things were strange about that part of the letter. It was the final part and had nothing to do with the body and theme of the letter. It was almost an afterthought. He knew about Chief Garrison and his relationship to the family.

"No, no, something is all wrong," Michael said to himself. "Why would a dying man write a letter to his son telling him how proud he was of him, and then direct attention to Gauge and Garrison?"

As he continued to stare at the last paragraph, a horrifying realization cut him down. He sank back in his chair and chugged the rest of his scotch. He then went quietly into his bedroom and woke Bettina.

"Hey, wake up, honey, and come with me into the study."

"Michael, what's wrong? Why are you still up?" Bettina asked.

"I'm sorry, but please come with me."

Bettina dragged herself behind her husband, unamused by the nocturnal disturbance. Michael shut the door behind them. "Sweetheart, please find me a letter, any letter, from my folks to us."

"Why do you—?" Bettina began asking.

"Bettina, please, this is important," Michael interjected.

Michael looked for additional letters from his parents. "Bingo, here is one from Dad congratulating me on getting the Cathedral job."

"I've got one from your mom here, honey. It's a letter she wrote to me after you proposed. It's very sweet."

"Give it here," Brandon insisted. He looked attentively at each letter, then he turned pale and fell forward, bracing his hands and arms against the desk.

"Baby, what is the matter?" asked Bettina.

"My father didn't write me this letter. It was my mom."

"What?" Bettina said.

"Here, see for yourself," Michael said and handed his wife the letter.

Bettina looked hard and could clearly see the handwriting in the two letters from the Congressman was not the same. More telling was the similarity in handwriting between the father's final letter to Michael and Mrs. Brandon's letter to Bettina. This new evidence might not play in court, but Michael knew the score. For reasons unknown and unimaginable, his mother had played him.

"Michael, what are you going to do?" Bettina asked.

"Confront Mom and get the truth. The whole story. Too much weird shit has happened, Bettina. And it has to all be related somehow. My sudden introduction to a stepbrother at age 40. My getting sucked into three murder investigations, all of which have an indirect family connection. All the troubles with the Bishop, who just happened to disappear from the scene, and now this letter."

Michael knew his mother was somebody not to be trifled with, but he now harbored feelings that she actually might be dangerous.

It was Michael's father, though, who ran the Brandon Family Trust containing both his and Patricia's money. That trust owned several units in Southern Towers condominiums, including the one from where Robert Martin was killed. The trust owned them through a holding company called Lighthorse. Brandon went to bed with another gut feeling that would have to be addressed immediately the following day.

Tuesday, February 19

Bettina's car had been recalled to the dealer, due to a transmission problem, so Michael would be driving his wife to work for the week. She could walk to her office from home in 20 minutes, but it was wintertime, and the early evenings were dark; so, he insisted that he take her and pick her up.

He dropped her off early at 8:15 a.m. He then went home, where he had eight or nine hours to research documents and computer files. He was not buying the story that John Gauge's tenant was having his rent paid by Open Door Development, aka Robert Martin. He began to search the public real estate records for the City of Alexandria. Frustratingly, no tenant information was on file, only owners and purchases. He only had a fraction of the family trust real estate documents, the ones his father gave him.

"How am I going to find out?" Michael said, speaking to himself.

He remembered something vividly all of a sudden. The Congressman took controlling interest of Open Door Development the previous year. He and Rector Thompson were involved in breaking up the company and giving it all, minus legal fees, to the Episcopal Diocese of Virginia. But not for 10 years. Patricia and the Congressman could easily have used the Open Door name somewhere in a public record. After all, it was Chief Garrison who told everyone that fact. And he controlled the investigation.

Brandon lay down on the sofa mentally exhausted. It was only 1 p.m. Breathing heavily, he took into the inner reaches of his psyche these last revelations, which fit his already held suspicions like a glove. In all likelihood, his parents paid the rent of John Gauge's tenant, the mystery man who Allison Peters thought capable of assassination.

That day's discoveries, coupled with the father's letter which was actually written by his mother, and the case kicker — Harry Penrose, killed in Brandon's church, was blackmailing the family, definitely with Smalls and probably Martin.

"Mom, what have you been up too?" he said aloud.

Michael was quickly running out of people to turn to. He did not trust his half-brother, the Chief. His mentor and friend, Rector Thompson, was still both to him, but the Rector would never side against Patricia. And Michael suspected the Rector had been conspiring with his parents all along. And Chief Garrison was Rector Thompson's son. And then Michael thought, he could call Detective Grimes. But then Julie could be privy to damning evidence.

He could talk to his wife, which he would anyway, but she should not be dragged into such a family squabble as this. As he made himself lunch, he resolved upon a course of action. Bettina called him around 4 p.m. to be picked up. Michael got his files in order, picked up his wife, and took them back home.

As Bettina closed the bedroom door to change and get ready for a shower, Michael placed a call.

"I know what you did. I'm coming to the house now," he said.

His thoughts raced out of control, torment to torment with no relief between.

"Who else did Mom kill?" Michael said to himself. "Was it her and the Rector who were involved, or just her? Did they do poor Dad in just so they could be together?"

Michael had deliberately waited to leave until Bettina hopped into the shower to avoid a very certain argument over her not being allowed to go with him. He had no idea what to expect from the impending encounter, and he did not want his wife anywhere in proximity. He shouted to Bettina that he was going out for few minutes. Brandon grew angrier as he drove, the anger being far preferable to the heartbreak he also felt. For whatever was about to transpire, his relationship to his family would be permanently altered.

As he was halfway to Dungannon, his phone rang. It was Bettina. He pushed a button and sent her call to voicemail. It rang again, then again.

Brandon began to sweat and shake, nearly panic stricken he lowered his window in order to get his breath.

As his phone lit up with text messages, the whole of the last year came front and center into focus as if it were only seconds in time. As he caught his breath and calmed a bit, he called Bettina.

"I'm sorry I had to run out like that," Michael told her. "I'll explain when I get back. I'm sure you are pissed at me, but I have to do this alone. Just be there when I get back, and I'll tell you everything. No, don't worry, I'll be okay. Love you!"

As he turned off the interstate, Michael noticed he was being followed. He only had several miles to go before he reached Dungannon.

"My esteemed stepbrother, the cop," he muttered.

It was the Chief behind him and, looking carefully in the rear-view, Michael could see he was alone. In one swift motion, the priest reached into the center console and pulled out a pistol, which he placed in the large inside pocket of his jacket.

"What a farce, what a shitshow," Brandon said to himself. "A mother and her live-in friend, possible criminal masterminds, a crooked cop, and a priest with a gun. I should fucking write a book!"

As he approached the estate, Brandon was all business; he was no longer joking with himself. As always, the beauty and serenity of Dungannon overwhelmed him, and for a moment he convinced himself that this home with the sweet older lady inside could never be the source or the realm of anything nefarious. Then, an immediate reality check. As he pulled up to the house, he could clearly see Chief Garrison behind him. Ignoring that fact, he let himself into the house and found Patricia and Rector Thompson sitting in the front parlor.

As he greeted them, Garrison came in and stood between his parents. As Michael began to speak, he noticed Garrison fiddling with his jacket, the part of the jacket where a shoulder holster might be. He carefully glanced at his mother and, through his peripheral vision, saw Garrison touching his jacket again. With lightning speed, Brandon drew his pistol from inside his jacket.

"Drop your piece, Garrison, and toss it over here," Michael said.

Patricia gasped and nodded affirmatively to the testy and anxious policeman, then turning toward her younger son.

"Michael, put down that gun," she said. "Have you taken leave of your senses? Nobody here is going to harm you. Sit down and I will tell you a story."

Brandon eyed the room like a trained detective while Garrison took out his pistol and holster.

"This is the only one I have with me brother," the Chief said as he placed it on a footstool. The Chief's gun had been attached to his belt on the opposite side of his jacket. Michael began to feel foolish and a little crazy, so he put his gun away and sat down next to the wet bar. Of course, he helped himself to the scotch decanter.

"I'm all ears, Mother," Michael said.

"I am not particularly long-winded today, dear," Patricia said. "I will relay the substance of the business. Then, if you have any questions—"

"Just let me have it straight," said an anxious Michael. "You owe me absolute candor, Mom. When I went to seminary and became a priest, I left the world of power and politics and money behind. You encouraged me in this endeavor, more than anyone else. But now I've been sucked right back into this sorry world. What kind of shit is that, Mom?"

Rector Thompson chimed in, "Don't address your mother that way, Michael. Your parents told you the score when you got in. There is always power, politics, and money in anything of consequence. And didn't your mother, your brother, your father, and I try to keep you out of it all? It was your recklessness that got you where you stand right now. Who told you to beat James Smalls half to death? Who told you to mess around with Detective Grimes? We have set you up in position to do something grand with your life, and we have protected you at every turn."

"All right, enough!" shouted Michael. "I want to hear it all from her."

"Very well, son," Patricia began. "You know all about your father's deals and his blackmailers. Well, it was Penrose, Smalls, and Martin. All three were behind it. Your father had felt sorry for Penrose, who needed the money badly. How I found out about the other two is immaterial, but I assure you that they extorted your poor father into an early grave. When I finally told you about his strokes, it was too late for him. Two years ago, after a stroke which I did not tell you about, our doctor told your father he had very little time to live. When I inquired as to the cause of it all, I expected to hear that it was his heaving drinking these many years. The doctor looked at me intently and said it was heavy stress. That his condition was brought on by what had to unbearable, unrelenting stress. It was the blackmail, Michael. These men killed your father! And so, I killed them. Had them killed."

Patricia sat staring at her youngest son, indignantly.

"So, you three planned it all?" Michael said. "Were you the trigger man?" Michael pointed to Garrison.

"Do you take me for an amateur? Of course not," said the policeman.

"I told you the what and the why. It's better you don't know anything about the how," said Patricia.

Despite a couple of drinks in his system, Michael could not stop fidgeting. "If avenging Pop was your motive, then why try and kill Matt Robinson?"

"We don't know anything about that," exclaimed Patricia. "Though it was a nice gift when he resigned in favor of our dear friend, Governor Bland."

"And the last killing, the banker?" Michael said.

"Nothing to do with it," said Garrison. Michael looked back and forth at all three of them in disbelief. They looked back at him and just shrugged.

"This is all neat and tidy, isn't it?" said Michael sarcastically. "What about John Gauge? Was he some kind of patsy, as they say?"

"The evidence all points to Gauge, four murders and one attempted murder," declared the Chief. "The case is closed, brother. That's our version and the official version."

"Now, son... What do you intend to do with this information?" Patricia asked.

"You know damn well I'm not going to do anything, or you wouldn't have told me in the first place," Michael said. "Do you have any more of this?" Michael pointed to the empty scotch decanter.

"Careful, I might have to pinch you for drunk driving," joked Garrison.

Patricia and the Rector joined him in a hearty, irreverent bought of laughter. The tension and the dark comedy circled the parlor like a storm cloud. Michael had two more scotches and assured everyone he was safe to drive. It was all he could do to politely refuse his mother's offer to spend the night. Perhaps more than ever, he had to get home as fast as he could to his wife. The only person he could now implicitly trust. He rose from the sofa and stretched. Then he sighed heavily.

"As of now, I can consider the evidence buried," he said. "I endorse the official version of things. But you can have your party without me. I don't wish to see any of you for a while. Do not contact me, I will call you when I'm ready. No more plots or scheming. No more targeting people. It ends right here, right now. That's the price of my silence. And I don't want your money. Give it to your true son." Michael pointed at Garrison.

"You are my true son, Michael," said Patricia.

"He is more like you than I am," Michael said. "Far more than I ever want to be. Please remove me from the will. If you leave me any substantial money, I will give it to the church, liberal or traditional. I don't care.

I will make sure some good comes out of this."

He threw down the last of the scotch and turned toward the foyer. "Oh, and one last thing," said Michael, looking back intently at all three of them. "Alexandria could use an honest cop, high-up in the ranks. Make Julie Grimes a Captain. And pay her a five-figure starting bonus."

"Of course, dear," said Patricia.

This time, Brandon walked slowly from his mother's house to his truck.

The night of February 19, 2010 would be a watershed evening for Michael and Bettina. The anger and hurt she felt for him leaving her behind earlier instantly subsided when he entered their home and she saw how pale and despondent he looked. Any negative feelings she harbored were replaced with womanly compassion and the desperate love of a wife toward her husband.

As Michael removed his jacket, they stood and hugged each other for minutes, then sat down together, not relinquishing their embrace for one second. Michael told Bettina the whole sordid tale, at least all that he knew. In addition to the anguish he felt over his family's crimes, he had been terrified at how his wife would react, what she would think of them, and of him.

When Michael finished, they both sighed and fell back into the sofa and stared at each other. As Bettina moved over and took his face into her hands, Bettina simply said, "You drink too much, Michael. I'm worried about you."

Bettina placed her fingers on his lips and told him not speak. And they went to bed.

The next day, Michael tendered his resignation to the vestry at Christ Church. He privately told the Senior and Junior Wardens that it was a combination of a nervous breakdown and heavy alcohol use for which he was seeking treatment. Whether or not they believed him was immaterial. They were very sad to see him go, and he was beyond melancholy at having to leave. He was no longer a priest. No more sermons, no liturgical leadership, no counseling. Apart from being a husband, he woke up every day for the next few weeks with no sense of purpose and a greatly reduced sense of self. Unbeknownst to Michael, Patricia had set up a trust fund immediately after their confrontation. The fund would pay Bettina Brandon $500,000 a year for 30 years. Surprisingly, there was little tension when Bettina told him. Patricia knew her son well enough to know that though he might refuse her if the money went to him, he would not deprive his wife of financial security.

"This money will give us comfort and time to decide what we can do with our life together, sweetheart," Bettina said. "It is a blessing. You can choose another career. Hey, you can be an author like you said you always wanted to be. And maybe we can adopt a child. As long as we're together, baby, we can make a life. We can be happy!"

Brandon smiled at his wife and touched his hand to her cheek. "Whatever happens, Bettina, you're the most important person in my life, ever."

Whatever benefit their new income spike had, it was overshadowed by Michael's sense of being a purposeless, directionless failure. Worse yet, his mind was being assaulted by a sense of dread. With the loss of his vocation, he could not shake this sense of dread that with the priesthood went his spiritual and intellectual life. His psyche was in a quiet sense of turmoil and Bettina continued to worry about him. He wasn't exercising. He hadn't gone hunting in months. She didn't see him reading his books in the evening as much as he normally did. One day, she became desperate and called for help.

Tuesday, April 8

Bettina was at work and Michael was home. It was early afternoon, and he was reading a book for the first time in weeks. He was also drinking gin. He was just reaching the climax of his book when the telephone rang and announced a visitor.

"He wants you to come down, Mr. Brandon."

"Who?" Brandon asked.

"A Mr. James Thompson," replied the receptionist.

Michael's depression had made him too tired to fight with anyone, especially those who had been close to him. He grabbed a jacket, put on his shoes, and went downstairs.

"Hello, my boy," said the Rector as he stretched out his hand. Michael nodded hello and shook hands with Thompson. "It's a nice day. I thought we might take a walk."

Bettina got home around 5 p.m. and saw Michael on the sofa reading. She smiled and gave him a kiss. As she hung her coat up in the closet, Michael gently chastised her, "I should be angry with you, you know? I wasn't sure if I wanted to speak with Thompson ever again."

"How did it go?" Bettina asked.

"Not bad, actually. He disarmed me, as usual, telling me that it's my decision when and if I assume a relationship with my mom, with my brother, or with him. Then he asked me a question to which he already knew the answer. He asked, 'Have I ever given you anything but good advice since we've known each other? Spiritual or otherwise?' Of course, I had to agree with him."

"What did he tell you, honey?" Bettina asked.

"He reminded me that I was still young, that I had not lost my gifts, that for someone with my talents and blessings to give up on life would be a horrendous crime. He also told me that I had not lost God's love and favor. That's when I almost lost it and wanted to tell him that ministers of the gospel don't get involved in contract killings. But I didn't. In a weird way, the Rector ministered to me at the moment like he was a saint. I mean, Bettina, there was no guile in it. It was pure."

"There are mitigating circumstances, honey," Bettina said. "Your mom was defending your dad, and the Rector was standing by your mom...and your brother, in a dark sort of way, was being the dutiful son. This is all hard for me to process, so it must be excruciating for you. But don't you feel a little better after talking with Thompson?"

"I don't know. I don't know, sweetheart. But thank you for caring so much."

Bettina teared up as she went into the kitchen to cook dinner.

Rector James Thompson was that rare individual who could compartmentalize his spiritual beliefs and ethics and his willingness, like Patricia, to defend loved ones and sacred things from the evils of this world. Even if the means used would outdo Machiavelli himself. Michael, in the end, could not so easily reconcile those things, hence his resignation.

Patricia admitted to him the hiring and directing the killings of Robert Martin, Harry Penrose, and James Smalls. She explained precisely why she did it: because of the years of the blackmailing of her late husband, Congressman Brandon. She told Michael she had no involvement in or knowledge of the attempted killing of Governor-elect Matt Robinson, or the final killing of the bank executive. So, there we have it. One killing and one attempted killing unresolved, though Chief Garrison made sure the official report connects them all to John Gauge.

How to account for such a discrepancy? Well, that should be obvious, unless the Brandons were the only Virginian Blue Bloods with the moxie to hire a hitman. Incidentally, the use of the word "killing" instead of "murder" means to suggest that depending on who you ask, not all killing is murder.

* * *

In an undisclosed island country where the weather is usually pleasant, one of the best riflemen in the world was surf-fishing on the beach.

It was twilight, so his fair complexion did not prevent him from enjoying the sand and the ocean air. He had two poles and lines staked out next to his towels and blanket. Sitting in a folding chair, the man took out a photograph as he sang the Frank Sinatra song "My Way" that he had heard at the tiki bar earlier in the day.

"Regrets, I've had a few..."

Humming the rest of the verse he stared at the picture of a striking young woman in a yellow summer dress.

"Well," he said to himself. "Maybe one regret."

Allison Peters always looked so devastating in yellow.

EPILOGUE

Religion and politics have always been the two impolite topics of discussion among strangers. They breed discomfort, even suspicion among Americans today. They only get passing mention in contemporary fiction. And yet, what would Michael Brandon's story be without them? Religion and politics are like business here in America. Just as nearly everything here in the States is some kind of business, so all organized human activity is politics. And as long as we all fear death, there will religion be, trying to answer the questions which philosophy asks: How did we get here, and where do we go when we die? Why do we have something (a universe) instead of nothing?

These questions are difficult, as is the question of whether or not we may have a civilized society without a common belief in an objective reality and an objective morality. We cannot. Michael Brandon was raised to believe that we cannot. Patricia and Congressman Brandon knew this indisputably, as did Rector Thompson.

They and their cohorts went to war against the postmodernist culture and its advocates, a prime example being the deposing of Bishop Burroughs. Yes, she was a threat to Michael professionally, but an almost greater motivation for our favorite blue blood cabal to depose her was her type, one who savagely waged a crusade against tradition. A ghoulish proponent of societal upheaval. And she was a Bishop of the

Church. She had to go, and she went.

Congressman Brandon was surely right when he admonished his son to pay attention to the politics in his own church. No matter how much we may say we want nothing to do with politics, politics wants much to do with us. Wherever several or more people gather, there politics awaits, even in the church. And some agendas must prevail over others. What is best in life, secular or religious, must be preserved. Some things must be handed down through the generations unchanged. To the Brandons, not all ideas are equal.

It is one thing to bluster opinions and to organize to defeat one's adversaries at the polls. But hiring a contract killer to destroy the lives of one's adversaries tends to demonstrate that you are serious. Granted, our particular blue blood family went after those who were extorting from them. But at this point in the story, the reader should know just how serious these illustrious families are, and at the lengths with which they might go to prove the issue.

Reverend Brandon had been a good priest. He was a wonderful preacher, a kind of warrior-poet of the church. He was a family man and a loyal friend. And his love and fidelity toward his wife would be admirable until the day he died. The man of passion had come to realize that he had to live with himself. He had to give himself the gift of peace. The conflict of the human heart is the most mysterious of all conflict, and in the end, he had chosen purgatory.

If heaven were turning his mother, brother, and mentor into the police and remaining a priest, and hell being to fall on the sword for his family, burying their secrets, and yet remaining a priest, living a contradiction each day he went to work. No, purgatory. He chose the middle ground. Heroic? Perhaps not. Loyal? To his family, certainly. His church? Yes. Resigning his priesthood was a personal decision, but one could argue that his act was one of loyalty to the church. No matter what the young rector's ability, his decision to aid and abet his mother had hopelessly compromised him in any pastoral position. He knew that deep down, and he decided to protect his church from himself.

Michael would forgive and be reconciled to his mother and to Rector Thompson. To his brother, he would hold no grudges, but they would never be close. As for Michael's internal needs, sense of self-worth, and the need to shine again, he would need to lean on someone very special. Fortunately for him, he had his better-half, Bettina.

One of the blessed things in this life is to be yourself, be true to yourself, and get away with it. You would think the Michael Brandons of the world, with a powerful family and fortune behind them, would not need to prove the issue like the rest of us. Except the very opposite is true. He, more than most people, needed to prove he could do and be something on his own. He needed to be someone he could respect, deep within himself.

* * *

Months later on a hot summer evening, Michael sat down at his computer and wrote a clever title to his book. He then wrote a gripping opening paragraph, then another one. Then he rubbed his eyes, stretched out his arms, and breathed deeply.

Michael looked behind him and smiled at the pretty picture of his wife cuddling the 5-year-old, adorable little girl they adopted from Uruguay. And then he wrote some more. Three hours later, he had an introduction and a first chapter to accompany the title.

Michael Brandon was now a writer. He was being true to himself. And his depression began to lift.

www.ingramcontent.com/pod-product-compliance
Lightning Source LLC
Chambersburg PA
CBHW030247030726
47493CB00023B/876